FAMILY SECRETS AT THE INGLENOOK INN

HELEN ROLFE

Boldwood

First published in 2022. This edition first published in Great Britain in 2022 by Boldwood Books Ltd.

Copyright © Helen Rolfe, 2022

Cover Design by Chapman & Wilder

Cover Photography: Shutterstock

The moral right of Helen Rolfe to be identified as the author of this work has been asserted in accordance with the Copyright, Designs and Patents Act 1988.

A CIP catalogue record for this book is available from the British Library.

Paperback ISBN 978-1-80415-526-4

Large Print ISBN 978-1-80415-527-1

Hardback ISBN 978-1-80415-524-0

Ebook ISBN 978-1-80415-529-5

Kindle ISBN 978-1-80415-528-8

Audio CD ISBN 978-1-80415-520-2

MP3 CD ISBN 978-1-80415-521-9

Digital audio download ISBN 978-1-80415-522-6

Boldwood Books Ltd
23 Bowerdean Street
London SW6 3TN

For my family

1

RUPERT

The Inglenook Inn, an elegant brownstone in the heart of Greenwich Village, New York City, had been Rupert's workplace for the last few years. Whereas some people worked hard for the financial reward and largely because they had to, Rupert couldn't deny that his job as the chef at the inn was a sheer pleasure. Even getting up at an early hour and starting his working day long before most people would didn't bother him.

A little before 6 a.m., Rupert had already done most of the breakfast prep, and without any guests demanding his attention just yet, he headed out of the inn, down the steps out front, and after waiting for a taxi to pass, crossed to the next block and his favourite coffee shop.

The sidewalks weren't too crowded yet, but they soon would be, with people out and about either for work or leisure and probably, much like him, savouring the almost non-existent humidity. A rare occurrence, at least by New York standards, in the warmer months. Rupert loved the seasonal shifts – he could never live anywhere like Florida with its constant summer. Growing up in Vermont had meant having all the seasons, just as he experienced in New York. He liked the changes, whether subtle or as big as they could come. He loved that winter brought crisp frosts, heavy dumps of snow, and an icy landscape, and on days like today, he loved that spring brought with it a flourish. After months of sweater weather and being stuck indoors, the Manhattan streets were beginning to fill again, cherry blossom bloomed, and the leaves on the trees reappeared as though they'd always been there and fall had never happened.

At the coffee shop, Rupert grabbed himself and his boss Sofia a coffee. She'd been at her desk situated in the communal lounge of the inn almost as long as he'd been in the kitchen. These days, the Inglenook Inn never had much of a lull in bookings, so it was simply a case of being busy or busier.

Once he'd got the coffees, Rupert headed back to the inn and took the steps two at a time to the entryway at the top of the tall stoop flanked with wrought-iron railings. Enormous planters, filled with delicate violet blooms mixed with mustard yellows and deep verdant green foliage, framed the dark double doors.

'It's perfect weather, Sofia,' he announced, letting the front door close behind him as he expertly balanced one takeout cup on top of another. The longer he worked here, the more informal they got, and Sofia felt more like a friend, or even family, than a boss. 'It's fresh this early on, but the sun is out... it's going to be a great day.'

'Here's hoping,' she called over from the desk at the far end of the lounge.

Rupert swore they had a similar conversation most mornings and it had come to be a part of his day. He handed her one of the coffees. 'One oat milk latte for you.'

'My saviour.' She briefly looked up from the computer screen. This was where she usually started her day – checking any new bookings, responding to guest queries, and managing the various tasks when it came to running a boutique hotel. He occasionally stepped in to help out but mostly this was her domain; the kitchen was his.

'You know where I'll be,' Rupert said brightly as he set off from the lounge, along the hallway, past the staircase, and all the way to the back of the brownstone. He briefly glanced into the dining room that was adjacent to the kitchen to make sure it was all set up for breakfast – he'd done it himself last night, but it didn't hurt to double check everything was as it should be.

Breakfast service started at 6.30 a.m. and was flexible, but today he had a family of five who were checking out in a couple of hours. Usually breakfast worked as menu service and guests could make their mind up at the last minute, but given the time pressure, the Tompkins family had not only elected to reserve the biggest table in the dining room; they'd already put in orders for a full cooked breakfast each.

Rupert opened the window in the kitchen. Soon they'd be able to open the balcony doors in the dining room for guests to enjoy the spring breeze, but it wasn't quite warm enough yet. A few more days or perhaps a week, he thought to himself as he had another mouthful of coffee.

When he heard the tell-tale sign of voices in the dining room, he had a sneaky look through the hatch – a little feature at the inn he hoped would never disappear – and knew it was almost time to start cooking. He didn't like to do so until guests were seated – nothing worse than reheated eggs. He checked his list again – the family was split in their choices; two wanted eggs sunny side up, three wanted their eggs poached. They all wanted toast and hash browns, and nobody was sure whether they'd have pancakes or not. Rupert had made the batter and put it in the refrigerator anyway because someone always wanted pancakes.

In the dining room, he took orders for morning coffees, tea –

herbal or traditional – and juices, and then, with that sorted, lost himself in the task as he cooked in his kitchen. Cooking was his therapy and he was soon whistling as he popped sliced bread into the toaster, flipped eggs, cracked other eggs into boiling water and served everything up in the professional manner people associated with the meals at the Inglenook Inn.

The Tompkins family were content with their breakfast feast and so it was on to some clearing up in the kitchen before anyone else showed up. Every now and then, he could check for other guests by peeking through the hatch and he chuckled to himself, wondering what he would do if it wasn't there. Would Sofia have installed one to make things easy or would he have to continually dash out of the kitchen and into the dining room to see who had appeared, who had left, who needed something else? Guests could, although rarely did, open the hatch themselves to make requests. Usually it was kids who opened it, wanting to watch Rupert in action. He didn't mind but he was grateful he had the ability to lock it on one side as he'd had to do when the terrible twins came to stay. They weren't terrible really, just inquisitive little boys, but when they started pushing toys through to the other side, he'd had to spoil their fun. He often lined food up along the counter near the hatch and he had visions of a piece of Lego landing in a fruit cobbler and some unsuspecting guest discovering it.

A quick peek through the hatch and Rupert knew he had more guests to see to. He began the customary routine of dashing from kitchen to dining room and back again, whipping up breakfasts and serving with a smile. He didn't have any room service requests this morning, so at least he wouldn't be running up and down the three flights of stairs in the brownstone. They were a challenge, but they kept him fit, especially when he delivered food to the top floor. The entire top floor of the brownstone was home to the most palatial apartment of all and it had gone from being rarely rented out to getting a constant influx of corporate clients. Furnished with vintage brown Chesterfield sofas in the lounge area, it had pocket doors to pull out to create an extra bedroom if required, plus an ornate fireplace with a beautiful mantel, above which was a giant mirror. The apartment had a luxury bathroom with a roll-top tub and a master bedroom with a deluxe super king bed as well as a chaise longue at one edge of the room that had a view across the rooftops of Manhattan. The rest of the apartments in the Inglenook Inn were spread between the first and second floors.

Back in the kitchen, with a lull as the last couple of guests vacated the dining room, he went through the current list of everyone staying at the inn to check he had indeed provided breakfast for every guest apart from the couple in apartment four – they'd chatted with him yesterday afternoon at the small bar area in the lounge and on their request, he'd filled the refrigerator in their apartment so they could fix their own breakfast and set off bright and early this morning for their trip to the Hamptons.

Rupert finished clearing the kitchen as Sofia came in. 'Six guests have confirmed they'd like an evening meal tonight,' she told him.

'Sure thing, boss,' he winked. They'd always had an easy rapport. Some guests mistook them for a mother and son team and he hadn't minded at all. Neither had his mom, Verity, when he'd told her – in fact, she'd come to visit last year and really hit it off with Sofia, telling her as though Rupert were thirteen, not thirty-three, that she was glad Rupert worked somewhere that felt so much like a home. Both women had sat in the lounge and over several large glasses of wine they'd put the world, or at least the hotel sector, to rights, saying how big hotels could very easily become impersonal and weren't a true slice of New York. Not like the Inglenook Inn.

Rupert smiled to himself. He always felt like this was a slice of true New York, working in a brownstone, a classic environment of the city if ever there was one.

He watched Sofia now as she glanced in the refrigerator, one hand on her tummy.

'You're hungry.' He was pretty astute when it came to women, or at least he liked to think he was. With a mom and four sisters, he figured that gave him a reasonable amount of insight. 'French toast? Pancakes?'

She smiled. 'If it's not too much trouble.'

'Course it isn't. Sit yourself down.'

She settled herself onto the high stool as he made the egg mixture. 'It's nice to take a breather for a few minutes.'

But her breather and their chat was short-lived when someone rang the stainless-steel call bell at the front desk, which was surprisingly loud. Sofia disappeared and came back a minute or so later to tell him another guest would require the evening meal.

At the Inglenook Inn, breakfast was provided to all guests but with this being New York, where there was a plethora of wonderful restaurants, many chose to have their evening meal elsewhere. Sofia did her best to remain flexible, but as a relatively small establishment with varying clientele, they tended to ask guests to confirm around breakfast time whether they wanted dinner. It meant Rupert could ensure the freshest of ingredients, stocking up on produce from familiar vendors at Chelsea Market and the Meatpacking District as required, either late at night or in the morning depending on the inn's demands. He'd got into the habit of buying a little more than he really needed to so they could cater for last-minute bookings. It also meant that quite often, he had enough for extra portions to provide Sofia and himself an evening meal.

'Remind me what's on the menu tonight?' Sofia prompted as he lifted the pieces of bread from the egg mixture into the hot skillet.

Rupert reeled off the two main courses guests could choose from. He was making a spring vegetable lasagne using fresh silky pasta he'd make this afternoon, vegetables he'd selected from the markets late last night, and a couple of firm cheeses he'd sourced, one a particular favourite for this dish with its infusion of black truffle and one that would create the perfect gooey texture for the menu option. He was also making steak with onion relish and potatoes served in a choice of two ways.

'Which one are you hoping is leftover?' he asked as he set the plate of golden-brown French toast in front of her and prompted her to wait while he grabbed the maple syrup. His mom had brought a big bottle all the way from Vermont as a present for the inn's owner when she visited last year and their supply hadn't run out yet. Rupert had decanted it into several smaller bottles to make the pouring easier.

Sofia drizzled the syrup over her French toast. 'Do you really have to ask?'

'The lasagne,' he concluded, adding, 'it's the cheese.' He carried on washing the last of the pans. 'I'll head out again later and pick up the seafood for tomorrow – I'm thinking swordfish or lemon sole, not sure yet.'

'You're a true gift to this kitchen.' She'd lifted her fork to direct the comment in his direction, even though there was no doubt who it was for.

When she was done with breakfast, Sofia rinsed her plate and slotted it into the almost-full dishwasher. 'I'd better get on with housekeeping and check which apartments need supplies replenished.'

Each apartment, for guests' convenience, had a kitchenette with all the necessities – a coffee machine, a kettle, a small refrigerator, a cupboard with basic provisions. At the inn, they also prided themselves on providing complementary additions like a basket of fresh fruit or packets of cookies and usually during a guest's stay, they got to know preferences. There was little point adding to a fruit basket that went untouched yet the cupboard was cleared of cookies and vice versa.

'Just give me a list,' Rupert said before he caught her eye. 'Are you positive you don't mind me being under your feet?'

The Inglenook Inn had six separate apartments in total, one of which was Sofia's. Rupert had been staying at the inn while his own place had necessary repairs, but a guest had called yesterday wanting a last-minute booking. As one of the strengths of Sofia's business was that she was adaptable, prepared to go the extra mile to accommodate sudden requests, he'd moved into Sofia's spare room to free up the smallest apartment.

'Don't be daft, of course I don't,' she said with a smile as she left him to it.

Rupert dried one of the pans he'd washed by hand. It was hard to think that Sofia had ever considered selling her beloved inn, but she had. She sometimes referred to that time as her *moment of madness*. And he for one was glad she hadn't gone through with it, not only because he loved his job but because this place and Sofia just fit somehow. He wasn't sure whether one would ever be right without the other.

Sofia nipped into the kitchen during housekeeping time to remind Rupert that he had to make a packed lunch for the woman in apartment one today. Once he'd seen to that, he cleaned the kitchen surfaces until they were gleaming and ready for round two, which was either snacks made to order throughout the day or it would be the dinner tonight.

Rupert took his break in the lounge and settled on the sofa to enjoy a long glass of freshly squeezed orange juice and a slice of coffee cake. He closed his eyes briefly, savouring the rest, but the respite didn't last long because Sofia came back into the room and he knew straight away that something was up.

'What's wrong?' She looked so distraught he put down his glass and went over to her. 'What's happened?'

'I just had a call.' Her voice wobbled and she was shaking as it all came tumbling out. Gabriella, her daughter, had been in an accident. Gabriella's husband had called Sofia from their home in Switzerland to let Sofia know that Gabriella was in hospital but he didn't seem to know whether her condition was stable yet.

'What can I do?' Rupert's voice was firm when she looked like she was going to crumble.

'I need to get to her.'

'Of course you do.'

'I need to go, Rupert.'

'I know. So let's get you organised.'

'But...'

He knew her thoughts went to this place: her business, her livelihood. 'I've got it all in hand.' He didn't. He'd never had to manage the place on his own before. Sure, he'd done it for a day or two here and there and it was exhausting. But more than that? Never.

He went over to the computer and pulled up an extra chair for her to slump into. 'First of all, let's get you a flight.'

With the beauty of technology, Sofia's flight was organised and booked for a few hours' time. 'Go and pack your things.'

'But Rupert, this place, I'll have to close.'

'And send everyone home?' He smiled at her, more confident than he felt. 'No chance. I'll make some calls, get some help. Your priority is your daughter.'

She didn't need telling twice. She went to her apartment to pack her things because he knew full well that if it was a choice between the inn and Gabriella, she'd let this place go to ruin. It was what you did, wasn't it, when a family member needed you? Regardless of the consequences, you dropped everything.

But Rupert wasn't about to let the Inglenook Inn crumble in her absence, nor was he going to cancel anyone's bookings.

He stood up tall from the desk, hands interlinked behind his head, rubbing his palms up and down the back of his head as he puffed out his cheeks. How the hell was he supposed to do this? He might have said he could manage, he'd be fine, but already he wasn't so sure.

There was only one person who could help him now.

He took out his phone, found the number in his contacts, and made the call. 'Darcy... it's Rupert. I need you. I mean, *really* need you. Call me.' He only hoped she would. And soon.

2

KATY

Katy released her wavy blonde hair from its low ponytail, the ponytail she only just managed to fashion given it wasn't really quite long enough to tie back. But her job required smart dress at all times and hair was to be pinned up if it was long, which hers apparently qualified as.

As Katy trudged down the street, well away from work, she tugged the discreet clips from her hair that she'd used to keep the stray wisps under control. It didn't matter what her boss thought of her hair now, did it? Because, after a few weeks working her notice, she'd just finished her job as the front desk clerk at a large hotel in Manhattan. Along with a dozen others working various jobs for the hotel chain, she was a victim of what was commonly known as a *restructure*, code for *job losses* in Katy's opinion.

Being out of a job wasn't great but right now, Katy felt free, finally out from under the cloud she'd been working beneath ever since she'd been handed the news in a formal letter. Morale was low amongst staff; even those who still had a job feared it wouldn't be long before the rug was pulled out from under them too, and some had reacted badly by phoning in sick or simply not turning up. Katy was one of the few who'd stuck it out.

She made her way to her favourite bagel shop, in need of some comfort food. She'd been on the early shift today so was finished by lunch time and she was famished. Handily, this place was on the way home. Home. What even was that nowadays? An apartment with her dad when she was twenty-nine years old, not the family home she'd grown up in, but a residence he and she had both escaped to when they desperately needed change. And now her dad had a long-term girlfriend, which meant everything was changing again.

The waitress smiled warmly as Katy placed an order for a bagel with breaded chicken, tomato sauce, and melted cheese. 'Good to see you, Katy.' She came in here often, and when she did, either ordered this or the smoked salmon with cream cheese and capers. 'You work the early shift today?' the woman added as she heaped on a generous amount of fillings to the wonderfully fresh bagel.

'Yeah, for my sins,' Katy joked. She wasn't about to tell her it would be the last early shift for a while unless she found more work soon.

Great flavours, fantastic service with a smile and the best bagels ever, thought Katy as she sat down. But, before she unwrapped the lunchtime delight, she checked her emails again. She'd put out feelers about jobs weeks ago but hadn't had even a whiff of interest yet. And she was starting to worry.

She groaned. Still nothing lurking in her inbox. And so she tried to focus on the good food in front of her right now, rather than the fact she was jobless. Katy hadn't been out of work for years. She'd gone from a retail assistant to a kitchen hand, worked behind a bar, waitressed in more than one café, and upgraded to a restaurant before she moved to hotel work, where she'd held various positions in housekeeping. She'd worked for different employers in the suburbs and in Manhattan and it was to those she'd mainly sent her resume in the hope that her past record might help, but so far nothing.

When she was halfway through her bagel, and her tummy was no longer grumbling at the lack of food, she took out her phone again to scroll through social media. She saw her now ex-colleague Jane had already scored a job as a waitress at a top-end restaurant; Shannon, who had been on the housekeeping team, had shared a picture of her and her boyfriend in Brooklyn along with a caption which read *it's going to be a lazy summer*; and Paul, who had worked as a concierge, had posted a photo of airline tickets. He'd talked about returning to England and his family and he was finally doing it. She left a comment against Paul's post with an emoji of the British flag and her well wishes.

The next post she scrolled to was a sponsored ad for a stunning venue called the Corbridge Hotel out in Inglenook Falls, Connecticut. It looked beautiful, complete with amazing views and a spa. Of course, it was advertising for guests rather than workers, but perhaps it was something to think about: going further out of the city. She was about to click on the ad and see if there were any links to human resources when another ad caught her eye beneath it, this time for a smaller establishment in the same locale. The Inglenook Lodge in Inglenook Falls wanted waiting staff for a two-week period to cover a wedding celebration and Katy knew she was perfectly capable with her experience. It wasn't long-term but it didn't matter. Something was better than nothing.

Katy didn't hesitate to call the number on the advert to speak with the woman who ran the place, someone called Darcy. She didn't get to speak to Darcy directly, but she did leave a voicemail and despite it being garbled, having not planned what she needed to say in her desperation to show an interest and get in quickly, at least it was done. Perhaps later on this evening she'd have to start

extending her search and accept that a commute was very much
on the cards unless something came up close by.

As she enjoyed the last part of her bagel before she really got
back to reality and went home, Katy people-watched, eyes
widening at the man who had fish flip-flops on his feet and
wondering where he'd found those. She watched two elderly men
chatting by the window, one of them laughing so much he was
wiping tears from his eyes. She loved the busyness of it in here and
already felt the pressure of too much time hanging around the
apartment if she didn't have a job to go to.

She drank a large Coke, the fizz making her burp discreetly,
and giggled at the thought of doing that at the front desk. That
wouldn't have gone down well at all. Some workers had altered
their behaviour in their annoyance at being laid off, but Katy was
smarter than that. It was hardly a decision made by the people on
the ground, as it were, and besides, she needed the money she'd
earn until her last day and she definitely needed the reference.
There'd be no burning of bridges, otherwise she'd never be able to
get her own place. It was high time and had her mom not died five
years ago, it might have happened sooner. But Katy had stayed
with her dad after her mom passed and they'd become a close-knit
team, the pair of them. At least they had been until her dad, Wade,
found Stephanie. These days, Katy felt more like a spare part,
because even though Stephanie had her own apartment, she was
usually at theirs.

And home wasn't quite as spacious as it once had been. They'd
swapped a grand Tudor-style house with old-world charm, nine-
foot ceilings and custom mouldings at the end of a leafy street in
Scarsdale for a two-bedroom, two-bathroom condo with oversized
windows, a twenty-four-hour doorman, and a live-in super on the
Upper East side of Manhattan. Katy hadn't hesitated to make the
move with her dad either because with her mom gone, the old

house had no longer felt like home. Moving had been an adventure, a change that finally allowed them to feel a shift in their melancholy to a happier state. An apartment in the city was well away from the constant reminders that her mom, Judy, would never again call up the stairs to say dinner was ready; she would never be reading a book on the porch swing late into the evening, only giving up when the natural light did; she'd never again wrap her arms around Wade in the kitchen the second he got home from work, as though she couldn't bear to be apart from him for too long. All of those things were memories, sewn into Katy's heart, into Wade's too, and the move to the city was a fresh start for both of them.

They said when you lost someone you loved there was a before and an after, and they were right. Katy's life, as well as her dad's, had a very clear dividing line. And now Katy saw another change giving them a *Before Stephanie* and an *After Stephanie*.

Before Stephanie, Katy and her dad had watched movies together with big bowls of popcorn, a lot of which had been found the next day down the side of the couch. It had been watching the Super Bowl together and yelling at the screen when it didn't go the way they wanted. *Before Stephanie* had been lazy breakfasts together on the days Katy's shifts allowed. They'd go to a café they'd never been to and try out the house special. Big holidays had involved heading out into the city to explore something new. One Easter they'd ended up laughing away at the acoustic oddity of the Grand Central Terminal Whispering Gallery. One Christmas they'd discovered the Garland Street Markets and had both known Judy would've spent a fortune there, especially at the knitting stall. Last Fourth of July weekend, they'd taken a picnic over to Brooklyn Bridge Park, where they'd stayed to watch the Manhattan skyline and the Brooklyn Bridge become a magnificent backdrop for fireworks.

Then came the *After Stephanie*, when things changed rapidly.
Movie nights were for three, not two. Stephanie wasn't into
sports, but had arranged for all three of them to watch the Super
Bowl at a restaurant. Katy's dad explored the city with Stephanie,
who knew all the hidden places, having lived here for many
years, and holidays were now shared. Katy had almost been able
to imagine her mom frowning and telling her to give Stephanie a
chance, to appreciate that she really was only trying to do the
right thing. But life had been Katy and her dad for so long, with
all the baggage the family had in their wake, and Katy found it
hard to admit she was struggling with the shift. Part of that was
because she knew she was being unreasonable – her dad
deserved to choose who he spent time with, he should be happy
– but her protective guard had gone up the moment Stephanie
came on the scene. She hadn't expected the union to last, if she
was entirely honest, she'd thought they'd have a bit of fun and
they – or rather Stephanie – would get bored. Wade was almost
ten years older than her, and Katy had thought they wouldn't
have much in common at all. But they never seemed short of
things to say, they laughed together, and they both regularly
went to the driving range at Chelsea Piers, although so far, Wade
hadn't persuaded Stephanie to accompany him for a proper
game of golf at the country club he'd been a member at for
years.

Katy hoped that whatever the future held for Wade and
Stephanie, nothing would come between her and her dad. She'd
lost enough family as it was.

* * *

When Katy arrived back at the apartment, Stephanie must've
heard the door and came out of the kitchen, into the narrow

hallway of the two-bed condo that was fine for dad and daughter, but these days felt cramped.

'Hey, Katy.'

Katy switched on a smile and tried to talk herself round to being more open and conversational. 'Hey.' She dropped her house key into the bowl on the table and hung her bag on a hook against the wall.

'How was work? Wade said it was your last day.'

Katy bristled as she kicked off her shoes. 'Busy,' she answered. She'd told her dad when she got given her notice but she'd avoided talking about it ever since. This was the first time Stephanie had mentioned that she knew and Katy supposed she should feel grateful she hadn't been grilled before now.

If Judy was still alive, Katy would've probably talked to her mom about it every single day. She had a knack for conversation, they both did, and their lengthy talks were one of the things Katy missed the most. They could go on for hours, batting around ideas, moaning about big things but also the little niggles in life if they felt they needed to. They'd talk about everything and nothing at the same time. Wade had found it fascinating they could go on for so long. Nowadays he did a good job with talking, but he had always been quieter than Judy; he was the one who disappeared into his thoughts the most, happy in his own company. Katy's bond with her dad lay in other things like watching the game or getting excited to try a new restaurant or coffee shop that had opened up. Or at least it had *Before Stephanie*.

'You've got something on your shirt.' Stephanie stepped closer and pointed a nude-painted nail towards something in a slightly darker shade on Katy's cream top. Stephanie was a savvy dresser. She wasn't skinny, she wasn't a big woman either, but she wore things that flattered her curves and showed off slender legs. And rather than disguise her greys, the colour of her mid-length hair was a faded caramel with streaks of grey allowed to show through in such a way that it looked incredibly natural.

Katy plucked it off. 'Bagel.' And she added, 'Thanks.'

'Was it good?' A piece of bagel definitely wouldn't look good on Stephanie's sky-blue, light-weave top.

Usually Katy would harrumph and head for her room. But she was an adult, she knew she should try to be mature about her dad's relationship. 'Very good. Lashings of melted cheese, breaded chicken.'

'You're making me hungry, haven't had any lunch yet. I'm about to have a milkshake, though, would you like one? It's strawberry.'

She followed her into the kitchen. This was what made Katy feel worse. She might think that Stephanie was all wrong for her dad, but she couldn't truly point out many reasons why. 'No thanks, too much with the bagel. But I appreciate the offer.'

Stephanie whizzed the blender and eyed Katy as though confused as to why she was hanging around and not leaving the room as soon as she could, so Katy took out a glass, adding lemon slices from the fridge and ice from the dispenser before filling it with water. She stood beside the floor-to-ceiling window that had a view of the street, a view she couldn't imagine ever growing tired of. If you stood in the centre and looked between the buildings opposite, you caught a glimpse of green, a little sliver of the magnificent Central Park that lay beyond.

'Dad not in?' Katy asked when the blender came to the end of its task.

'He'll be back soon. He's out for a run. I'll have one of these ready for him to enjoy after his shower.' She poured the mixture into the two waiting glasses and slotted them both into the fridge.

'You're not drinking it?'

'I'll wait for Wade.'

Katy frowned as a thought came to her. 'I didn't think Dad liked milkshakes. He always said milk should taste like milk.'

'That was until he tried one of these.'

'Oh.' She zoned out as Stephanie began talking about the fruit she'd added, the scoop of some funny powder that had special properties and did something or other.

Katy's dad had only dated one other woman since his wife died, a woman he'd gone on a blind date with after a well-meaning friend set them up. That woman had left him wondering what the point of dating even was. He'd never looked happy after they'd been out and after the fourth time, he'd called it quits. Katy had been beyond relieved; they'd even managed to laugh about it. Perhaps it was time to trust her dad's judgement and maybe notice the little gestures Stephanie did that proved she wasn't out to hurt Wade. He'd lost the love of his life, the woman he thought he'd grow old with, and Katy had no idea what it must feel like for him. All she wanted was for him to be happy.

'I'm going to get changed,' Katy said when Stephanie had hovered beside her, taking in the view long enough for it to feel a little uncomfortable being so close to one another. 'I might head to Central Park for a walk around.' It was one thing losing her job, but quite another to be confined in the apartment all day.

'Good idea. The April showers appear to have passed; we've already had some glorious May days.'

Katy managed a smile in Stephanie's direction before she headed to her bedroom to change, but rather than going straight into the en suite to freshen up, she flopped down on her bed on her tummy, her head turning to focus on the picture of her mom in the silver-plated frame on her nightstand. The photo showed her mom some twenty or more years ago, pushing Katy on a swing in the park, her smile as big as her daughter's. And every time Katy looked at it, she could hear the laughter, her own giggles, the warmth of her mother's presence and bond.

'I wish you were here to talk to, Mom.' She kept her gaze on the photograph as her fingers toyed with the intricately set pearl of the rose-gold necklace her mom had given her for her eighteenth birthday.

She leaned over, pulled out the bottom drawer of her night-stand, and took out the pink suede photograph album her mom had made and given to her alongside the necklace on her eigh-teenth. The pages of the hardback album contained the story of her life from the day she was born, and she flipped through the special memories.

'I don't know what I'll do next,' Katy said out loud to the photo-graph of her at age nine holding her mom's hand as, dressed in a bumblebee costume, she went door to door, trick or treating. 'You'd know what to say to me, wouldn't you Mom?' She smiled. 'I bet you'd make my favourite cookies, for comfort purposes, of course.' She was speaking quietly, knowing she'd sound mad if Stephanie overheard, but she did this often and it helped. She missed her mom, the pain an ache that no medicine could ever get rid of. It had been five years and she'd give anything for just one more day with her, twenty-four simple hours to be together.

Before her mom got sick, Katy had been working in Manhattan for a couple of years, doing the commute between the city and Scarsdale. She'd soon started dating Shaun after meeting him at a bar at Rockefeller Center. They already knew each other from years before but had never been romantically involved until that day. And then everything seemed to go wrong at once. Katy and Shaun had talked about moving in together but had realised they were better suited as friends. It sounded like an easy break-up, but it had still been an adjustment and Katy had just got her head around that when her mom found out she was sick. One minute

Judy had been in great health, the next she wasn't. Or, at least, that was the way it had felt. And Katy's world had slowly begun to crumble.

What had started off as a small mole on Judy's scalp and seemed so inconsequential that nobody even went with her to the dermatologist to get it checked out had turned into the start of something big. Judy was diagnosed with melanoma, stage 4, and it had already spread, invading her body and her organs, taking her from them less than a year after diagnosis.

During the time her mom was sick, Wade had to keep working – the medical bills were piling up and the only thing that would cover them was his high-paying job. Katy had eventually taken a leave of absence and become the one who spent the most time with Judy apart from health visitors, and she'd known then, and still knew now, that she wouldn't have changed it for the world. Shaun had carried on their friendship, he knew their family well, and even though they were broken up, Katy couldn't imagine having got through it all without him. He'd stopped by to cook dinners or bring takeout, he'd been there to talk to and for Judy to chat with when Katy simply needed a break, and he'd helped Katy make her mom's final days as stress-free as they could be under the circumstances. He'd taken her dad out for the occasional beer to support him when Judy begged someone to get Wade away from the house because he was moping around as though the world was ending. Katy had tried to point out that his world *was* ending without her in it. But she hadn't needed to. Her mom knew it already.

Katy puffed out her cheeks, put the photograph album back into the drawer, and closed it as she brought herself back to the present, back to reality.

Katy had joined the workforce the moment she finished college and now she felt like an epic failure for having no job to go to and absolutely zip on the horizon. In her early twenties, not having a job for a time wouldn't have stressed her out, she'd have been fully confident about finding something else, but given all her enquiries this time had come to nothing, she was beginning to doubt how easy this would be.

She freshened up in the en suite before grabbing a casual top from its hanger and pairing it with denim pants. She pulled on her white sneakers and took a lightweight cardigan from the wardrobe. She'd only just opened her bedroom door when she heard voices and realised her dad was home.

She was about to go say hello when she zoned in on the conversation not meant for her ears.

'You said you'd talk to her, Wade.' It was Stephanie's voice.

'I will, I promise, I'm just putting it off,' Wade replied, and it went so quiet Katy sensed they were having a moment.

Katy made a bit of unnecessary noise closing her bedroom door to announce she was around – she didn't want to go in mid-conversation – and once she was in the kitchen, smiled at her dad as though she hadn't heard any part of their talk, even though she wondered what her dad was putting off.

She had a sinking feeling that he was going to ask her to move out. That couldn't be it, could it? She knew it was time, but he'd never rushed her before. Not *Before Stephanie*, anyway.

Her dad was drinking the milkshake Stephanie had been making him earlier and she was enjoying hers at the same time.

'I thought you only liked plain milk,' Katy pointed out as soon as she joined them.

But Wade shrugged after another glug of the thickened liquid. 'Turns out I like milkshakes. Who knew?' And he planted a kiss on Stephanie's cheek as though she'd been the one to invent the concept.

'How was the run?' Katy registered the sweaty T-shirt and

shorts and tried to keep the conversation light. She was deter-mined not to let it show that anything was bothering her.

'Best time yet.' He had muscular legs, never seemed to put on much weight around his middle, and even though his once-thick hair had thinned on top, it suited him. 'Not bad for someone who didn't take up running until recently.'

And that was another thing. It wasn't only milkshakes Wade had been introduced to. He'd never run before, at least not since his college days; he was a golfer and a walker and that was the extent of it. *Before Stephanie.*

'Are you sure you don't need the go-ahead from the doctor?' Katy frowned. 'Shouldn't you get a clean bill of health before intro-ducing something as strenuous as running?'

'I'm still standing, aren't I? I don't know, Katy. You worry too much about me. I'd hug you and tell you I was perfectly okay if I wasn't so sweaty.'

'I think I'll pass.' She tried to make light of it, but she'd meant what she said. Was running really a good idea when he hadn't pushed himself that much in years?

And now she had to ignore her dad messing about as he pretended he was going to hug Stephanie and she did that girlish giggle that said *don't come near me* but really meant she was enjoying the flirting.

Her dad turned his attentions back to Katy and noted the bag she had with her. 'Are you going out somewhere?'

'Walking,' she said. 'Central Park.'

'Well, it's a beautiful day,' Wade concluded as Stephanie refused his help and pulled over a step stool so she could climb onto it and put the blender jug away in one of the uppermost cabi-nets. 'Winter is over.' Now he'd set down his empty glass, he put up his arms as though he were part of the spectator crowd at a sports event.

'Oh, Wade, winter has its benefits.' Stephanie took his outstretched hand as she climbed down once again and put the step stool away between two of the cupboards. 'Cold weather is cosy; we can take romantic walks in the snow, go away to a cabin for the weekend, and build a campfire.'

Katy didn't want to think about her dad and his girlfriend having a romantic interlude anywhere, whether revoltingly sweaty in the heat or at a winter temperatures so cold that it could turn your breath into mist every time you spoke.

Wade took his sunglasses from the top of his head where they were still nestled, having only just come back, and he put them on. 'Give me sunshine any day.' He began to make a joke about making Stephanie go to Florida all winter and Stephanie batted back that she'd prefer ski lodges and hot cider.

Katy filled her water bottle at the sink and as she turned around, she didn't miss the look her dad exchanged with Stephanie after he'd put his glasses back on top of his head. It was clear the exchange between the pair had to do with the part of the discussion Katy had overheard moments ago and whatever it was that Wade was putting off telling her.

'All right, you two,' she said in a tone that sounded like roles had been reversed, with them the minors and her in charge. 'What's going on?'

Stephanie said nothing but looked to Wade.

Wade reached out and took Stephanie's hand in his.

Here it was. They were going to announce they wanted Stephanie to move in and that it was time Katy moved out.

'The thing is, Katy...' Wade stumbled. 'Well, Stephanie and I...' He looked at her and smiled. 'We're getting married.'

Katy felt like a walker on a pleasant stroll who'd just been knocked over by a runner who hadn't been looking where they were going.

'Married?'

'I asked Stephanie last week and she said yes.'

Katy eventually looked at Stephanie, but she couldn't smile, she couldn't say much at all. Eventually she managed, 'But it's... quick.'

'I know it's quick, but we've thought this through. And we wanted to tell you first. It won't be a big affair, something small in a week or two; as soon as we find a suitable venue we'll let people know.'

Katy's mouth went dry. 'Did you say in a week or two?' Surely he meant months rather than weeks.

'Yes, I know it's soon but we've been thinking about it for a while. There doesn't seem any point in waiting and Stephanie wants her best friend Marnie to be there before she heads overseas with work for a couple of years.'

Katy felt hot, then cold, then numb, then in pain. She felt nauseous, confused.

'Katy...' Her dad waited anxiously for her to say something.

'It's soon,' Katy babbled.

'Yes,' he said as though hoping merely establishing the fact might help her understand what was happening. It didn't. The proposal was one thing but a wedding in record time wasn't something she could make sense of.

'I'd love Marnie to be there,' Stephanie put in. 'I don't want her to miss it and we have thought about this. I promise you.' She looked to Wade who had hold of her hand and gave it a squeeze in reassurance. 'We both want this, we're both sure.'

'Right,' said Katy. She stared at them both and then, despite her dad having been for a run, she stepped forward and put her arms around him. 'Congratulations,' she mumbled against his neck. She wasn't even sure she'd said it loud enough for anyone to hear.

'Oh, look, I'll ruin your outfit,' he grumbled when at last she let go of him and stepped back. 'I'm all sweaty.'

'Congratulations,' she repeated, this time to Stephanie before she looked away and said, 'I'd better go.'

'We'll talk later,' Wade called out to her before she'd made it out of the kitchen. When she stopped he suggested, 'Dinner tonight? Stephanie is dining with friends in Brooklyn this evening. We could go to our favourite Japanese restaurant if you like or get a takeout. Or I'll cook. Your choice, Katy. It's up to you.'

He was sounding desperate to smooth things out with her now and Katy would console him if she had it in her. But she didn't, not right now. 'Sure, Dad. Dinner would be good.' She put the bottle of water into her bag. 'I'll see you both later.'

And she didn't let her smile slip until she was outside the apartment.

She greeted the doorman downstairs warmly as though nothing were wrong at all and enquired after his grandson Hugo, who had just started at Princeton.

Eventually she emerged with considerable relief back into the sunshine and the hustle and bustle of New York life. She made her way through the streets and towards Central Park, intent on a leisurely stroll in the spring sunshine, but with every step, she upped the pace and ended up in more of a march around the Jackie Onassis Reservoir. Every step bore her frustration and she barely slowed her pace until she'd completed the lap when she stopped and took a few swigs from her water bottle. She leaned on the fence, looking out across the water.

They were getting married?

She hadn't expected that. At all.

Asking her to move out might have been easier to process.

At a slower pace, her energy levels as well as her enthusiasm for anything flagging, Katy changed direction and made her way towards the Great Lawn.

She'd lost a job and was on her way to gaining a step-mom in a matter of days.

Right now, nothing seemed fair at all.

3

RUPERT

Rupert came out of the kitchen during a break in breakfast service, with four guests currently ensconced in the dining room enjoying plates filled with sausages, egg, hash browns, and mushrooms. He wanted to check on Darcy, who was not only a good friend but someone in the hotel trade who knew her stuff. Darcy had jumped right in with the job, having managed the Inglenook Inn in Sofia's absence once before, and shared as much knowledge with Rupert as she could. She'd gone through everything from laundry requirements and the computer system used for guest records to reordering soaps and little extras for the apartments. He'd always helped out with more than chef duties but never to the extent he'd need to do now. It might seem like a small establishment to most, but for the Inglenook Inn to run smoothly, what they really needed was another pair of hands. And Darcy couldn't do this the whole time Sofia was away. She'd been dividing her time between here and her own inn in Connecticut, and they both knew that it was a very temporary solution.

'How's it all going?' he asked as he found Darcy at the front desk in the lounge.

'Not too bad.' Her blue eyes lit up with her smile but faded when she added, 'I'm afraid I haven't had much luck finding anyone to work here yet. I'd thought a couple of my contacts might come through, but...' She picked up her phone as if to check again but set it down pretty quickly afterwards.

'Have you spoken to Sofia since she got to Switzerland?'

'Not yet.' She pulled at the ends of her shiny dark hair as she worried. 'I don't want to hassle her.'

'Gabriella is your best friend from school, Sofia like a second mother to you. I don't think it's hassling and she wouldn't mind.'

'You're right, she probably wouldn't. But I'm sure she'll call when she has news. I texted to say I was thinking of her and that I was here with you.'

'I really appreciate this, Darcy. I didn't know who else to call. I panicked because I told Sofia everything was in hand, but I'm not sure why I did that when clearly I've no idea what it takes to run this place single-handedly.'

'Don't be defeated,' she encouraged with a smile. 'And what are friends for?'

'Friends are there to check whether you're okay.' He leaned on the door jamb of the communal lounge so he could see whether any more guests came down the stairs for breakfast. 'Are you? Okay, I mean.' If she needed to, she spent the night in Sofia's apartment, but they rarely had much downtime to chat and he could see this was all, unsurprisingly, taking a bit of a toll on her, even though it hadn't been going on much more than a few days.

'Keeping busy is the best way for me to be right now.' Her voice caught mid-way through her sentence.

'Ah, so you're using me to keep your mind off Gabriella,' he joked, hoping humour might help her feel less stressed. 'Wondered why you leapt in so eagerly to help me.' When her shoulders relaxed, he assumed his comment had gone some way to lightening the tension. 'And you're really sure Myles doesn't mind you being here rather than at your inn full-time?'

'Myles is on top of things at the Inglenook Lodge, don't you worry.' She was rummaging in the bottom drawer and looked up to add, 'Assuming responsibility is no problem for him; he enjoys it.'

Her husband Myles had gone from investment banker to joint hotelier with Darcy and from what Rupert heard, he didn't miss the rat race one bit. 'You two are taking the hotel trade by storm.'

'And you need help.' She waved the folder she'd pulled from the drawer. 'I should've thought of this before.'

'What is it?'

'It's a list of people who have previously worked here on a casual basis. There aren't many but I can make some more calls.'

'That would be a godsend.' Jill, part-time cleaner at the inn, had already called in to say she'd got two of her sick grandchildren with her for at least a couple of weeks, so she'd be off work. No Jill and no Sophia meant an even more demanding workload and therefore a problem for him and the inn.

Before Rupert could say more, he heard guests' footfall on the stairs. 'I'd better get back to the kitchen.'

After he'd given the latest arrivals to the dining room a chance to peruse the small menu on their table, Rupert went through and took the order for two lots of pancakes and two portions of waffles. Back in the kitchen, as he poured the batter into the pan and tilted it to spread the mixture to the edges, he hoped they could find someone else to help out here. There was no way he could do it all on his own when Darcy returned to her own inn full-time. Last night, he and Darcy had cleaned two of the apartments ready for check-ins this morning. They'd removed all the bedding and sorted out loads of laundry, remade beds and all of that while they took turns to go downstairs if they heard the bell at the desk announcing a guest needed their attention. It didn't sound all that time-consuming, but it was if you did it properly, the way it was usually done, and no way did he want standards to slip in Sofia's absence.

Rupert didn't pause in the kitchen for a good hour before he left the clearing up and went to see Darcy again. He found her at the front entrance at the top of the stoop directing a guest to the Guggenheim Museum. Rupert helped another guest hovering in the lounge, waiting for Darcy's return, and noted down their request for a late check-out tomorrow. It wasn't always possible, but he told them he'd see what he could do. They didn't appear confused that a man in a kitchen apron complete with grease spatters was helping them rather than the lady in the smartly cut pants with a pristine white blouse; Rupert supposed people might soon have to get used to it if it was just going to be him. He had visions of his kitchen becoming chaos, the floors of the inn and the entrance wouldn't gleam like they did now, the apartments would only get a basic clean, and he'd probably have to halve his sleep to keep up with everything.

When Darcy came inside, she beamed a smile his way.

He held out his arms in expectation. 'Tell me you have good news.'

'Two interviewees coming in the next half an hour.'

'Fantastic. Thank you, Darcy.' That was another thing she'd taken on board: the interviews, which were time-consuming to arrange and deal with. He hooked a thumb over his shoulder to let her know he had to get back. Leaving the kitchen a mess was something he never did and it would play on his mind until it was done. 'You're one in a million!' he called back as he set off down the hallway.

'Don't thank me yet,' she replied.

But he refused to think of it as anything other than positive. In what felt like no time at all, but had probably taken him a long while, he had the kitchen sparkling. And next it was on with any special requests. He had a request for a couple of packed lunches, so he prepared a gluten-free pasta salad which could chill nicely until midday, he selected the fruit he'd use for a colourful fruit salad and set it aside to prepare at the last minute, and after he'd cut up a selection of crudites, he made a non-dairy dip with lemons, anchovies, and mustard.

By the time Rupert ventured out of the kitchen again, Darcy was mid-interview in the lounge. She was sitting in one of the armchairs by the front window to talk with the candidate and Rupert thought the young boy looked passable.

When Rupert's phone sounded, he quickly turned back the way he'd come and pulled it from his pocket. In the dining room, he answered with, 'Hey, Ma, how's it hanging?'

'I wish you wouldn't say that, Rupert,' she admonished, but he detected a light note in her voice. He could imagine her in her floral print pinafore apron, standing in her kitchen next to the range. It was her favourite place, she said, and he'd always known her love of cooking had been passed down to him. She wasn't a chef or a professional cook, but home baking was something his mom had been born for. She baked for all the local school fairs despite the fact that her children had left education a long time ago, and if ever there was a fundraiser, she was supplying baked goods almost before the organisers had had a chance to notify the locals.

'It's our greeting,' he grinned as though she could see him all the way from Vermont.

'You're not wrong there,' she sighed.

He frowned and stopped folding up the corners of one of the tablecloths that needed taking down to the laundry in the basement. His mom wasn't a woman who sighed; she was a doer, practical, not one to sit around and ever feel sorry for herself. 'What's up?'

She hesitated just a moment and he wondered whether she'd dismiss the suggestion that anything could possibly be awry.

'It's Natalie.'

Of course it was, Rupert thought. He was one of five Gray siblings, him being the oldest, with twin sisters Maisie and Amy only eighteen months his junior at thirty-two, his sister Cameron, who had just turned thirty, and a fourth sister, Natalie, who was twenty-eight and often in trouble. She'd been the only one of them to ever be suspended from school, she'd broken curfew more times than any of them, and she never seemed to have much direction when it came to what she wanted out of life. She'd finished school and then bounced from office clerk job to office clerk job, never sticking in one position for long. Sometimes he had to wonder how his parents, Verity and Frank, had ever managed to hold it together with five kids all so close in age and one still at home with them.

'What's she done this time?' Rupert asked when his mom offered nothing further. His little sister might have been in a bit of trouble over the years, but he loved her to bits and she was fun, kind-hearted, and spirited. He wondered if it was because she was the youngest that made her trials and tribulations seem so much worse now the rest of them were older. And in the same way everyone assumed he as the eldest was strong, capable, and knew what he was doing, with Natalie being the youngest, everyone assumed the very opposite: that she was disorganised and only one step away from messing up.

'It's a long story,' Verity confessed. 'Do you have time for a chat? I mean, I know you're at work.'

He was about to say of course he had time when he noticed through the open door that Darcy was showing the interviewee out. 'Listen, Mom, I hate to do this, but can I call you back another time?'

'You're busy, I'm sorry.'

'Don't be, never too busy for you, Ma, you know that. Well, apart from now, just that we're in crisis mode.' He briefly recapped about Sofia and Gabriella, the accident, the dire straits they were in if they couldn't get some more help.

'Oh, poor Sofia, do please let her know she's in my thoughts. I'll let you go. I'll call you again in a few days when things have calmed down.'

'I can call tonight.'

'No, don't be silly. You've got your work. I just get frustrated with your sister, that's all. Reminds me of myself at her age.'

'If you're sure that's all it is?'

'Of course. We'll talk soon, promise.'

When he hung up, he wasn't so sure of his mom's claims that it was nothing and he also wasn't so sure it was a good thing if Natalie reminded his mom of herself at her age. From what Verity had told her kids, she'd been a bit wild before she settled down with their dad and started a family. She'd told them snippets here and there about how she'd joined a band, gone on the road, and partied in places she would never allow her kids within a hundred feet of.

He'd have to talk to her about Natalie again later but, right now, as he made his way to the communal lounge, his heart sank. Darcy's face said it all about the interviewee who just left. In the absence of phone calls or guest requests, she was sitting at the desk, leaning back in the chair and looking up at the ceiling as though it could supply the solution to the problem.

'He wasn't what we're looking for.' She shifted her gaze from the ceiling to Rupert. 'I mean he was polite, friendly, he had references, but he stank of cigarette smoke and chewed nicotine gum the entire time we talked. I saw it churning around in his mouth.'

'I saw it too, even from a distance.' He pulled a face.

'I can't inflict him on guests; it won't do much for the reputation of this place.' She checked her watch. 'I've got another due any minute, let's hope she's a bit better.'

'I'm going to put one of the tablecloths in the wash and then, if it's all right with you, I'll duck out to the market for food supplies.'

'Of course. I'm here all day and it's important you keep ahead with the food side of things.' She ushered him away but not before she asked, 'What's on the menu tonight, out of interest?'

'A favourite of yours – fresh tuna.'

'You doing extra?' she asked hopefully.

'Of course I am.'

'You know I love it.'

'Exactly right, and you've stepped in so heroically, I had to make it. You'll get to enjoy it as well as the five other guests who have ordered a dinner. And myself, of course.'

'Off you go to the markets, I'll let you know how the next interview goes.' But when her phone rang, she pressed answer and told him it was Sofia.

As she spoke with his boss, Rupert heard voices coming from the hallway and two guests came in to announce they were having trouble with the bathroom door in apartment five. He went upstairs to check it out. The door had been temperamental for a while and now it had dropped a fraction more to make it difficult to close. He hoped it was merely a case of tightening the screws on the hinges, which wasn't a big job at all and one he could manage easily enough rather than calling in a handyman, which might take days.

'I'll have it sorted for you soon,' he told the guests, and rather than go to the markets as he'd intended, he went straight down to the basement to grab the toolbox. He felt as though he'd begun his work here as a chef and over the last few days had expanded his working repertoire to include receptionist duties, a role as a cleaner and now, a handyman.

They really needed some extra help.

He got what he needed and back up in apartment five, it was as he'd predicted. Once the screws were tightened, the door closed easily enough.

Back downstairs, Darcy had finished her call.

'How's Sofia? And Gabriella?' He set down the toolbox.

Darcy exhaled, clearly relieved at the news. 'Gabriella is going to be fine. She's recovering well by the sounds of it – battered and bruised but she'll be home in a day or so.'

'That's a relief.'

'Sofia sounded like she'd just had the weight of the world taken off her shoulders.'

'I'll bet. Did she give any idea when she might be back?' He puffed out his cheeks. 'That sounds selfish of me to ask.'

'No, it doesn't, and Sofia is fretting about this place herself, which is how I know she's less worried about Gabriella and that Gabriella will be fine,' she smiled. 'Sofia told me she needs to stay a while longer; perhaps it'll be a few more weeks but she didn't specify. I don't think even she knows. At this stage, it sounds as though Gabriella will need help with everything from bathing to getting up the stairs to bed.'

'Her grandkids are still very young too.' He definitely felt selfish now. Sofia must be run ragged physically as well as emotionally.

'Gabriella's husband has apparently been great but he'll need to get back to work soon. Sofia says his parents have agreed to fly out there in a few weeks but until then, I think Sofia has had such a big shock that she needs to be sure they'll all be okay when she leaves them to it.' She was smiling again, the good news about her best friend having its effect. 'The grandkids are wearing Sofia out but in a good way, if you know what I mean. I think she's embracing the time with her family.'

'She's got enough energy for them all, that's for sure.' And then he added jokingly, 'I thought I might at least get a hello from her or maybe an enquiry as to how I was managing.'

'Are you feeling neglected?'

'Actually, it's nice that she trusts me. Not sure she should. I'm panicking slightly at how I'm going to manage all this.'

'She does trust you. And don't panic, that won't do any good at all.' She let out a sigh. 'I didn't tell Sofia we have no cleaner and nobody to help you out when I head back to Inglenook Falls full-time. I left out those tiny details.'

'She has enough to worry about.'

Her eyes at last fell to the toolbox; he gave her the gist of the problem and what he'd done to fix it.

When the front door went, they both looked up, but it was a guest rather than the other interviewee and by the time Rupert had been down to the basement to put the toolbox away and returned, they still hadn't turned up.

'Well, time-keeping obviously isn't their strong point,' Darcy grumbled.

'How long can you realistically help me out here?' Rupert thought he might as well get straight to the point.

'Honestly? A couple more days at most. Myles and I have a wedding party in three days' time and he'll need me there full-time for that. We've been advertising for extra help for a while.' She put her index finger in the air as though she'd just thought of something. She picked up her phone and as she clicked on a number and put the phone against her ear, she told Rupert, 'Myles has started the interviews, let me see how he's getting on.'

Rupert hung around eavesdropping because he knew where Darcy's mind might be going. If they had a list of workers and found one for them, perhaps there would be someone on the list for the Inglenook Inn too.

'If you're happy with who you've chosen, don't factor me in, Myles, I trust your judgement.' Myles must've said something amusing as Darcy laughed before asking, 'Anyone else on the list?' She crossed her fingers and met Rupert's gaze. 'Uh-huh, uh-huh, uh-huh...'

Rupert was about to leave her to it when she ended the conversation with her husband and put both thumbs up. 'We have a contact.'

'We do?'

'Myles found someone for us already, but he had another applicant who lives here in the city. She left a number and it sounds like she has the right experience. He's sending me the contact.' Her phone bleeped to prove the point and she immediately clicked on the contact details her husband had sent her. 'I'll call her right away.'

He listened to Darcy leave a voicemail explaining who she was, how she'd come to have the number, and what they were looking for at the inn.

'Fingers crossed she calls me back,' said Darcy.

'And let's hope she turns up too,' he said, heading off to make the list for what he needed from the markets.

'Positivity, Rupert!' Darcy called after him.

He was trying.

4

KATY

Katy had been on her way out of the New York Public Library when she switched her cell phone off silent mode and saw the display announce she had a new voicemail. She'd called the number the woman left right away and spoken to Darcy, the owner of the Inglenook Lodge, who was here in the city at the Inglenook Inn – which Katy had never heard of – and wanted her to come for an interview as soon as possible. Katy tried to schedule it for tomorrow, but the woman had insisted it be today. Then she'd tried to get it in a few hours rather than immediately but at that point, Darcy somehow read her mind and told her it didn't matter whether she was dressed for it, they really needed to recruit someone, and fast.

Katy had headed straight there.

The tree-lined streets and hub of cafés, bars, and restaurants amongst traditional brownstones gave Greenwich Village a definite charm. Katy turned a corner, then another until she was in the street she needed. She was a good ten minutes earlier than she thought she'd be. And it didn't matter that Darcy had told her to come as she was; Katy still wished she'd had a chance to head back to the apartment and change out of her ink-blue, casual top with button embellishment down the sides, a top that had once been smart but now was verging on the side of worn-too-many-times. She also had on denim capri pants that had seen better days and she never would've worn them in a workplace, let alone to an interview where she needed to impress.

She ran a hand through her hair, tugging at a slight knot at the back, which must've formed as she walked around Central Park and then strolled the city streets before ending up in the library. Inside its walls, she'd felt like a woman of leisure, browsing the book aisles and flipping through novels at whim and in all honesty, she hadn't minded it too much. But when she'd got the call from Darcy, it made her realise she didn't want too many days of freedom and now she kept everything crossed that this would be a good interview.

Katy made her way along the brownstones and when the sign for the inn was in view, she'd almost reached it when she heard someone call out her name from across the street.

Using both hands to hook her hair away from her face, she focused on the man coming towards her. 'Shaun?'

The beaming smile of her ex-boyfriend met her as he scooped her up in a bear hug. When he finally put her down, she asked, 'What are you doing here? I thought you lived in Dubai these days.' It felt so good to see him.

His blue eyes danced, his blond hair catching the sun. 'I moved back a few months ago. Too much heat, you know, missed the winter.'

She reached out and pushed his arm jokingly. 'You did not. You're like Dad, you hate the snow and the cold.'

'Time to be back with family and all that,' he said before grinning again. 'I meant to get in touch but moving countries is a crazy time, I'm afraid I hadn't got around to it. It's *so* good to see you, it really is.' He hadn't aged much at all. Perhaps a hint of crow's feet around his eyes when he smiled back at her, his skin was golden as it always had been every summer, and he looked good in a well-cut, grey suit he wore with a pink shirt that might not look right on a lot of men but sure did on him.

'The family are all well, I hope.' She wanted to excuse herself and get to the inn. Already she was imagining Darcy looking out on the street and concluding her latest applicant had no sense of urgency. That wouldn't do her much good.

'They are. Still getting on my back about settling down.'

She began to laugh. 'They were always going on about that, I remember it well. Listen, I—'

'How have you been?' She could tell by the way he said it that he was asking how she'd been since her mom passed away.

'It was a long time ago.'

This time, he reached for her, picked up her hand, and squeezed it. 'It doesn't matter, and I know how close you were.'

'I can't believe I haven't seen you since the funeral,' said Katy, realising again that he'd already left America at that stage, that he'd only come back for the funeral, for her, even though they weren't together. She could vaguely remember his words of comfort, encouragement she'd get through it, but it had all morphed into a bit of a blur. She'd got to the end of what felt like the longest day of her life, attempted to accept condolences when all her and her dad wanted to do was close the door and grieve in private. And the one person they'd both hoped would be there hadn't been and it had added to their heartbreak with a vengeance.

Katy checked the time. 'Listen, Shaun, I've got somewhere I need to be.'

'You look good, Katy.'

'Now I know you're lying,' she smiled. 'And I really do have to go, I have a job interview.'

'Yeah?' He eyed her casual attire. He knew her well enough to know she didn't have a problem looking professional.

'I know, I don't look dressed, but it was last minute.'

'How about a coffee after? It would be great to catch up if you have some time.'

'Today?'

'Sure, why not? I don't live too far and I'm working from home for the rest of the day.' He took out his cell. 'Give me your number and I'll text, then you'll have mine. Let me know when you finish and we'll arrange it.'

He hugged her goodbye and it felt familiar, welcome, a comfort after so long. 'See you soon. And good luck.'

'Thanks.' She wished she could catch up with him now, but it was time to focus.

She really needed this job and she was going to have to come across exceptionally well to detract from her scruffy attire.

* * *

Darcy finally took a seat across from Katy in the communal lounge of the Inglenook Inn, situated at the front of the classic brown-stone. Katy had arrived and been shown into this room by someone called Rupert, who was the chef. He had kind, brown eyes and the sort of hair that had a fringe which flopped in a stylish way, despite the fact he must be used to the temperature of a kitchen. Most men didn't end up with hair like that unless they had the help of styling products, but she couldn't quite imagine the inn's chef doing that. He'd brought two coffees – one for Katy, one for Darcy – before he'd left them to it and Katy had waited for Darcy to finish checking someone in. It had given her a chance to take in the ambience of the inn, which was so delightful. She couldn't believe she hadn't known it existed until now. From the outside, if the name of the inn wasn't there, you might be forgiven for thinking the classic brownstone that stretched a good three floors above this one was somebody's home. Inside, certainly in this room, the furniture was classic and comfortable, two armchairs positioned in the slightly curved bay window with a long sofa stretching out in the room in front of a coffee table.

'I'm sorry I'm not dressed a little smarter,' Katy began. She wanted to make sure this woman understood that she knew how to dress appropriately, despite their earlier conversation on the phone. 'You caught me when I was out and about. I don't feel very professional.'

'I'm just grateful you came as soon as you could,' Darcy smiled warmly. 'And I feel it my duty to warn you that this might not be the most professional of interviews because we may well get interrupted by the phone, a guest, who knows. It's unpredictable.'

'I understand.' Already Katy liked her. The relaxed atmosphere made her feel a little better about her casual appearance.

Darcy closed her eyes and sipped her coffee in a way that suggested this might be the only chance she had to grab a bit of respite. 'Right... now I've had that very much-needed mouthful of coffee, let me introduce myself properly.' She explained again how she didn't usually work here but out in Inglenook Falls and had stepped in last minute when the owner had been called away unexpectedly. 'Sofia was willing to let the inn close, but Rupert rightly refused to let that happen. It's exactly what I would've done.'

'The chef?'

'Chef, general dogsbody at the moment, I'm afraid. So far, he's not only cooked but cleaned, checked guests in and out, answered calls, and carried out maintenance. To say this has put a lot of weight on his shoulders is an understatement. Which is where you come in.'

Katy was ready to list her experience, but Darcy seemed to want to give her the lowdown first and told her a bit about the inn itself. She recounted a bit of her own history in the process – she'd worked in hotels for a long while, travelled to various countries to do so but had come home here to Manhattan.

'I think it's always nice to know a bit about a place where you're thinking of working,' Darcy added.

Thinking of working? Katy would chew Darcy's arm off if she was offered this position. She hated the thought of being out of work. Today had been fine, wandering around the city and the library, but she couldn't be out of the apartment all day every day avoiding talk of her father's impending marriage. And a new job would not only give her a much-needed financial injection but also a place to be until she figured out what to do next.

'Do you have any questions so far?' Darcy took the chance to take another sip of her coffee.

'Could you recap on what my duties might be?'

But before they could continue, they were interrupted and after a mouthed apology, Darcy went to help a guest who needed directions to Pier 61.

'Sorry about that,' Darcy smiled when she came back over.

'You did warn me.'

'I did. Right... duties. For a small establishment, there's a lot to do here and with Rupert in the kitchen, we need someone front of house as much as possible – responding to guest queries, making sure emails are answered, the phone, there's the check-in and check-out process. Then on top of that there's a bit of cleaning involved... with your experience, I assume cleaning isn't usually in your job description. Are you still interested?'

'Of course. It really isn't a problem.'

'There's an evening turndown for some guests, perhaps

helping out with dinner service depending on how many guests are booked in, making sure the inn is presentable at all times.'

'How long do you expect the role to last for?'

'I'm afraid I can't be exact, but I would imagine at least a couple of weeks, perhaps more.'

Katy wished it was longer but at least it was something to tide her over.

Darcy picked up her coffee again. 'I don't have your resume, so why don't you give me a rundown of your experience and previous positions... it'll give me a chance to finally finish this.'

Katy recapped her work history, listing roles and responsibilities, and hoped she'd made a good enough impression. During her recount of her working life to date, they were only interrupted twice more – once by a guest saying a simple hello as they headed out and the other by a delivery that Darcy brought through and dumped by the desk far back enough that nobody would trip over the cardboard box.

'Now, anything else you'd like to ask me?'

This question usually tripped Katy up in interviews that felt like they were coming to a conclusion unless she had something prepared, but Darcy had made her feel so welcome, her words seemed to come naturally now as she said, 'Perhaps I could take a look around and you could talk again about what happens here on a daily basis.'

They started in the kitchen, where Rupert took a moment to say hello. He shook Katy's hand firmly, meeting her gaze, and she couldn't help but note the strong chiselled jaw accompanied with the slightest hint of stubble, nor his muscular forearms as he went over to the sink to wash up a large pot. Darcy talked for a while in the kitchen, explaining breakfast service, snacks on request, and dinners. Katy listened while Rupert went back to cooking whatever it was that smelt so good. Before they left, he smiled at her again and she wondered whether it was a *nice to meet you* smile or a *thank goodness I might be getting some help soon* smile. Darcy had already explained that she couldn't be here full-time or indefinitely with her own inn to manage.

They checked out the dining room and Darcy talked more about the actual inn itself. 'It's a walk-up building so no elevator unfortunately.'

'I guess it keeps you fit.'

'It definitely does that. Sofia briefly considered whether to forego this dining room and have a suite in here for anyone who couldn't cope with the stairs, but she needed the space for breakfasts and dinners. Now, if she ever gets requests for accessible rooms, she points guests in my direction out in Connecticut – I have an option for guests to use a room on the ground floor. They don't always want to be out of the city, but we've had a few who've told me that actually it proved to be the best thing for their holiday. They came and saw the bright lights of Manhattan but also had the taste of small-town living.'

As they made their way all the way up to the top floor, Darcy explained they were at full occupancy. Passing each apartment, Darcy gave a rundown of what was behind the door and as they chatted, Katy felt a rising desire to get the job. They finished their tour in the basement where there was an extra refrigerator and freezer, the electrics, the laundry, and lots more storage.

'So, what do you think?' Darcy asked her as they went back up the stairs.

'Of the inn?'

'The inn, the job?' She led the way back to the lounge at the front of the brownstone and they settled into the armchairs once again.

'It's a gorgeous place, the job sounds just what I'm looking for.'

Her brows knitted together in confusion. 'Shouldn't I be asking you what you think of me?'

Darcy began to laugh. 'This has not been my most professional of interviews. I'm usually prepared with questions, I don't give away such a sense of desperation.'

'I can go away and come back later if you like.'

'Oh, no, don't do that. We can't lose you!'

'So I've got the job?'

'Yes, you have the job,' Darcy smiled. 'If you could forward your resume to me, that would be great.'

'I can do that now,' said Katy, holding up her phone, 'it's in my email.'

'Great.' Darcy shared her own email address so Katy could forward the document. 'I'll print it out, keep it on file. Sofia does that with people who've worked here; she keeps their details and in case of emergency like this, we usually have a pool of former staff to contact. Didn't work out this time, none of them were available, but I'm so pleased you were. And before I forget: I know you live in the city already but with the unpredictability right now, and with Rupert so busy in the kitchen, is there any way you'd consider living in?'

Katy thought she might have to pick her jaw up off the floor. It all felt too good to be true. 'How much would it cost me to live in?'

'It won't cost you anything. The smallest of the apartments here is occupied at the moment but our guest checks out today and then we've not got anyone booked in for a while. It's very comfortable,' she added as though Katy needed more convincing. 'There's a small refrigerator in the kitchenette and a newly installed en suite.'

'As long as it has a bed, I think I'll be set,' Katy smiled.

'I'm afraid there may well be very late nights as well as early mornings. You and Rupert can juggle them between you, of course, he's not work shy at all, but as I said...'

'His main job is chef, I understand.'

'It's not that you won't get a break,' she added quickly. 'Just that some days it might be erratic – you know what it's like in the hotel business, work doesn't always spread itself out through the day. It might be a case of adjusting to the needs of the inn,' Darcy added, unsure.

'I can be flexible, not a problem at all.' She suspected Darcy meant she might not be able to plan evenings or weekends or anything in between but she didn't mind. She just wanted a job, even a temporary one, as soon as possible.

'It's a lot to ask for you to have this much responsibility along-side Rupert, but I do hope the rate of pay compensates for that.'

They'd discussed the hourly rate and it was slightly more than Katy expected, especially living in, but she'd assumed that was down to the open-ended nature of the job.

'Does Rupert live in too?' Katy wondered. She wasn't sure how she'd feel if it was just her.

'He does at the moment. He usually goes home to his own apartment but while his place was having work done on it, he'd moved in the small apartment which will be yours, then we needed it for a guest and he went into Sofia's spare bedroom – her apartment is number three – and now he's staying at Sofia's until she's back. The guest in the apartment you'll be using checks out in about an hour's time. I can show you it then, you'll see it's a nice space.'

Katy smiled. She felt as though Darcy were the one on trial here rather than her. 'You honestly don't need to sell it to me any more. I'm *very* interested in both the job and the opportunity to live in.'

'I don't mean to sound desperate...' Darcy went on, ignoring the phone ringing at the desk and waving to Rupert, 'but when can you start?'

Katy shrugged as Rupert went to answer the phone. It really was all hands on deck in this place and Katy kind of liked it. It was smaller than a hotel, personal, friendly. 'Whenever you like.'

'Is now too soon?'

She was about to laugh at the joke but then realised Darcy was actually serious. 'I'll need time to go home and pack my things, but I can be back in a couple of hours.'

'Just bring all the formal bits when you come back – some ID, social security number.'

'Sure.' She shook Darcy's hand as closure for the interview.

'Thank you, Katy, I'm so pleased you applied to the Inglenook Lodge and ended up being able to fill in here instead. Now, if you'll excuse me, I'd better go help out.' And she went over to the desk.

Katy was making her way to the front door when Rupert, who must have followed her out of the lounge, called over to her. 'Welcome aboard.'

She was smiling as she opened the front door to the inn and looked back at him. 'Thank you. I'll see you later on.'

And he lingered in the hallway, leaning on the door jamb of the lounge, muscular arms folded in front of him. 'Yeah, see you soon.'

* * *

Her head filled with the excitement and relief of a new job, Katy made her way home. When she reached the apartment block, she remembered Shaun, so before she got into the elevator, she sent him a text to say she had the job with an immediate start and couldn't do coffee. She added *Another time* because she meant it. He knew her, her history, her family... all of it. She didn't have to explain herself, make excuses for the way she dealt with things, because he just knew.

'Is that you, Katy?' Her dad's voice came from the kitchen the moment she went into the apartment. Today's events had been a good distraction to stop her thinking about her dad and Stephanie's announcement, but now the pooling of dread in her stomach was back. She was fretting that this was fast, that her dad was rushing into something. The shape of their family was about to change yet again and she couldn't rid the sinking feeling she'd felt ever since she was told about the engagement and the sooner-rather-than-later wedding.

Katy found her dad at the kitchen counter, poring over a recipe book, apron on. 'I thought I'd make us something, that we'd stay home and talk.' He was smiling until he saw her reaction.

Katy put a hand to her head. 'I'm sorry, Dad. I forgot I said I'd have dinner with you tonight.' And he was cooking? That was something he'd have baulked at *Before Stephanie* – once upon a time, he would've leapt at the chance to get takeout, but slowly she'd been encouraging him to have more cosy meals at home.

'You're not cancelling on me, are you?' He said it as though it couldn't possibly be the case, but her face told him it really was. 'Look, I know—'

'Dad, it's not your news, that's not why I'm cancelling. It's just... well, I have a job.'

'Already?' His smile was back and he wiped his hands on the drying cloth before coming to give her a hug. 'Congratulations, Katy.'

'Thank you. It's an immediate start.' She laughed. 'Like now.'

'Now?' He whistled between his teeth. 'That really is immediate.'

'They're totally desperate.'

'They'll be glad to have found you, then.'

'Let's hope so.'

'Katy...' His voice stopped her from leaving the kitchen. 'We really do need to talk.'

'We will, Dad. I promise.'

'Are you angry? Upset?'

'Dad, I really can't talk now, I need to get on and pack.' And avoidance was welcome until she could sort through her emotions in her own head.

'What do you mean you need to pack?' He was following her out of the kitchen, back along the hallway to her bedroom.

She turned to face him and gave him the gist of the inn, the owner's predicament. 'It's a live-in position so I am available as much as possible.'

'Just you?'

'Me and one other, Rupert, the chef there, except he's more than just the chef, he seems to help out with most things but obviously can't do it all on his own.'

'I suppose it'll be a good experience to add to your resume.'

She'd gone into her bedroom and was down on her knees, pulling a suitcase out from underneath the bed. 'Let's hope I do well at it.' As she packed, she told him more about the inn and what her responsibilities would be.

Her dad left her to it and, once Katy had freshened up and changed her clothes, she emerged to see him hanging around. 'Can I at least take you?' he asked.

'No need, I've ordered a cab.' She waved her phone in the air as if to prove her point.

'Well, at least let me help you take all these bags downstairs.'

'Now that you can do.' She smiled. Wade and Katy: they'd been a duo for so long, the two of them taking on anything that came their way.

When they reached the foyer, Katy explained to Eric the

doorman where she was off to when he asked and he congratu-
lated her before her dad hugged her yet again.

'Can I at least have the full address?' Wade prompted.

'Dad, don't be dramatic. I'm still in the city, I'm not all that far
away. And I'll text you the address as soon as I get in the cab.' Eric's
deep rumbly laugh that always lightened a situation sounded
when she looked at him and said, 'Anyone would think I was going
for good.'

Wade helped her into the cab, Eric doing the honours with the
rest of her bags. And, after waving to them both, she sat in the back
seat as the car made its way through Manhattan amongst the traffic. She felt bad that her dad was going to all the trouble to cook a
special meal, disappointed they wouldn't share an evening just the
two of them, but also relieved that she didn't have to talk to him yet
and try to be completely honest when it came to her feelings about
his impending nuptials.

Because if she was totally honest, he might not like what she
had to say.

She wanted him to be happy, but he was beginning to change –
in little ways for now, but how long before he changed so much she
barely recognised him?

Was that really what she wanted? What he wanted?

And were either of them really ready for Stephanie to become
a member of their family?

That was something Katy wasn't sure she'd ever be able to get
her head around.

5

RUPERT

Rupert washed the pile of plates that hadn't fitted into the dishwasher earlier, swirling around the soapy water on each one to ensure they were back to the way they should be.

'I think they're clean,' said Darcy. He hadn't realised she was right behind him filling a jug of water and slicing up a lemon to go in it. 'Thought I'd put this out at the bar. It's only spring but the days are warming up; guests will appreciate the refreshment.'

'I'll bring some glasses through when I've finished in here,' he told her. He'd been in a world of his own and slotted the last plate into the rack by the sink before pulling out the plug to let the water escape. His mind had been on the newest recruit at the inn: Katy.

Katy was pretty but more than that, there was something about her – her smile, her demeanour, the way she'd looked around the inn like it could be more than merely a place to work. He was excited to see her again.

He shook himself. Maybe it had been way too long since he'd been involved with anyone and that was why the sudden interest. The last woman he'd dated, Siobhan, had been on-again, off-again, the type of relationship that suited them both for more than a year until they called it quits. Now he had friends in Manhattan and back in Vermont, he had a big family and he had his work, which left little to no room for anything else.

Rupert took through a tray of small glasses for Darcy to put next to the water jug.

She looked up from her desk. 'I just spoke to Sofia – she says hello and apologises she didn't get to talk to you again but she'll reply to your email. She wasn't on the phone long – she had to go help Gabriella in the bath.' She let out a slight laugh. 'Gabriella would've hated that. She doesn't even like having her hair washed at the salon, says they spend a weird amount of time massaging her head.'

'Most women love that part.' His mom did. She had a monthly trim and blow dry at the local salon and refused to have it any other way. 'Isn't it called an Indian head massage?' He was sure he'd heard one of his twin sisters talking about it.

'No idea, but I'm more than happy when I get my hair done – the longer I get to relax, the better.'

He wiped down a spill at the edge of the bar he'd somehow missed attending to last night, although he'd also been putting on another load of washing as well as folding sheets, tasks being added to his repertoire whenever required. Was it any wonder his duties were all over the place? 'Between you and me, I think Sofia, despite being worn out with the grandkids, is enjoying taking a step back from this place. She sounds quite happy in her emails.' She'd been eager to check up on him, that he was coping, and of course he hadn't given her the slightest hint that he had any worries on that score.

'I get it. She works hard and when it's your own place, you never let up. It's hard to admit when you might need a rest. I'm really surprised she'd never hired more help here before, you know.'

'She's always said it was unnecessary, apart from the odd time it got crazy busy or she needed a holiday. The good news is she doesn't want to sell the inn, but I think this emergency dash overseas has made her want some help on a more permanent basis, if only to give her a day or two in the week to herself.'

He leaned against the corner of the desk while Darcy scrolled through something on the screen. 'Maybe the new girl will work out.'

She looked up at him.

'What?' he said. 'What's that smile?'

'You know…'

'No, I don't. All I'm saying is that you obviously really liked her, she's got the experience and presence this place needs.' From the look on her face now, he was only making it worse.

'I saw the way you looked at her when she came in. And the way she did a double take when she saw you, for that matter.'

'The poor girl was flustered, having been summoned across town by you,' he defended. 'I wanted to help, I only brought out coffees.'

'All right, I believe you. And it *was* a great coffee, a much-needed one for me.'

'You'll always be nice to me when there's coffee involved,' he joked before he left her to it.

* * *

Once the kitchen was put back to rights, Rupert got his list and at last was able to set off for the markets. He liked to have everything as fresh as possible and so far, he timed his visits for when Darcy was at the inn so there was a contact point in his absence, something Sofia prided herself on. There was nothing worse for a guest than not being able to speak to someone in charge.

Rupert sometimes liked to linger at the markets – it didn't feel like work choosing ingredients, musing over what recipes he could use or experiment with, talking with the vendors – but today he had to cut any chit-chat short, even with the woman who sold him the freshest Yellowfin tuna. He was keeping tonight's dinner menu simple – no point trying anything too fancy when he couldn't spend his whole time with his head in the kitchen. They had a new member of staff in Katy – at least they would if she showed up, people had been known not to – but she'd need a settling in period to know what was what. Rupert's motivation wasn't only because he liked her, probably more than he should when they would be working in close proximity; he wanted her to work out for Sofia's sake and Darcy's. Darcy needed to get back to her own inn full-time, but she was such a good friend to both him and Sofia that she was doing her utmost to make sure he was sorted first. She also had another vested interest, however, and that was more on the sentimental side. Not only had Darcy co-managed the Inglenook Inn a while back; it was also where she and her husband Myles had fallen in love.

When he got back to the inn, Rupert took a call from his sister Amy. Usually Amy was the sister who got straight to the point, but she'd started the conversation asking how he was, a sure way to tell there was something on her mind and she was gauging how to talk about it.

He set the shopping bags down at the top of the stoop and sat down, leaving room in case anyone wanted to go in or out of the doors. 'What's up, Amy?'

'I'm worried about Mom.'

After his last phone call with his mom, he'd texted to check up on her and arrange a time to chat but she'd brushed away his concerns and said she was far too busy baking cakes right now for the library fundraiser. He sensed she'd regretted troubling him with her worries the first time round and was now trying to avoid doing so. From memory, there'd be no getting into the kitchen or having a conversation this week if she was baking her renowned carrot cake with thick frosting that made your mouth water and her famous lemon blueberry cake, which had just the right amount of sweetness and tang. Verity's focus now would be right where she wanted it – on something she could control rather than whatever was going on in the family.

'I got the impression something was up with her,' Rupert confessed to Amy. From where he was sitting, he could just about make out a few bruised clouds through the trees. 'She seemed worried about Natalie.'

'That girl.' Amy's frustration was evident but then she'd never bothered to hide her exasperation with the youngest sister of the Gray family. 'You know she came home drunk, again? At least I think that's what has Mom all over the place. She must have been bad, right? For Mom to react this way.'

'What way?'

'Having an opinion but not really sharing it with the rest of us. That tells me Mom is worried.'

Rupert had always got on with Natalie and sometimes he thought the others were a little hard on her. She was the youngest; it was easy to forget they'd been through many of the same things. 'She's always partying, I don't see how this is any different, but I'll talk with Mom once she can drag herself away from baking.' He ran a hand through his hair, which probably needed a cut – he didn't want to ever risk the dreaded hair in the food at the inn. 'For now, let's try not worry too much. Natalie is single, she's enjoying herself. Nothing different to what you or I have done.' He'd done this a lot too, reasoned with one sister or another, calmed them in a crisis. 'And definitely no different to Maisie before she settled down with Noah, remember how bad she was? She could out-party the lot of us.'

'She really could.' She managed a laugh, but it didn't last long. 'I saw Natalie the morning after when I turned up at the house. She looked bad, Rupert. It looked like more than a hangover.'

'Are you sure you're not mothering her a bit too much?' That was another thing his sisters tended to do with one another. Perhaps, as the only boy and the oldest, he'd escaped being treated in the same way.

With a sigh, Amy told him, 'You've always been blind to her faults.' He could imagine Amy with her chocolate-brown hair, so thick it needed a couple of clips to pin it away from her face every day in her job as a kindergarten teacher. She had a no-nonsense attitude and if something was wrong, she wouldn't hesitate to say so if she thought she was being fair. And clearly she did in this case, doing it out of concern for her family.

'I love *all* my sisters,' he assured her, imagining her flushed cheeks at the emotional declaration.

'I know you do, same,' she said, matter-of-factly.

When a guest came out of the door to the inn, he made sure he shifted over a little more and gave them a smile and a wave. 'Listen, Amy, I'll call Mom again soon and I'll sound her out, work out what's going on.'

'I'm sorry, this call is all about Natalie and Mom and I know you're having a tough time. Mom said your boss has had to fly overseas unexpectedly.'

He recapped on the story a bit and appreciated the support. 'But as of this afternoon, we will have a new member of staff, which is a relief.' And a pleasure, he hoped.

When they finished the call, he thought he might get a few minutes inside to call his mom now, but a smiling Darcy greeted him alongside a guest who had a late request for dinner this evening. 'Not a problem,' he told them. This was why he bought plenty of everything. And this was what Sofia prided herself on here at the Inglenook Inn: being able to adjust to guest requirements in the blink of an eye. He wasn't about to let the standards slip, not on his watch.

In the kitchen, he got going with the prep straight away. He didn't always, but with other tasks to do in Sofia's absence, he wanted to get ahead as much as he could. He portioned the tuna, covered it, and put it into the fridge. He made a vinaigrette dressing with vinegar, garlic, herbs, and a touch of chilli, washed the mixed salad leaves, and prepped the runner beans and a generous number of potatoes. He was so ahead of time, he whipped up a simple vanilla cake that he'd drizzle with icing and add sprinkles to, always handy to offer guests and staff. Things like this were never on a specified menu but coffees could be requested, teas, or cold drinks, and he and Sofia had agreed it was nice to offer a variety of things. Some days it was biscuits, either made here or store-bought, other days he made something, as he was doing now.

Once the cake was in the oven, he took a tall glass of orange juice into the lounge for Darcy. It felt like the least he could do.

'Thank you,' she enthused when he delivered it to the desk. She took a few sips before telling him, 'While you were out, I cleaned the apartment for Katy and made up the bed.'

'I told you I'd do all that.'

'No time. We don't want her to arrive to a mess. She might run for the hills.'

'True,' he laughed. 'I'll be sure to replenish supplies in the refrigerator for her.'

He was about to head back to the kitchen when he heard a noise at the front door and when he looked, he saw the outline of someone standing on the other side.

He pulled it open and a smile spread across his face at the sight of Katy. 'You came back.' If it was possible, she looked even better than she had when they'd met earlier. Instead of pants that finished above the ankle and hugged her figure nicely, she had on a pair of inky denim jeans and a smart white shirt with a design of intricate pale blue flowers. The same rose-gold necklace with a pearl in its centre he'd noticed earlier sat in the dip between her collar bones and he wondered whether she ever took it off. It looked too delicate to sleep in or shower with it on. The thought of her showering had him clear his throat and give himself a stern reminder that she was a co-worker.

'Of course I came back.' A bulging bag over her shoulder, she smiled as much as he had and Rupert got a good feeling about her, about them working together. When she turned to get a suitcase and another bag from the stoop, he stopped her. 'Let me grab those.' He picked up both items, neither of which were too heavy, just cumbersome, and headed inside. 'Tell me you didn't walk with all of this.'

'Of course not. Cab all the way, my dad's treat. It's like he paid to get rid of me.' She pulled a strand of wavy blonde hair from the side of her mouth that must have blown there from the spring breeze.

'I sincerely doubt that.' The words he'd said under his breath almost gave away the attraction he felt but he distracted her by calling to Darcy that Katy had arrived.

Darcy came out of the lounge with Katy's key to hand over.

'Why don't I put your things in your apartment?' Rupert suggested. 'You two talk.' He gestured for Katy to loop the bag she was carrying onto his arm and as she did so, he told her, 'The apartment is clean, the bed is made up, provisions are in the refrigerator, and I expect you even have chocolates on your pillow.'

'Wow, I feel like a guest.'

'I can't guarantee you'll get the same treatment every night, but welcome to the Inglenook Inn.' He smiled back at her as he started up the stairs.

In Katy's apartment, he set down the suitcase and bags. It was a compact space but enough for one in the short term. It had a double bed, which was more than comfortable, a small en suite bathroom with a shower, a kitchenette with a few cupboards and a refrigerator, and a window that had a view of the street. The single panel radiator kept this place warm enough in the winter and the window he'd left ajar kept it cool enough in the spring, before summer brought with it the need for the small aircon unit. Darcy had made up the bed with a more feminine set of bedding than he'd had when he stayed in here, this one duck-egg blue with pink flowers – neither Darcy nor Sofia wanted standard white hotel bedding throughout; they thought the Inglenook Inn deserved a more personal touch. Darcy had also left miniature soaps in the bathroom, a hand soap and hand cream in the kitchenette, a welcome basket of fresh fruit on the side along with other treats like pancakes, maple syrup, and luxury chocolate. The chocolate gift extended to the pillow; she'd placed a small see-through bag of pre-wrapped chocolates there.

He closed the apartment door behind him and, back down in the lounge, handed the key to Katy. Darcy was on the phone again and Katy told him, 'She's already shown me how to book a guest in – she did it when she was on a call. And she's done some printouts with idiot-proof notes for me.'

'I doubt you'll need those.'

A heart-shaped face looked up at him. 'I'll be slow but hopefully get the hang of it quickly. New systems are always tricky until you're used to them.'

'From memory, whenever Sofia has the tech guy come in if she has issues, she tells him to keep it simple. I think if she had any choice in the matter, she'd ditch the technology and go back to paper, but she's a savvy businesswoman and she knows that won't work in the long-term.'

'She sounds like a good boss.'

'She's the best boss I've had and I know it's cliché in some businesses to say this, but she's like family.'

'No, I get it. Some places I've worked I would *never* say that but in other places, sure.'

A moment's pause hung between them. 'Anyway,' said Rupert, 'any issues and you can always ask me, I'm here most of the time and if I'm not, I'm never far away.'

Darcy finished up on the phone and must've caught the tail end of their conversation because she said, 'Rupert can help you with anything, Katy. Just ask, he doesn't bite unless you get in his way in the kitchen.'

Rupert pretended to be shocked. 'I've never bitten, Darcy, you know it.'

'True, he's as gentle as they come,' she batted back.

'Will you need me in the kitchen?' Katy asked.

'I haven't needed a kitchen hand yet,' said Rupert. 'Even when it's really busy and we're at maximum occupancy, the most Sofia has had to do is take meals out to guests. She's tried to offer help plenty of times, but it's not needed.'

Katy smiled. 'Well, you know where I am if you need me too.'

'Good to have you on board.' When Darcy took another call, he prompted Katy. 'Go check out the apartment.'

'Thanks, I will.'

Rupert went to take the cake out of the oven and set it on top of the cooker to cool. Back in the lounge, he watched as Darcy talked on the phone with someone while simultaneously slotting the papers that were sitting on the printer into a folder for Katy. Darcy had to be one of the most organised women Rupert knew and that was saying something, growing up in his household of seven. His mom was similar. She'd run their house like a military operation. Their family home was so organised that even his dad's garage and shed had proper shelving and storage to keep things in order.

Unlike the rest of the Grays, Rupert and Natalie had been the messy rebels of the family. It had taken leaving home for Rupert to sort himself out when it came to being organised and a little bit – okay, a lot – neater. When you were independent with a career and not living under the family roof any more, it was time to take control and once he'd done that, he'd realised he liked it that way. He wondered now whether his mom was just getting frustrated with Natalie and wanting her to move out, stand on her own two feet, and take a bit of responsibility. But it wasn't anyone else's responsibility other than Natalie's, so she had to get there on her own, and it wouldn't be a suggestion his sister would take kindly to if it came from him or any of her sisters.

Katy was back soon enough. 'It's perfect,' she said.

'You don't want to unpack?'

Darcy apologised when the phone rang and Rupert told Katy, 'Go upstairs and do some now if I were you, while Darcy is around. You might not get another chance.'

She didn't hesitate for long. 'You've probably got a point.' And he did his best not to watch her go back up the stairs to her apartment.

Darcy finished up on the phone. 'Myles is wondering when I'll be on my way back.'

Rupert nodded. 'I think we've got it from here.' Although he wasn't really so sure. Darcy had a calming presence and, having worked here before, knew the place inside out, but it wasn't her responsibility now. It was his. And Katy's. 'Darcy, you came and saved my ass, you got me Katy and she seems like she'll fit right in.

You've shown me everything, I have your details and Sofia's if I need to ask anything. You can go home.'

She smiled. 'You can do this.' But as she looked once more at the folder she'd put together for Katy with information he'd used a few times himself already, her worries kicked in again. 'Are you totally sure?'

'Not at all,' he chuckled. 'But time to cut those apron strings and let us take it from here.'

'You're a good man, Rupert.' And she looked relieved at his confidence, whether it was put on or not. 'It's a shame I'll be missing tonight's dinner, you know I love tuna, but I can't wait to get back to my inn. *My* inn... even though it's been the case for a while now, it still feels good to say it. And our first hosting of a wedding party there is an exciting step up for us, I can't wait.'

'I'll bet. When Sofia's back, I'll head over to Inglenook Falls again and see the place for myself again, perhaps get Myles out on a run.' Darcy's husband had loved New York when he first came here, running through Central Park, on the High Line.

'We'd both like that – he needs reminding to take a break sometimes.' She'd collected a couple of bits and pieces from the desk. 'Let me go and organise my bags and I'll come back to talk with you and Katy before I leave.' He was about to say no need, but she added, 'Just let me run through what needs to be done one more time.'

'Fair enough. Now go get organised, I'll stay here and hold the fort,' he told her when the phone rang yet again.

'That'll likely be the electrician... there's a buzzing on the light switch on the top landing.'

He took the call and, sure enough, it was the electrician confirming he'd come tomorrow morning first thing. He let the woman staying in the apartment on the top floor know – they'd already asked her not to use the light switch to be on the safe side and put a table lamp outside so she could better see at the front door – and he offered her a complementary room service breakfast to make up for the inconvenience. She'd merely laughed and said there was no need for any fuss at all because they were hardly putting her out.

Darcy had just come downstairs with her things when Katy returned from unpacking.

'Right, you two...' Darcy spoke as though she might be talking to a couple of kids.

Rupert shared a quick smile with Katy as Darcy recapped some of the daily chores and where things were kept until eventually she ran out of steam. 'Are you absolutely sure you no longer need me?' she finished.

'We're more than capable of handling this place, aren't we, Katy?' Darcy had checked this girl's references and she really did come with glowing recommendations.

Katy smiled tentatively. 'Sure, we've got it from here.'

'Darcy, go.' Rupert got the impression if he wasn't blunt, she'd never leave them to it. 'Go back to Myles, back to your inn, and I promise we'll shout if we need help. Did you order a cab?'

'I'll hail one outside.'

'I can do that for you.'

'Oh, no, you don't. Plenty of cabs go past or at the end of the street.'

He hugged Darcy tightly. 'Thank you, thank you, thank you. You saved me, you found me help. What else can I say?'

'Say you'll come to dinner soon, that's all I need.'

'You're on, I'd love to.'

Darcy said goodbye to Katy and the second the door to the inn closed, a couple of guests came down from upstairs and Katy was right on it, finding a leaflet about the Empire State Building on request and recollecting rough prices. 'I went there not so long ago,' she explained when the guests went on their way. She seemed buoyed with having stepped in already. And when her phone rang, she apologised, took it out, and rejected whoever the call was from.

'I usually have it on silent at work,' she said, her cheeks flushing slightly.

'No need here, unless you're helping with dinner service or speaking with guests. And you'll be here from morning until late in the evening, you'd be pretty incommunicado if you switched it off until you were in your apartment.'

'Not always a bad thing,' she smiled.

His phone interrupted them this time. 'My turn. Don't these people know we're busy?' When he took his phone from his back pocket and saw his sister Natalie's name flash up on the display, he rejected it the same way Katy had with her caller.

'That was my sister,' he admitted. 'One of them, anyway.' And he didn't have time for any extra drama just yet; the inn and its smooth operations were too important right now.

'How many do you have?'

'Four.'

'That's a lot.'

'Sure is. How about you?'

'No sisters, no.'

'Brothers?'

She hesitated and then shook her head. 'It's just me.'

There was something else there, he wasn't sure what and he didn't know her well enough to ask, so he hooked a thumb over his shoulder in the direction of the kitchen. 'I'd better get on. I've got an earlier dinner service tonight. There'll be plenty of extra food for you too – I don't know whether Darcy mentioned it but it's the usual arrangement: I buy enough to make extra meals in case of last-minute bookings and when they don't happen, usually there's enough food for myself and Sofia or Darcy or whoever else is here.'

'Count me in, if that's okay.'

'Of course it is. Any allergies?'

'None, but I do have a strong dislike for parsley, so you'd better warn me if you're putting that in anything.'

'Will do, I promise. Tonight it's fresh tuna with a leafy salad and vinaigrette dressing, roasted lemon potatoes, and fried green beans. Absolutely no parsley whatsoever.'

With a smile, she said, 'I only hope I'm not too busy to eat.'

'You'll make time. I'll be sure to remind you – had to do that with Darcy more than once.'

Rupert returned to his domain and with the dinner prep all done, he finished off the cake by drizzling it with icing before adding sprinkles. He also whipped up a chocolate mousse and put it into individual glass pots ready for dessert. It was an easy recipe, one people seemed to enjoy, and it meant it was already setting in the fridge ahead of time and he wouldn't be so pressured in the kitchen this evening. Fewer dinner guests and keeping it simple were a good idea when it was him and Katy handling everything on their own for the first time.

He soon headed to the front of the inn to check whether Katy was coping all right and found her sitting in the same armchair she'd been in for her interview, giving a guest the lowdown on some of the most talked-about museums in Manhattan. Rupert greeted Miss Davenport when she came downstairs from the top floor and made her a Cosmopolitan at the bar in the corner of the lounge as Katy continued to share her local knowledge. It was a definite added bonus of having her here – he knew enough about the city, but he'd only been here a fraction of the time Katy had.

Rupert left Katy chatting away and went back to the kitchen, satisfied she didn't need his help for now. He cut some chocolate shards ready to put on top of the mousses when they were set enough and was whistling the same tune as the one playing on the radio a while later when he heard Katy knock on the kitchen door.

Without turning around, he pushed another chocolate shard into one of the mousses, concentration required with the delicate treat. 'I'll be with you in a minute.'

Having her in his domain felt more personal, somehow, than anywhere else in the inn.

He turned around once he was finished with the last mousse. Katy was hovering at the door, her hands on the frame as she stalled from coming in. And before he could tell her it was fine, the door flew open, almost taking her with it, and in came Natalie. Arms outstretched, she barrelled towards her brother and wrapped him in a hug.

'Natalie! What are you doing here?'

'Well, don't sound too pleased to see me, will you?' she admonished.

'It's not that, just a surprise, that's all.'

And when he looked at the doorway, Katy had already made a sharp exit.

Perhaps she was even better at sensing impending drama than he was.

6

KATY

Katy was glad to have a job. And a live-in one at that. But she hoped whoever this arrival was with Rupert in the kitchen right now wasn't going to cause trouble. She hadn't banked on sharing the inn with his girlfriend – she wasn't confident in a job she'd only just started and for all she knew, he'd got in extra help, got rid of Darcy, all so he could kick back with his girlfriend and lay all the blame on the new girl's shoulders if the inn didn't function as it should in Sofia's absence.

Rupert and whoever the girl was appeared shortly after Katy had sat down at the desk in the lounge and Katy tried to rid the frown from her brow at the latest development.

Rupert wasted no time introducing them. 'Katy, this is my sister, Natalie.'

'Your sister?' Katy, trying not to make her relief obvious, straightened her shirt and stood up, holding out a hand. It made sense now she could see them both side by side. They each had the same olive complexion and brown eyes, but while Rupert's looked trusting and kind, Natalie's seemed to hold a sense of mischief and trouble. Or perhaps she was reading too much into it when they'd only just met.

'Yes, for my sins,' Natalie smiled. 'He's older, waaaaaay older.'

'Enough of that,' Rupert joked.

Katy could tell he and his little sister meant the world to one another and she felt a pang of envy. 'Well, it's good to meet you properly,' she said before looking at Rupert. 'She didn't want me to spoil the surprise earlier, so she didn't want to say who she was.' Katy had asked Natalie to wait in the lounge while she went to tell Rupert he had a visitor, but her request had been ignored.

'I had no idea she was coming,' Rupert whispered in Katy's ear when he passed the desk on his way to the bar. He asked his sister whether she'd like a drink.

'Do you have root beer?'

He nodded. 'Coming right up. Katy?'

'Nothing for me, thanks.'

Natalie had gone over to the sofa and slumped down onto it as though she'd had a long journey, which maybe she had, and Katy went over to Rupert. 'Is she staying here?' She kept her voice low as she sensed Natalie might not appreciate being talked about.

Rupert dropped ice cubes into a glass from the bucket on the side of the bar. 'She hasn't booked in, so I assume she's staying in the city.' But the uncertainty in his voice gave away the fact that he had no idea. 'Don't worry, she won't get in the way.'

While brother and sister caught up, Katy responded to a couple of online queries. She still wondered whether she needed to pinch herself – she'd taken Darcy's call, had an interview, been offered a job and started it as well as moved into a different apartment all in less than twelve hours. Katy had already unpacked most of her things in the apartment upstairs and for a small space, she had a surprising amount of storage, or perhaps that was because she really hadn't brought all that much. At her dad's apartment earlier, she'd shoved as many of her toiletries into washbags as she could and collected bits and bobs from her bedroom, including her photograph of her mom and Samuel, the teddy bear her parents had given her when she went away to college.

She'd been grateful to Rupert for helping with her luggage. He was kind, he was courteous, and Katy watched him now in the lounge as he sat with his sister. On the surface, he seemed pleased to see Natalie but at the same time Katy picked up some hesitation and she wondered whether he was asking himself why she'd turned up out of the blue. Rupert was surreptitiously watching Natalie rather than humming or whistling like he had on the other occasions Katy saw him. He'd told Katy that Natalie wouldn't be a problem, when surely that wasn't how you introduced a family member. Katy didn't have to know much about a family to detect tension; she'd had enough of it in her own to know that these were clear signs.

Rather than thinking about brother and sister, Katy tried to turn her focus to familiarising herself with the information Darcy had collated: the details of daily and weekly tasks at the inn, the checking in and out system, which earlier had looked easy enough. But she couldn't help overhearing some of the conversation in the room, or at least the tone of it. The body language had altered too – rather than sitting back and relaxing, Rupert was leaning forwards with muscular forearms stretched along his thighs, hands clasped together as well as a knot of frustration on his brow. And Natalie had left the sofa in exchange for standing up and gazing out of the window at the front of the brownstone.

'Can't I visit my brother without anything being wrong?' Natalie asked him, seemingly oblivious to Katy's presence as her voice rose.

'Of course you can,' Rupert replied. 'It's great to see you. But if you'd warned me—'

'Yeah, well, life doesn't always go according to plan, does it? Not like you and the rest of our family seem to think. In your organised worlds, I bet nothing much ever goes wrong.'

Rupert scratched the back of his head. 'I wouldn't say that. Take this place, for starters – my boss has gone to another country. I'm used to running a kitchen rather than an inn, and suddenly I'm responsible for both. I'd say that very much wasn't in my plan last week.' She seemed to mellow as he talked. 'Look, you took me by surprise, that's all. And I feel guilty that I can't take time off to show you a bit of the city.'

'I'm a big girl, quite capable of doing that myself.'

'Are you sure?'

Natalie thawed. 'Of course. I don't expect you to drop everything because I'm here. Is it okay to stay at your apartment?'

'Ah, can't, I'm afraid, I'm staying here while my place gets some urgent repairs. New York rentals,' he added with a roll of the eyes. 'Expensive and fraught with problems that crop up at the least convenient time. So I'm here. I'm sure if I ask Sofia, she won't mind you staying in the apartment with me for a couple of days.'

Natalie nodded but then said to her brother, 'How about a couple of weeks?'

'A couple of weeks?' The frown was back and Katy wanted to reach out and erase it for him, as if it was that easy. She hardly knew him, but she recognised a kind nature when she saw it. Her dad was the same way. Always happy to mediate, to help others, unlikely to make a fuss about much even if they were put out.

And it was then Natalie must've registered they weren't alone because she looked uncomfortable as she met Katy's gaze. 'Tell me if it's a problem, Rupert.'

'I'll have to clear it with Sofia. But if she's okay with it, so am I.'

'Thank you.'

'I need to get back to the kitchen. Come chat?'

'Would you mind if I go have a lie down?' She let out a sigh. 'I've been travelling for what feels like forever and let me tell you, buses are not comfortable long distance.'

'You came by bus?'

'Cheap,' she said, one hand rubbing her lower back.

Rupert took out his phone. 'Let me send Sofia an email now. You can make yourself comfortable upstairs.' He led them out of the lounge with an apologetic look Katy's way.

Katy swept a hand in the air to tell him it was no bother. She hoped his sister showing up wouldn't be a problem. Perhaps she'd be out sightseeing soon enough and they'd hardly see her at the inn. Then again, this girl seemed to have her brother wrapped around her little finger, so who knew what would happen in the time she was staying here. Katy was hardly an expert in sibling relationships, was she?

While Rupert and Natalie were upstairs, Katy spent time going through Darcy's well-laid-out instructions again and followed steps on the computer to review the booking system and check who was in which apartment. She liked to know the names of guests and which apartment they were in to give her a sense of familiarity with who was staying here.

When one of their guests, Mr Moss, came downstairs, she helped him choose a museum to visit. He'd been to Manhattan a few times and so she filled him in on some of the lesser-known places before he decided to venture to the Bronx Museum of the Arts. Having not been herself, she told him to find her when he came back and let her know all about it. She was used to doing that; she liked the social side of the hotel business and it had the added bonus of gathering unexpected information for herself and future guests.

Once she'd helped Mr Moss, Katy went through the lists of tasks for the inn, hoping to commit as many to memory as soon as she was able. Along with daily tasks, there was a tick-box sheet of paper that was similar to others she'd used previously and required marking off jobs once they were done so you knew you'd remembered everything. She never really forgot – it was more a checklist for management – but it was handy to have, despite the inn being a lot smaller. It would be easy to assume that smaller meant a lot less work, but there was still a lot to do and, of course, a smaller establishment meant fewer staff to handle the workload.

Checking the time, Katy knew dinner service would be underway before too long and sure enough, when she ventured down the hallway, she found Rupert in the kitchen. 'There are six guests eating this evening,' she confirmed as a reminder. She'd just looked on the system.

He looked across at her from his position at the cupboard where he was pulling out a big pile of perfectly white plates. 'I thought it was four.'

'Definitely six.'

'I'm already forgetting things.' He consulted a pad of paper on the surface beside the refrigerator where he presumably left himself reminders. 'Thank you. You're right, it's even written down. Could've been embarrassing to not make enough. This is what I was worried about in Sofia's absence: the little mistakes.'

'That's what I'm here for: hopefully to make it easier.'

He looked at her again. 'Fingers crossed. But I'd been hoping to have enough to feed us both. There should still be enough for one extra portion.'

'I can grab takeout.'

'I wouldn't hear of it. You get the dinner, I'll get takeout for Natalie and some for myself, it's honestly no bother.'

'Well, I appreciate it on my first night.'

'It's my pleasure.'

When he held her gaze, it made her a little flustered until he turned his attention to pulling out the cutlery and a pile of napkins.

'Do you need me for the dinner service?' She was still hovering in the doorway.

'I can manage it this evening, but I appreciate the offer.' He'd changed into a chef's jacket and besides looking handsome, he really looked the part – as though he was in an upscale restaurant. He must have noted her looking. 'Sofia likes me to wear this for the evening meal, mingle with the guests. They like to see the chef when they can, know where their food is coming from.'

'Well, you know where I am if you need me.'

* * *

The time seemed to fly and before she knew it, Rupert appeared in the lounge to tell her that dinner service had ended and there was a meal waiting for her in the dining room.

'I'll wait for you to eat then head out to get our food,' he said as she took the opportunity to head to the dining room and eat now before she got busy again or a guest needed her attention.

'You should try some batch cooking with that huge freezer in the basement.' She sat down at one of the tables. 'That way, you don't have to resort to takeout.'

'I can usually whip up something from ingredients I have left but with the busyness of the last few days and with my sister showing up, I don't have the energy to be creative this evening.'

She knew how family dynamics could deplete your emotions, leaving you with little room for anything else. 'This all looks so good, Rupert. I'll try not to be too long.'

Rupert manned the front of house while she ate. 'Compliments to the chef,' she told him when she took her plate out to the kitchen and met Rupert coming towards her along the hallway.

'Compliments accepted. Mind if I head out now?'

'Sure. What do I do with this?'

He took the plate. 'That's mine to deal with. Can I make you a coffee before I go?'

'You really do look after everyone, don't you?'

'I try my best.'

She didn't doubt it. Rupert was the opposite of a lot of the chefs Katy had met during her time working in hotels. Some could be really ratty, the heat of the kitchen getting to them, the pressure of working with such precision and timing, open to criticism from all angles. But Rupert seemed calm, settled in his job, and went with the flow.

'I appreciate the offer,' she said, 'but it's a bit late for coffee for me – I'll probably make a herbal tea later on. Go get your dinner.'

While Rupert was out, Katy solo managed the inn and nothing unexpected came her way thankfully. As soon as Rupert was back, she ventured down to the basement, careful on the crazy steep stairs, to put on another load of laundry, this time mostly towels and drying cloths. She'd have to wait for a convenient time to do her own load; she didn't want to get in the way of the hotel's needs. She folded up the waiting sheets which had been through the dryer and took those upstairs to put away. She got the wrong cupboard at first, and again a second time, but found the right one eventually and knew it wouldn't be long before it all became second nature.

With the time marching on and the daylight already looking like it might begin to fade away, it was time to get organised for turndown service, which had once been an optional extra but was now included in the price of the stay.

After she'd gathered everything she needed from the basement, Katy took it all in a big straw basket and started at the top floor first, the floor with the most palatial apartment.

She had a brief look around. The businesswoman staying here was certainly neat and there wasn't any need for a quick vacuum. She pulled out her list of what turndown required and followed it carefully. It differed from hotel to hotel – some went all out with luxury, others did a basic service. Emptying the bins was first on the list and Katy unrolled the garbage bag and emptied the wastepaper baskets in their various spots in the apartment. She pulled the drapes closed at the window in the lounge area and in the bedroom and switched on the table lamps dotted around to create a soothing atmosphere for their guest's return. She took a moment to absorb the beauty of this apartment, the nicest one at the Inglenook Inn, with enough room for a family but often booked for business customers, Darcy had told her. She'd mentioned her husband Myles had stayed in here once and Katy had wondered what their story was: how they'd gone from inn worker and guest to husband and wife.

Katy smiled at the next thing on the list – the small packet of handmade chocolates wrapped in cellophane and tied with a neat bow that went onto the pillows. After Katy had remade the bed and plumped the pillows, as well as turning back the corner of the sheets, she placed the packet of treats on top of the pillow, remembering she had the same in her apartment. She took the empty carafe from the kitchen, went downstairs to fill it with water and ice cubes to keep it cool, and found Rupert in the kitchen once again.

'Did you and your sister have your dinner?' she asked him as he set a dessert glass onto the drainer with a collection of them he'd already washed.

'We sure did. Thai red curry. Haven't had that in a while, sometimes make it here, although curries are a tough one with guests: some love them, others hate them.'

'How do you decide what to make?' she wondered.

'When guests book in, I put some regular items on the booking form and they're asked to indicate likes and dislikes. It's not high tech but it gives us an idea of what or what not to make. Most seem to just be happy with a meal that's reasonably priced and convenient if they've been out all day and only have to venture downstairs.'

'Like a home away from home.'

'Exactly.'

When he flipped a drying cloth over one shoulder, he leaned against the counter facing her and nodded towards the carafe she was still clutching as though she had no idea why she'd come in here. 'Want me to fill that for you?'

'Sure, thanks. Just water and some ice, for turndown.'

He went over to the freezer and took out a tray of ice cubes before looking back at her. 'I know.'

'Sorry, I forget this is all familiar to you.'

'Chefs at the bigger establishments wouldn't be involved in turndown but things work a little differently here.' He filled the jug with water. 'I jump in when I'm needed.'

'I'm beginning to see. And it's a good thing, I like it.'

When he handed her the filled carafe, she didn't miss the way the tendons in his strong arms braced as though carrying something much heavier.

'I'd better get on. Thanks for this.' She left him in the kitchen and got back to turndown duties.

Once Katy was finished on the top floor, she picked up her basket of things, ready to head to the two apartments on the next level down. When her phone sounded, she took it out to see Shaun's name flashing on the screen but she rejected it again; he'd been the one to call earlier. Though she knew she didn't have to go totally incommunicado here at the inn, it felt right to do so as she tried to find her feet.

When Katy finished on that floor, she progressed down another flight of stairs to see to the one remaining apartment aside from hers and Sofia's – or rather Rupert's, as it was at the moment. She could hear Rupert laughing with someone downstairs in the hallway and suspected that much like her, it would be a while before he got to the end of his day.

Once she was done, Katy put everything she hadn't used back in the supplies cupboard in the basement and by the time she came upstairs, Rupert was showing the man he'd been chatting with out of the front door.

'Someone enquiring about a Christmas function,' he told her as he joined her in the lounge.

Katy pulled a face. 'It's May.'

'I know. But they had their Christmas meal here last year and the year before so wanted to get in early to book. I vaguely know how to make the booking, but I've just taken notes, thought I'd leave all his details with you.'

'No worries, I'll do that now.' She headed over to her desk, still shaking her head. 'I feel like winter has only just finished. I can't get my head around anything remotely Christmas-like.'

'Me neither.'

She looked up from the note he'd left her before she got on with making the reservation. 'Tell me you get help in the kitchen for the festive season.'

'If it's a big party, then I can draft in an extra pair of hands or two.' His smile was kind and held something else behind it, which had her wondering what he was thinking when he looked at her. Whatever it was it left her more flustered than she wanted to be with so much responsibility on their shoulders.

She turned her attention away from the handsome chef. 'Let me get these details in now and email the client confirmation.'

By the time she was done, Rupert was hovering in the hallway near the kitchen and this time he was having a heated conversation on the phone. There was no sign of Natalie, who must have turned in for the night already.

'Everything all right?' she asked him when he finished the call and came into the lounge. Katy was wiping down the bar top, even though it wasn't all that dirty. She just wanted to make sure everything was shipshape for tomorrow morning when she'd be up first thing.

'Another sister.' He waved his phone in the air to indicate the source of both his call and his frustration. He came over to take the cloth from her but nodded approval when he realised he couldn't help because it was all spotless over here.

'You're in demand because you're the big brother?'

'Something like that.' He sighed. 'I don't want to overshare.'

'But...'

He laughed. 'Usually Sofia or Darcy would hear me vent when it comes to family.'

'Will I do in their absence?' She dropped the spent cloth into the tub that could go down to the basement for washing.

'You'll do,' he said. And then added, 'I told this sister that I wasn't the go-between and suggested that if she wanted to know what was going on with Natalie, she call Natalie herself.'

'Sounds wise to me.' He looked tired, which could be the late night, but Katy suspected it was more likely to be family troubles.

'She won't do that. She might text Natalie, but I doubt she'll try to call. Those two have always clashed.' But he must have registered how little they really knew one another because he changed tack. 'Tell me, how's the first day... or part-day been?' With a shake of his head and a cute smile, he added, 'An interview, a job offer, and starting here all in one day. You've got to be exhausted.'

'Do I look it?'

He leaned against the bar. 'Far from it; you look a part of the place already.'

'I am pretty beat, though, I think it's the adrenaline.'

'I promise it won't always be non-stop like today. Half of your time you've spent learning the way we do things, so that won't always be the case. Why don't you get to bed and I'll stay here in case I'm needed? I'll turn in around 11 p.m.'

'No, you go, you deserve a rest and I'm still buzzing a bit, first day and all.'

'Listen to us arguing over who gets to go to bed first.'

She was quite enjoying talking to him and she got the impression the feeling was mutual. 'You go on up. I'm happy here, grab the chance. Unless you're avoiding your sister.'

'Busted.' He didn't break eye contact.

It would be hard to get to sleep tonight if she couldn't stop thinking about him or his smile. 'Go on, I might not offer another night.'

'If you're sure.' He accepted the offer but turned when he got to the door frame of the lounge. 'Goodnight, Katy.'

Those words coming from him stirred something deep inside of her. 'Goodnight, Rupert.'

As it happened, the next hour or so went quickly. The only remotely stressful part was the text she received from her dad letting her know they'd heard back from a restaurant in the city to confirm he and Stephanie could hold their wedding there even at short notice. Katy had tried to block out the date making the nuptials less than a fortnight away – it was so soon - but she'd managed a brief text in reply to say how great the news was and that of course she'd be there. What else could she possibly say?

Katy took the used cloths from the bar downstairs for washing, left them there for the morning, unloaded the machine, and popped everything into the tumble dryer. She checked the kitchen even though Darcy had told her Rupert was meticulous when it came to making sure all appliances were off and equipment away at the end of a day. She ensured all the lights were off, the door to the basement locked, and finally it was her turn to head up to bed.

She barely had time to get her pyjamas on and clean her teeth before her body collapsed onto the mattress. She pulled the sheets up, hugged her bear, and drifted into her very welcome first sleep at the Inglenook Inn.

She'd done it. A successful first shift and not only did it feel good; being here at the inn rather than at the apartment felt like a break she hadn't known she'd needed.

7

RUPERT

Sofia had always been the best boss he'd ever worked for and when she'd emailed him back to say it was fine for his sister to stay here as long as she needed, he'd told her that as soon as his own place was habitable, he'd shunt her off there. It wasn't only for Sofia's sake either – he loved his little sister to bits but having her in his home and workplace, even temporarily, was more than he wanted to handle.

Rupert had started the game of musical beds again and this time moved to the sofa rather than invading Sofia's space by using her bedroom, even though she'd said it was more than okay. Natalie moved into the spare bedroom where she could stay for two or three nights until his apartment was ready and then he'd go back into the bedroom until Sofia's return. And despite his reticence at Natalie staying here, there was a certain pleasure in having her around. He was close to his family and didn't get back to Vermont as often as he'd like, so he tried to keep reminding himself of the positives rather than keep a level of suspicion that served well to stress him out.

It was a beautiful morning in Manhattan. It had rained first thing, but as Rupert traipsed back to Greenwich Village from the markets, there weren't many clouds in the sky at all. In fact, it looked as though it was going to be such a stunning spring day that it would be impossible not to bring a smile to even the most miserable of faces.

Back at the inn, he suspected Natalie wouldn't be up just yet. She'd be making the most of lying in bed until the very last minute and not being hassled – there was a certain element of that whenever you were living with your parents. She'd be up soon, though, because he'd enticed her with the idea of a breakfast she wouldn't have to make if she came down to the dining room at a reasonable time.

He went in through the doors at the front of the brownstone and found Katy looking as fresh as the spring breeze outside, dressed in a floaty fabric skirt with a thin blouse that formed a V-neck. She was filling the vase on the side table in the hallway with extra water to keep the purple irises hydrated and perky. This morning, Rupert had inspected the pots at the top of the stoop on his way out but due to the rain, they hadn't needed any more water.

'Gorgeous day,' she beamed at him when he said hello.

'I take it you slept well.'

'I don't think I moved from the moment my head hit the pillow until my alarm went off.'

'That well?' He nodded his approval. 'Some guests struggle to sleep in the city with the sounds going on as though it were the middle of the day, but I guess you're used to it.'

'I am.' The jug she was using empty and the vase filled, she remembered something before he walked on past towards the kitchen. 'I'm having a bit of trouble opening the little window in the lounge. I'm not tall enough to give it a big shove which I assume is what it needs.'

'Let me take all this through to the kitchen and I'll take a look.'

She'd put the jug down and was trying to take one of the brown paper bags he was holding in his arms. 'Let me help.'

'No need, honestly—' But she'd already prised the one from his left arm. 'Thank you.'

'I have a bit of an ulterior motive,' she tossed over her shoulder as they made their way along the hallway to the kitchen.

He began to laugh. 'Don't tell me, you're hungry.' When she'd turned and smiled at him, he had to remind himself not to stare. The natural lipstick she wore and a lick of mascara accentuated the features on her heart-shaped face but apart from the physical attraction, he couldn't deny he had a feeling she was as kind and genuine as she'd seemed from their very first meeting. And that was one of the most attractive qualities of all, that and honesty as well as loyalty.

'You guessed correctly.' They reached the kitchen, he dumped his big paper bag on top of the counter and took the one from her arms. 'I feel a bit cheeky, though.'

'You shouldn't. Darcy told you the deal – I usually whip Sofia up a breakfast, as well as for Darcy when she's here, so it's fine. And remember my job is to cook. I'm used to it and I also happen to love it.'

'Just some toast is fine – I don't want to leave the desk unattended for long.'

'A girl has to eat. But first, let's see to that window.'

Back in the lounge, all it took was a good shove and the window opened obediently.

'Thanks, Rupert. I did look for a set of steps to climb up but couldn't find any.'

'There's some in the basement tucked down near the washing machine.'

'I'll remember that for next time.'

'Always happy to help. And now that's done, let's get you fed.'

She laughed at his description and followed him back to the kitchen where he carried on unpacking the groceries.

'Don't be too concerned about the front desk while you have your breakfast either,' he told her. 'It'll be fine for a while and if anyone needs you or me, they'll let us know.'

'What about security?'

'Don't you worry about that. I'm conscious of it too. That's why there's a computer in the lounge and not a laptop, I don't leave iPads or cell phones lying around, and the bar has a locked lift-up section.'

'Ah, I wondered why that was the case. I tried to go behind the bar to get a cloth and couldn't access it.'

'It's easy enough, the catch is on the opposite side underneath. Not enough to keep anyone out if they have a bit of time in there to figure it out, but we usually keep toing and froing between us so the room is rarely unattended. If it is, we ensure the front door is closed. Then at night-time obviously guests have the key code to get in.' He slotted a carton of cream into the refrigerator, a couple of fresh lettuces into the crisper.

'Talking of unattended, I thought I might duck out this morning some time and get some more flowers for the lounge. The ones in front of the fire are past their use by date I'd say.'

'That bad?'

'They're looking a bit sorry for themselves. There's a florist a couple of blocks away, thought I might head there.'

'Go for it. Now, let's get some food sorted for you. We can't have you keeling over with hunger, that wouldn't create a very good impression, would it?'

'I meant to grab some bagels for my apartment so I could eat before I started work but I totally forgot yesterday.'

'Understandable, there was a lot to do on day one for you. And listen, there's no point making things in your apartment when I have a perfectly good kitchen here and do breakfast service. Like I said, it worked the same way with Sofia and with Darcy. Ask either of them.'

'I'm really not putting you out?'

'Not at all.' He took the stripy apron from its hook and popped it over his head before doing the ties at the back as he asked, 'Now what'll it be? You can eat now before service starts. Nobody has come down yet for breakfast, lazy lot,' he laughed, 'get in quick. I can do toast with eggs, pancakes, waffles, bacon or all of the above.'

The sound of her laughter pleased him almost as much as her smile. 'That won't be necessary. Maybe just the eggs?'

'Two poached on toast, do you? I offered the same to my sister last night in an effort to make sure she doesn't spend all day in bed. I told her it's either that or she fixes something herself. I'd be amazed if she didn't show in...' he looked at his watch, '...a maximum of twenty minutes, as this is the time slot I heavily suggested she made use of before I'm too busy.'

With Katy back at her desk while he cooked, Rupert knew he probably wouldn't have whistled his way through the poaching of eggs and the toasting of sourdough bread if Katy hadn't been getting one of the portions. Sure enough, his sister showed but she looked like she had the weight of the world on her shoulders. Whatever had happened at home before she came here had to be more than the usual partying, didn't it? Perhaps she'd ended up here for a bit of support from her brother and maybe when the dust settled, she'd be ready to talk about whatever was so bad it had sent her hundreds of miles to him and nowhere else.

When the eggs were ready, Rupert opened the hatch to tell Natalie. He'd covered the other portion with a silver cloche for Katy in case she was in the middle of something.

'This smells amazing, Rupert.' Natalie gratefully lifted her plate to take over to a table.

'You sleep all right?'

'Not bad. But the city is loud.'

'You get used to it.' But before she could tuck in, he asked her to go through to the lounge and tell Katy her breakfast was waiting for her in the kitchen.

'Sure thing.' She still had her pyjamas on, with a big baggy cardigan over the top. He supposed at least her pyjamas didn't really look like that's what they were, given they were part old college T-shirt and part sweatpants, but he wasn't sure he could have her looking quite so scruffy outside of this early hour. He sighed as he wiped some water droplets from the counter. Perhaps he should focus on finding out what was up with her rather than looking for new things to moan at her about.

'I can eat this in the dining room,' said Katy when she came through, at least ten minutes after Natalie had headed back to the dining room to enjoy her own breakfast.

He pulled out the stool in the kitchen, however, and tilted his head. 'I wouldn't hear of it.' He removed the cover from her food as she came to sit down. 'Enjoy it here. Away from everyone else.' There was a small part of the counter away from the prep area and a high stool where Sofia and Darcy had sat plenty of times. They didn't want to eat at the front desk for obvious reasons, nor did they want to mix with the guests, not when they were eating on the job.

'As long as I'm not in your way.'

He headed over to the sink and picked up some kitchen towel to wipe the mushrooms clean. 'You're not.'

Katy must have been hungry because she was almost halfway through the breakfast before she spoke again. 'How's your sister?'

'She says she slept well, that's something, still no idea how long she's staying but I guess it's nice to have her here.'

'Family is family,' she said.

It sounded more profound than perhaps she'd meant it to be but he couldn't work out the peculiar look on her face when he turned around, so he simply agreed. 'Yeah, it is.' And she got back to focusing on her eggs.

As Katy finished up, he heard noises from the dining room and peeked through the hatch again. 'Looks like breakfast service has started.' And it looked like Natalie had finished and left her plate out there. He'd definitely have a word with her about that.

'Rupert, that was amazing.' Katy put down her cutlery, satisfied. 'Thank you again.'

'Hey, all part of the service for the team here at the Inglenook Inn.'

As she brought her plate over to the sink, he didn't miss the pleasant aroma of the perfume he'd appreciated when she came for her interview. Something with a hint of spicy but not too much, along with an undertone of citrus zing. 'What are you doing?' he asked as she picked up the dishwashing liquid.

'Washing this?' She acknowledged the whirring sound of the dishwasher already on a cycle.

'Katy, there will be a ton of plates to do once this lot finishes breakfast, leave it, please. I'll put it in the next load.'

She looked about to argue but thought better of it. 'I'll head back out there then.'

'Sure thing.' He smiled. 'Off I go again. Breakfast service is like a long-distance race but not one done at a particularly steady pace. I'll see you on the other side.'

* * *

As breakfast service came to a close, Natalie appeared in the kitchen. 'I think I left my plate in the dining room.'

Rupert turned on the faucet to fill the sink and squirted in some dishwashing soap. 'You did.' As she began to walk away, presumably in the direction of the dining room, he told her, 'It's not there now.' Katy had helped him clear the tables before she'd ducked out to grab those flowers she wanted.

'Sorry, I wasn't feeling so good when I finished eating.'

He took pause. 'Not my eggs, was it?'

'When has your cooking ever been an issue for me?'

'That's true.' He felt as connected to her as ever when he was reminded of their growing up. He'd always liked to experiment in the kitchen and of all the siblings, it had been Natalie who'd hung around the most to keep him company.

'I think it's the travel, like I said, that bus journey wasn't for the faint hearted. It wasn't the cleanest.'

'It's been years since I braved the bus.' He usually hired a car and drove all the way or flew. 'You're not going to pass anything on to me, are you?'

'I don't think so, probably more tired than anything.'

And she looked it, but he wasn't about to say.

He turned off the water now the sink was half full. 'What are your plans today?' As he plunged a big pot into the soapy suds, his sister picked up a drying cloth, which he appreciated.

'Not sure. Hadn't thought any further ahead than breakfast,' she grinned.

'What's that look for?'

'You've always been a good cook but seeing you at work is something else. This is *your* kitchen, you're in charge. I'm proud of you, brother.' She was looking at him in the same way she had as a kid when he'd taught her how to ride a skateboard after she'd tried so many times and ended up crying tears of frustration. He'd had a patience with her that his mom sometimes had to dig deep for with so many of them in the family. There were five years between him and Natalie, and he could still remember her coming to watch him play baseball. He was a teenager and she and her friends would crowd together and cheer for him and his buddies, and it had given him the same buzz as her evident pride was doing now.

'I'm sorry I'm so busy,' he said as Natalie took the large stainless-steel pot to dry. It was so big she had to set it on the countertop to manage it – one-handed wasn't an option.

'I gave you no warning and I'm well aware you are working so please, don't worry about me. Being in your company is enough.'

Okay, now he knew she had to be hiding something. They'd always got on, but she was being far too nice.

'I'll keep myself busy,' she said, misreading his doubts as being concern that she needed him to spend time with her. What he'd really been thinking about was what could have possibly propelled her here when all his sisters lived closer and they all worked more sociable hours.

'I might be able to take an hour or so this afternoon,' he suggested. 'But I don't want to go too far. As I explained last night, Sofia's away and Katy is new so I need to hang around in case she needs me.'

'You know you've got that look on your face?'

'What look?'

'The same look you used to get whenever you spoke about, or anyone mentioned, Madison Ingles.'

Laughter rumbled from his belly. 'I do not.'

'Ah, so finally you don't deny you had a huge crush on Madison.'

'Do you think she knew?' he grinned. Madison Ingles had arrived shortly after Rupert's eighteenth birthday to stay with their family for four weeks as part of a student exchange programme.

He'd got flustered every time she spoke to him right from the time she arrived to the time she left. His sisters had teased him endlessly about having a crush, something he'd denied until now.

'Er... yeah!'

'Well, Katy is a professional and so am I, so while you're here,' he warned, 'don't make trouble.'

She put a hand to her chest. 'Me?'

They chatted their way through all the pots, pans, and utensils that needed attention and she decided she'd venture out and investigate the High Line today and the markets he went to on an almost daily basis. He wished he was going too because sometimes talking came easier if you were busy doing something else and maybe he'd be able to find out what was really going on with her.

* * *

'You've got everything you need?' he asked Natalie when she came back down the stairs from the apartment, ready to go.

Hovering at the front entrance to the brownstone, Natalie pulled down her oversized sunglasses from the top of her head and patted the floral bag she wore across her body. 'Yes, Dad.'

'Have a good time. I'll see you this afternoon.'

After he waved her off, he looked in on Katy, who was making an adjustment to the arrangement of red flowers she'd bought for the vase that stood in the hearth. 'You should take a photograph of those – send it over to our web designer, Dylan.'

She went over to the desk, picked up her phone, and took the photograph as suggested. 'What do you think?' She showed it to him for his approval.

'It's missing something...'

'What?'

'People. They make pictures more personal.'

She looked at him curiously. 'Oh... you want me in it?'

'Of course. Dylan can put something on the website that lets visitors know you're the newest member of staff.'

'But I'm only temporary.'

She had no idea how much he wished that wasn't the case. 'Doesn't matter.' He motioned for her to give him her phone and once she was in position, it took a few shots before she relaxed and they had a natural picture. 'Honestly, Sofia will love this, appreciate it too.'

Katy took her phone over to the desk, ready to send the pictures to Dylan. 'It must be hard for her to leave this place in the hands of others when she's so far away.'

'I think it is. When Darcy worked here years ago, she was fully in charge while Sofia went away and that was one of the first times Sofia realised she didn't always have to be here. That other people could jump in. I wasn't so confident we'd pull it off this time, not when it was such short notice for us all and without Darcy around full-time, but you seem to be fitting in.'

She looked up from what she was doing at the computer. 'I'm glad you think so.'

'I know so.' When she seemed to be pondering something, he asked, 'Problem?'

'I'm not sure what to say in the email. Sending a photo of myself feels a bit self-indulgent.'

He made a 'tsk' sound and went over to the keyboard. He moved it his way to enable him to type a basic message about their new recruit and before she could argue, he pressed send. 'It's great and, like I said, Sofia will love it.'

After a beat of hesitation, she asked, 'Where's your sister off to today?'

'She decided to walk the High Line. She's only been to New York once before, so she's got plenty to explore.'

'If you want to spend more time with Natalie, I don't mind, as long as I can contact you when I need to. I don't expect you to hold my hand the entire time.' When she realised she might well have hinted at a slightly intimate gesture, she got flustered and began moving papers around the desk. Rupert liked it; it showed a less serious side, the Katy she might well be beneath the professionalism. Someone fun, he suspected, and a Katy he'd love to get to know a bit more.

'You feel confident here?' He thought he'd better take the focus away from what she'd just said.

'Not entirely but any emergencies, I've got your number.'

'Maybe I'll go out for a walk in a bit then, see if I can locate Natalie, if she's got her cell switched on, that is. She's notoriously bad at responding to anyone. She usually has it on silent mode.'

'I don't blame her, I do it sometimes if I'm in desperate need of a little downtime.' When he looked doubtful, she told him, 'Trust me, it really helps you take a step back. Good for mental health. You should do it – just not when I need to get in touch with you,' she added with a hopeful smile.

'Promise I won't do that.'

When the phone at the desk rang, she turned her attention to what sounded like a new booking and Rupert returned to the kitchen to double check everything was there for tonight's meal. He'd already prepared the chicken and marinated it in a mixture loaded with fresh lemon juice, a choice of herbs, and a punch of mustard. He checked the variety of vegetables he'd roast to go with it and had a quick look in the pantry to be sure they had plenty of couscous to which he'd add some colour using scallions and chopped bell peppers.

His own cell rang before he'd had a chance to head up to the apartment to grab his wallet.

'Ma, how's it hanging?' Perhaps now they'd get a chance to talk.

She sighed and didn't bother to tell him not to say the familiar phrase. 'Are you busy?'

'Actually, Katy is very capable and so after a panicky couple of days, it's feeling calmer already. Still the usual busyness but she's even happy to handle things here while I head out to meet Natalie.' He was already in the hallway and could hear Katy laughing with a guest in the lounge, the sound bringing a smile to his face until his mom spoke again.

'Natalie? She's there?'

He'd assumed she'd know, but evidently she didn't. He rested an arm on the wall, his head on his forearm. 'I thought you knew.'

'We had a big argument, Rupert.'

'I know you did.' But then wasn't it only natural? Any twenty-something still living at home wasn't destined to get along with their parents, in his opinion. Both parties needed some space and he suspected their mom was fussing over Natalie when really she should back away and let her be the grown-up that she was at twenty-eight. Was it the youngest this happened with? Or was it whoever stayed living at home? Either way, he was glad it wasn't him. He loved his family dearly but distance and time apart gave a much better level of appreciation.

'I don't know what to do with her, Rupert.'

'She likes to party, that's all.' He headed back to the kitchen to have privacy. He wanted to add that she'd grow out of it and seeing her here now, he'd believe it was true if he didn't have his mom hinting otherwise. That had been what most of the arguments between their mom and Natalie had been about in the past – Natalie staying out late or all night, at bars, parties, never being serious about work enough to really find a career she could stick with. Some people never did; Rupert had friends who flitted from one job to another, but it suited them and their lifestyle. And none of them were living at home. As much as he wanted to stick up for his little sister and be on her side, even he could see Natalie desperately needed a focus or nothing would ever change and they could all be having this same conversation for years to come.

'She'll be here a while, Mom, then she'll come home and you can both take it from there. Maybe some time apart is what you need. What does Dad think to all this?'

'He buries his head. You know your dad, Natalie can't do much wrong in his eyes.'

Natalie was a daddy's girl – they were all loved equally, but his dad more than his mom didn't seem to want to let the youngest member of the family go. Rupert recalled the term 'empty nest syndrome', but he'd always assumed that was more applicable to women. Then again, their dad, Frank, had always been the more lenient one when it came to parenting. Frank had been the one to take them camping in the woods when they were younger and taught them how to build campfires; he'd let them stay up late into the night telling ghost stories and toasting marshmallows. They all knew why, too. Frank Gray was an Englishman in New York – the way he described himself – and he'd had a strict upbringing as a kid. He came from a family where his own father truly believed kids should be seen and not heard, and Frank had vowed even as a young boy that if he was lucky enough to have a family of his own, he wouldn't bring his kids up in the same way.

The only link they really had to that side of the family now was Rupert's name – he'd been named after his dad's favourite uncle, Rupert, who Frank said had been a better dad than his own. Uncle Rupert had taken Frank fishing on his days off, they'd laughed, he'd bought Frank his first beer, counselled him through school and a round of bullying when his dad was nowhere to be seen. Frank's mother had been detached from it all, preferring to let Frank's dad call the shots, something Rupert felt sure Frank had never truly understood and had therefore let his relationship with her fade away long before she died. Uncle Rupert had never visited America, but he and Rupert had met once in England. They'd known then that he didn't have long to live and when they left him sitting in his chair beside a window bathed in sunshine, Rupert didn't think he'd ever seen his father look so distraught.

'Dad needs to recognise you might need help on this one.' Rupert felt like a counsellor giving his mom advice on the phone. 'I know he thinks Natalie can do no wrong, but it won't help her in the long run either.'

'No, I don't suppose it will. And it's not that he thinks she's without fault. He just values all you kids and doesn't want anything to come between any of us.'

When his mom said nothing further, Rupert had his suspicions. 'Why do I get the feeling there's something you're not telling me, Ma?'

As he waited for her to deny it or admit what else she had on her mind, he realised his mom was crying. It broke his heart to not be able to fix whatever it was that was wrong. It always had.

Rupert hadn't heard Katy come in until he noticed her opening the refrigerator in the corner of his eye. She mouthed an apology as though realising she'd walked in on something very private and took out an ice-cold can of soda just as his mom spoke again.

'It's drugs, Rupert. Drugs. She took drugs,' Verity wailed on the other end of the phone.

Rupert swore, which had Katy looking at him before she reached the doorway. 'Drugs, are you serious?' he said quietly into the phone when Katy left him to it. 'Mom, that doesn't sound like Natalie. Do you know for sure?'

Her voice wobbly she told him, 'Randall dropped her home.'

'Randall?' Randall was his sister Cameron's husband and a police officer. And that didn't bode well. Rupert had a sinking feeling in the pit of his stomach.

'He told me he'd seen her stumbling around outside on the street near that bar you all seem to love so much.'

'Delaney's,' he confirmed. It was a favourite haunt for her and her friends. And it was where he usually went to meet the guys when he was home.

'Randall told me he'd pulled over and couldn't see any of her friends with her. He'd offered her a lift home, but she'd barely recognised him at first. Randall said he'd seen enough people on drugs to know the signs and he'd sat with her on the sidewalk as he wasn't about to leave her alone. As they talked, she must've got the impression he was thinking as a police officer rather than her brother-in-law because all of a sudden she got paranoid, she started begging him not to make a scene, not to go in to the bar and do a raid, not to call for backup. It was then she told him she'd taken something at a friend's house nowhere near the bar, she refused to tell him where, said she was experimenting and begged him not to call me or your dad.'

'Oh, Mom...'

'Randall drove her home – stopping on the way for her to throw up at the side of the road.'

'Shit.'

'I could tell this was more than just drink when she came home, Rupert. She had this horrible look in her eyes, not one I ever want to see again.'

He waited for her to compose herself.

'She wouldn't talk to me either. She ran upstairs, presumably to throw up again or escape me when I found out what she'd been up to. I wasn't even aware she was going out to a bar, let alone anything else. She'd told me she had a date. Obviously that wasn't the case. You know how much I hate lying, Rupert.' He could hear the tension in her voice from miles away, the sense of her head being all over the place, not knowing what to do.

'Has Randall told Cameron?'

'No, and he said he wouldn't.'

'And has he reported the drug use?'

'No, she wouldn't tell him what she'd taken or who'd given it to her. But he warned her he'd be keeping his ear to the ground. When Randall left, I went upstairs, she'd vomited everywhere. I asked her what she'd taken and she burst into tears.' Her voice wobbled. 'It broke my heart to hear her cry like that. I rocked her, she told me over and over that she was sorry.'

So it *was* true. Rupert had no idea how to react. Because being sorry didn't make it all right, it didn't make it better. But what he didn't understand was how his mom and sister had talked that night and yet Natalie was here now. 'Why did you argue? She didn't do it again, did she?'

'No... but she caught me rifling through her bag the next morning and freaked out.'

He scraped a hand through his hair and the front flipped obediently back into position.

'I grilled her about whose house she'd been to, I couldn't help myself. I was terrified that that wouldn't be the end of it. Seeing her with bags under her eyes, dark circles like a druggie you see on all those ads that tell you never to take anything, don't give in to pressure. She yelled at me, Rupert. Told me to stay the hell out of her business and then she swore at me.'

'Mom, I don't know what to say.' But he had an idea of how his next conversation with Natalie was going to go.

Verity's voice came out softly. 'I can't have drugs in my house, Rupert, I just can't.' She was panicking and it was painful to hear.

He hoped his composure would help his mom to calm down, at least for now. 'The main thing is she's here, she's not bumming around with whoever she was with before. She's together and in one piece.' At least she was until he got his hands on her. It was probably a good job she was out and about; he needed time to process all this.

When he finally ended the call, despite an assurance in his voice that everything was going to be all right, he was livid, the tension riding up his body from the hands he'd placed on the kitchen countertop. His shoulders that had never felt so tense.

Maybe he should've taken Katy's words of advice and switched his phone to silent, taken his own downtime. Because now he was as far from relaxed as he was ever likely to be with his sister in what could only be described as a total mess.

Rather than heading out, he took his frustration out on the kitchen floor in apartment two, since Katy had already informed him the guests had checked out and wouldn't be getting their full security deposit back on account of the state they'd left the place in. There was no way he wanted to meet his sister now because he wasn't sure he should let his anger show in public.

'Thanks, Rupert.' Katy took the cleaning box from him when he came back down the stairs. 'Everything all right?'

He was about to open his mouth when his sister breezed in the door. When Katy saw the way he looked at Natalie, she made a hasty retreat. He couldn't blame her.

'New York is amazing,' Natalie beamed as though she didn't have a care in the world. 'I love it! I walked the High Line, ate a New York bagel, I went to Chelsea Markets. There's so much to see here.' She took in his stance, the hands on his hips. 'What's up?'

'You really need to ask?'

She pulled a face as though she had no idea until the fury on his face must have given it away. 'You spoke to Mom,' she said. But when she opened her mouth to offer something else, he cut her off.

'Not here.' He ushered her down the hallway and opened up

the door leading down to the basement. He gestured for her to lead the way.

'You're locking me in the dungeon for breaking the rules?' Her flippancy almost had him shoving her down the stairs, but instead he warned her to mind the step.

'I really don't think this is necessary,' she grumbled as she slowly headed down into the basement.

'Oh, it's totally necessary.' He followed after her. 'It's one thing making a mistake and acting out when you're at home, but this is my place of work. I won't have you bringing this crap my way.'

'What crap?' Her voice rose once they were in the basement surrounded by the buzz of the refrigerator, the whirr of the washing machine, and gentle rolling of the tumble dryer.

With the responsibility for the Inglenook Inn resting on his shoulders and Katy's, the last thing he needed was his little sister causing trouble. It was bad enough she was doing it back in Vermont, causing no end of stress to his parents.

But she was here and she was family. What else was he supposed to do other than attempt to deal with the situation the best he could?

8

KATY

Katy had interrupted Rupert in the kitchen earlier and thought she'd heard the name Natalie and the word *drugs* in the same conversation. Instead of saying anything, she'd gone back to the linen cupboard and got on with her task: to make up the bed in one of the apartments she'd given a good clean. She had a new-found respect for the hard work cleaners did because it was back-breaking work. It was a shame Jill wouldn't be back for at least a couple of weeks, but she and Rupert would just have to manage it between them.

The minute Natalie had come in the front door after her walk, Katy had seen the way Rupert looked at his sister. She wouldn't have been surprised to see steam coming out of his ears. Katy had scurried off before either of them said a word. She didn't want to be party to whatever was brewing and she had to head down to the basement to get the sheets from the tumble dryer anyway. But Rupert must have come down to the basement with his sister, likely not wanting to have the conversation in Sofia's apartment where other guests might overhear. Little did they realise Katy was stuck down there and when she'd heard them, she'd hidden.

While Katy had pulled the bed sheets into position in the apartment upstairs as Rupert talked on the phone in the kitchen earlier, she'd decided she must have heard wrong. But now, in the basement, there was no doubt about it. She hadn't.

Katy was glad of the sound of the washing machine as well as the dryer because she really didn't want either Rupert or his sister to know she was here. She respected Rupert, liked him, she knew by the tone of his voice that he wanted to keep this personal matter private and would likely be embarrassed if he knew she could hear every word.

Katy's heart pounded as the revelations unfolded between the pair.

'Mom called,' said Rupert. Listening to the hurt in his voice, Katy's heart went out to him. They may not have known one another for long, but already she felt like she was on his side.

It didn't take long for Natalie to snap back with, 'And so now you think you know everything and are about to give me a lecture on the perils of partying.'

'What are you playing at, Natalie?' Exasperated, he added, 'Experimenting with drugs is hardly a rite of passage.'

The washing machine had reached its crescendo, but Katy could still hear Rupert when he went on, 'What have you got to say for yourself?'

'You're not my dad!' Natalie yelled back at him.

'No, I'm not, but I'm your brother. I care, and you're here with me right now.'

'What so while I'm under your roof, I live by your rules?'

'Yes!' he roared back at her. And then more calmly added, 'Mom is upset, she's worried. What were you thinking?'

The washing machine, having wound its way down, bleeped to announce the load was ready to remove. 'Seriously, have you really got nothing to say?' Rupert demanded.

Natalie's voice wobbled. 'I don't know what to say, all right?'

'Try telling me the truth.'

'I'm not proud of that night.' She sounded so close to tears that Katy almost felt sorry for her. But drugs? It was hard to feel sorry for anyone who took them, especially when it came to the consequences for everyone else. Drugs ruined lives, drugs tore families apart.

'So why did you do it?' Silence. 'Natalie...?'

'I don't know.' Her voice small, she wasn't offering Rupert much at all.

'You're staying in my boss's apartment, for crying out loud!'

'Are you kicking me out?'

'No, I'm not kicking you out. But I can't have drugs here, do you understand that?'

'I promise there won't be, Rupert. I'm not an addict or anything.'

'I'll bet that's what they all say. And the addiction has to start somewhere – you know that much, right?'

Katy couldn't see the looks the pair were sharing right now but neither of them spoke and so Katy risked leaning forward a little bit so she could just about see Rupert yanking the sheets out of the washing machine and dumping them into the basket. He pulled the fresh sheets from the dryer next and Katy hoped he wasn't going to come over and fold them all. But he didn't. He must have handed them to Natalie because Katy heard him say, 'Here, take these.'

Katy shrunk back again so she wasn't seen. She heard the dryer go on a moment or two later, presumably with the fresh load Rupert had put in there.

'If you're going to stay here,' said Rupert to his sister, 'then you can help.'

'You mean work here?'

'You got a problem with that?'

'No.' She sounded both surprised and relieved.

'Good. I'll clear it with Sofia, you'll get paid, we could use the extra help, so it'll be best for all of us. Take those sheets upstairs, fold them in the dining room, the lounge, in the apartment, I don't care where as long as there are no guests around. And I'll get you some other jobs soon enough.'

'Can I at least use the bathroom first?' Katy heard Natalie moan as the voices began to fade as brother and sister headed back up the stairs.

'Make it quick. Because you're about to get busy. Real busy.'

Katy heard the door at the top of the stairs open and fall shut before she stepped out from her hiding place.

She ventured to the top of the stairs herself and made sure she couldn't hear anyone around before she stepped out into the hallway.

Rupert must have headed to the kitchen and the desk in the lounge gave Katy solace while she digested what she'd heard. If Natalie was taking drugs, Rupert was fooling himself that this could be fixed by a stern brotherly telling off and making her busy at the inn. He had his work cut out for him and the worst thing was, he didn't seem to realise it.

9

KATY

Katy had cleared it with Rupert this afternoon to head out for her dermatologist appointment. She'd had it booked for months and the reminder had flashed up on her phone an hour or so after the conversation between Rupert and Natalie in the basement. She'd been unsure as to what kind of reception she'd get from Rupert or even whether to mention it or just cancel the consultation, but he'd been fine with it.

Back at the inn, Katy put her things in her apartment and headed downstairs to where Rupert had been chatting with a guest in the hallway. The guest had gone now and she thanked Rupert again.

'Sure thing. Everything okay?'

Katy hadn't enlightened him as to what the appointment was for, but she had stressed it was a medical consultation she really didn't want to miss. 'Of course.'

The problem with the dermatology appointment, the annual skin check Katy had without fail, was that it brought back memories of her mom's diagnosis and the great loss Katy would never recover from. She'd gone to a café right after her consultation and sat looking at nothing in particular, the city moving on without her beyond the windows as she drank her coffee. Once she was back in the right frame of mind, she'd made her way back to Greenwich Village with the knowledge that at least she'd got the all-clear from her dermatologist today, who was pleased to hear how meticulous she was about applying sunscreen and looking for any skin changes on a regular basis.

'I hope you don't feel like you're a prisoner here,' said Rupert and then by way of explanation added, 'I heard you on the phone earlier telling your dad that you're too busy for visitors. Just remember, even prisoners get visitors.'

She smiled at him. 'Dad wanted to stop by this evening but I'm still relatively new here, it wouldn't feel right.' Not to mention the wedding day was marching closer and closer and she and her dad were yet to talk properly about it since the announcement had been made.

'Katy, this isn't just your place of work, it's now your home while Sofia is away. I'd draw the line at a big party but your dad stopping by is fine.'

'If you're sure.' She'd already cleared with him that she'd need a few hours off for the wedding which was thankfully so local she wouldn't have to be away from the inn for too long at all.

'Of course I am. And it's much easier than trying to go out to meet him with things around here so up in the air. Show him the place, always nice to do that with family.'

'I'll tell him... perhaps he'll stop by soon. And thank you.' She supposed she couldn't put off talking to her dad about the upcoming wedding for much longer, much as she'd like to.

'Talking of family, I've asked Natalie to help out at the inn – Sofia confirmed it's all right to put her on the casual payroll.'

'We could sure use the help,' Katy agreed, trying to sound as genuine as possible when she knew the reasons Rupert felt the need to jump in and put his sister to work.

'I've had her folding sheets and towels and putting on more laundry. She's also helped with some of the dinner prep. And she'll be on hand to answer the phone if neither of us are around.'

'Is she up to it, do you think?'

'She's not that lacking in social skills.'

Katy tripped up her words a bit. 'Sorry... I didn't mean to imply... I just meant...'

'It's fine.' He seemed to have taken it in good humour. 'It's good you feel as responsible for this place as I do. But please don't worry about Natalie; she knows she has to do a good job on my watch.'

But what about when he wasn't watching?

He tilted his head in the direction of the kitchen. 'I need to get back to it, don't want to burn the cookies. Oatmeal and raisin, fresh from the oven, can I interest you?'

'Actually, my mouth is watering so I'd say I'm interested. But—'

He stopped her from stating the obvious by saying, 'The desk will wait.' And she followed after him.

The timer he'd set pinged the second they went in. He used an oven mitt to take out three separate trays filled with chunky golden cookies.

'They smell so good.'

'A few minutes cooling and they'll be set just enough.'

'Perfect.' A memory came back to her so vividly, he must've read it on her face.

'Are you wondering how to tell me you hate raisins?'

'Not at all. It... this... it reminds me of my mom baking cookies. If ever I was having a bad day and refused to talk about it, she'd make a batch, flavour dependent on what was in the pantry at the time, and sit me down with a few cookies fresh from the oven and a big glass of milk like I was five years old.'

He came over to where she was sitting on the stool now. 'And did it work? Would you tell her all your secrets?'

She looked up into mesmerising brown eyes like small pools of chocolate. 'Every time.'

'Does she still do it?' He moved across to the cupboards and took out a plate. 'Does she still think the way to get you to talk is through baking, which is a technique I fully respect, by the way?' He lifted two cookies and put them onto the plate.

But his enthusiasm faded when she told him that her mom died. 'Five years ago now.'

He looked at her and it was a beat before he turned and added two more cookies to the plate. 'Here, eat as many as you need, I can always make more.'

'Thank you,' she smiled. 'I think a couple will be my limit, but I appreciate it.'

'You must miss her terribly.' He shook his head. 'Stupid thing to say.'

'Most people don't know what to say. Some try platitudes, others try to avoid bringing it up in conversation.'

'And what do you prefer?'

'Today I'm good to talk. I mean, I wasn't earlier, but...' She blew on one of the cookies to cool it down before she took a tentative bite and smiled her appreciation at the delicious taste.

'What happened earlier?' He was leaning against the counter as she sat on the high stool.

'Can't you eat some cookies too? I'll feel less like I'm being grilled then.'

'Who am I to argue with that kind of logic?' He got his own plate and loaded it with four cookies just like her, raising his eyebrows at the conspiracy.

When she finished the first cookie, she told him what her appointment had been for. 'I go once a year, I check my skin weekly.' She went on to explain her mom's shock diagnosis, the very little time she had left once they knew.

'It must've been an awful time, I can't imagine.'

'It was pretty bad.' She hadn't realised her fingers were resting on her necklace the way they usually did when she thought about her mom, especially when she talked about her. She picked up a cookie again. 'These are making me feel so much better; they make me think about the good times.'

'Hey, anytime you need cookies, just holler, day or night. Well, maybe not night...'

'I'll try to keep requests to daytime hours.' She finished the second cookie and was done for now. 'I'll save these other two for later, if you don't mind. And you're 100 per cent sure it's all right for Dad to come over some time soon?'

'Are you guys close?'

'Very. We live together in the city – we left the suburbs after Mom died, needed a change, and we've been a unit ever since.' At least, it had felt that way until Stephanie came along.

When a guest knocked on the kitchen door, Katy got back to work and confirmed with Rupert that one more guest would be requiring dinner tonight. And then she headed back to the lounge and the desk to catch up on any emails that may have dropped into the inbox in her absence. She also texted her dad to suggest a time to stop by and he messaged back straight away, which made her happy.

Katy was kept busy until an hour or so before dinner service and when she looked up from the desk, expecting to see a guest coming into the lounge, she saw Shaun.

She came around to the other side of the desk with a smile for her very good friend. 'What brings you here?'

'I apologise for dropping in like this unannounced, but you're a hard woman to pin down.'

'Busy,' she said.

'It's going well?'

'Really well.'

He was looking around him, his ocean-blue eyes taking in the inn's presence, quaint and a little different to some of the hotels he'd stayed in for business, she expected.

When she heard someone swear loudly in the hallway, she excused herself and went out to find Natalie with a split garbage bag and a load of detritus covering the floor at her feet.

'Stupid bag split,' Natalie complained. She looked tired already, despite it being nowhere near time to knock off for any of them. 'Rupert wanted me to empty the bins,' she grumbled but showed no signs of bending down to pick anything up.

Katy found another garbage bag from the cupboard in the hallway. She crouched down but when Natalie didn't do the same, she shot her a look that had her helping pretty swiftly.

'Could you please watch your language?' Katy said softly. She'd been about to smile and add that it wasn't a problem for her, but guests might not appreciate it, when Natalie got in there first.

'The words were out before I had a chance to think,' Natalie snapped. 'What am I supposed to say, "Oh, fiddlesticks"?' She attempted to adopt a posh British accent.

'There's no need for sarcasm,' came Rupert's voice from behind them and Katy appreciated the interference.

She left Natalie and Rupert sorting the rubbish while she apologised again to Shaun for being dragged away and went to find a mop and bucket. She'd disinfect that part of the floor quickly given there'd been foodstuff amongst the garbage.

'Definitely busy,' Shaun smiled once she was done. 'Any way you can escape for a cup of coffee?'

'I can't. I've had an appointment this morning, so plenty to do around here. I'd feel like the worst employee if I added heading out for coffee into the mix. Rain check?'

Rupert had come back along the hallway without her realising and offered them coffees here at the inn. 'I'll fix them now.' He smiled with his whole face and she felt she could smile back at him for a lot longer than it took to have a simple conversation. She also wondered whether he was being overly accommodating given his sister's behaviour. Katy was pretty sure he wouldn't want this particular anecdote to work its way back to Sofia.

Shaun looked to Katy. 'That might work.'

'If you're sure,' Katy checked with Rupert.

Rupert kept his voice low as he said, 'Natalie being here isn't the most convenient for you no matter whether she's supposed to be helping. It's in my interests to keep you happy – if you abandon me, I'll be in trouble.'

Katy couldn't help but smile up at him. 'Then coffee would be great.'

'Two coffees coming right up.' He checked their preferences and left them to it.

'So that's the chef,' said Shaun the moment Rupert was out of earshot. 'He any good?'

'Very.' She recounted some of the food she'd already been able to enjoy and they talked more about her job here, only having to pause once to take a delivery package that Rupert came to pick up from the desk when he brought through the coffees.

'What's the chef like to work with?' Shaun asked, nodding approval at the beverage. 'He makes a decent coffee, I'll give him that.'

'He's nice, he's having to do a lot more than be in the kitchen with the boss away and his sister is doing a stint here too, which I guess helps when she's not throwing garbage everywhere and creating more work for me.'

'Sounds like a good guy.'

She didn't miss the teasing note in his voice. Perhaps he'd seen how close Rupert had stood to her earlier, the way they'd held one another's gaze as they talked. In an instant, she felt unprofessional. 'He's a very good guy. And we're friends.' Her tone suggested she didn't want to say anything else about it.

He took the hint. 'I'll bet your dad is missing having you around at the apartment.'

'It's weird not seeing so much of him.'

'I saw him a week or so ago, but he was on the other side of the street so we didn't get to talk. He was with a woman.'

'That'll be Stephanie. His fiancée.'

He nodded after another mouthful of coffee. 'I never expected that. Good for him.' He noted Katy's reaction. 'Or not?'

Katy puffed out her cheeks. 'It's not that I don't like her, it's just that Dad is changing.'

'In a bad way?'

The question surprised her and it made her think. 'Trust you to ask me that,' she grinned. She supposed there was nothing wrong with running and drinking milkshakes all of a sudden; it was whether the little changes became bigger ones that Wade didn't want. And she told Shaun as much.

'You do know it's up to Wade to decide what parts of his life will evolve, what will stay the same?'

'Sometimes I really dislike you,' she said with a shake of her head, 'because you're usually right.'

'Give it time.'

'I'm just not sure she's right for Dad, that's all.'

'She's got a high standard to meet. Your mom was one of the best.'

'She really was.' Her voice drifted a little and her head was in danger of doing the same.

He seemed to sense it and with one arm across the back of the sofa, he reached his other hand out to hold hers, right at the moment Rupert came back to get something from the desk drawer.

'Sorry, don't mind me.' Rupert made a sharp exit and it had Shaun smiling.

'I think the chef might well see you as more than a colleague.'

'Don't be ridiculous.'

He was nodding, his cropped blond hair not moving much at all; it wasn't long enough to do that. 'I'm telling you, the way that guy just looked at me touching you, he's interested, all right. Having me here might keep him on his toes if he thinks there's more between us than friendship.'

'Stop it,' she laughed because apart from the time they'd spent together as a couple, they really were just friends now. Very good friends.

She got him off the topic of Rupert and they talked some more about his family, his work, and looped round to talk about the inn again.

'This will be a great experience,' Shaun approved.

'It should look good on my resume if I do this right.'

'And why wouldn't you do it right?'

She made sure they were alone. 'Rupert's sister.'

'The girl with the garbage?'

Katy nodded, her fingers toying with the necklace again. 'He wasn't expecting her.'

'Katy, you're going to have to give me more than that.' He moved his hand in a circular motion as though to crank a handle and squeeze out more drips of information.

Lucky for Katy, a guest came down the stairs at that moment and she saw to their enquiry before she went back to Shaun. But he clearly wasn't going to let her off that easily.

'I overheard something, that's all,' she said, paranoid Rupert or

Natalie might overhear and think she was gossiping. 'And it wasn't good.' Katy told him what she'd overheard when she was in the basement.

'Jeez.' He scraped a hand across his smooth-shaven chin, his other hand resting along the back of the sofa. 'Any signs she's brought drugs in here?'

'Not that I've seen and I'm pretty sure Rupert will be on his guard. You should've heard how angry he was with her, but she's his family.'

She only had to look at him for him to say, 'It's a reminder, isn't it?'

'Yeah.' She hoped they wouldn't get interrupted because Shaun knew her history. He knew that not only had she and Wade lost Judy; they'd lost her brother too.

Natalie heard at the doorway but...

10

RUPERT

Rupert was humming away in the kitchen, putting the finishing touches to an admittedly over-the-top Death by Chocolate trifle. It was being presented in a glass dish to show off all the layers and he'd added the final toffee bits across the top to the whipped cream and dark chocolate layers with brownie chunks throughout.

He stood back, proud of his creation. At least he was until he heard yelling coming from the hallway and if he wasn't mistaken, it was his sister doing the shouting.

'What's going on?' He'd moved as quickly as he could from the kitchen to the doorway of the lounge.

'Ask her!' Natalie hadn't got any quieter in the last couple of minutes. 'She's accusing me of stealing.'

Katy, meanwhile, was frantically lifting up cushions on the sofa and running her hand down every crevice of the piece of furniture that she could find. She looked up as he went over. 'I didn't accuse her; I asked if she knew where my necklace was.' She looked upset and her voice was decibels lower than his sister's.

He turned to Natalie. 'Go, cool down and stop shouting. This is a place of business, in case you'd forgotten.'

'Might have known you'd take someone else's side, everyone does. You want to put me in the basement again?'

He almost roared himself. He wanted to ask her whether she was stupid to accuse him of not being on her side with all that he'd done for her lately, letting her stay here no matter what mess she'd got herself into. 'Go to the kitchen, I'll be in in a minute.'

When Natalie stormed off, Rupert could see the angst on Katy's face, the upset, the devastation. The way she always wore the necklace and touched her fingertips to it often was all he needed to know how special it was to her.

'I'm sorry, Rupert.' Katy had moved over to the desk now, opening drawers and rifling through. 'I shouldn't have even asked Natalie. I wasn't accusing her, though, I promise.'

'I believe you. Now let me help.'

But she shook her head. 'Go see Natalie. We can't have her yelling like that, no matter her reason. She already scared away one guest who was about to come and ask me something just after I asked Natalie whether she'd seen my necklace. She really over-reacted.'

'Sounded like it.' He frowned. 'She's got a lot going on – not an excuse, but it's probably why she assumed you were accusing rather than asking. I'll talk to her.'

In the kitchen, he found his sister looking at the trifle. 'Don't even think about touching that.'

'Not you as well,' she moaned, although at least she wasn't doing it loudly.

He moved the trifle to the refrigerator, out of the line of fire. 'She says she wasn't accusing you and before you say I'm taking her side, I'm not, she wears that necklace every day, so unless you've developed some seriously good techniques when it comes to stealing jewellery off a person wearing it, then Katy's common sense will tell her it must have come off by mistake.'

Natalie's silence suggested he might have made his point.

'Are you going to tell me what's made you so angry these days?'

'I'm not angry.'

He'd taken out a load of carrots to prepare for tonight's dinner and paused before he washed them at the sink. 'You were shouting at her, your language when you dropped garbage all over the hallway earlier was colourful, you barely manage a smile when you look at anyone.'

'I'm working here, that's why.'

'So you're sulking that this isn't the easy going holiday you thought it might be?' He shook his head. 'Should've known.' And with the carrots scrubbed to within an inch of their lives, he grabbed a knife to julienne them.

After some pretty speedy knifework on his part, she tried to get on his good side by making him smile when she told him, 'Go easy on those carrots, Rupert. I've no idea how long it'll take to get to an emergency room if you keep going at them like that.'

He had chopped them faster than usual. He took a deep breath in and let it out, hoping it would calm everything else he was feeling.

Nope. The two women in his life right at this moment obviously had their own issues and both of them clashing really was the sort of recipe he could do without.

'Could you go check in with the Garcias, who are already in the dining room playing cards before dinner – I think one kid wanted raw carrots rather than cooked, and the other wanted whole potatoes rather than mashed.' But when he looked, his sister was leaning against the cabinet on the far wall with her eyes closed and hadn't registered him talking to her. 'Natalie!'

She jumped. 'All right, no need to get angry. I'm trying, Rupert.'

'Did you hear what I asked you to do?' Since he'd confronted her about her partying and apparent drug use, he'd found it hard to be tolerant of anything she said or did. One more night and his apartment would be ready and she could go stay there but return here for work. It was the deal he'd laid out to her and she knew that if she didn't turn up at the inn when requested, then he'd be putting her on the next bus back to Vermont to face the music at home.

'I'm sorry, I didn't.'

He pursed his lips together briefly and maintained enough patience to repeat the request. 'Stop daydreaming; we work quickly here and I need you to do the same.'

She went off muttering something about fussy kids and slave labour with the odd swear word thrown in for good measure.

'Watch your mouth,' he said but almost to himself as he didn't want their conversation to travel. The last thing he needed was for word to get around that an angry chef ran the kitchens here at the Inglenook Inn. Reputation was everything in this business. And in the same way Katy boosted reputation, he suspected Natalie's behaviour would do the exact opposite.

Katy. His heart sank a little. He'd walked in on her and her visitor earlier and seen the way that guy held her hand as though they shared a history, as though he wanted to keep on doing it.

Natalie returned and detailed what the Garcias wanted with regards to potatoes and carrots and, leaving one portion of julienned carrot sticks to the side, he piled the others next to the pan of nearly boiling water ready to throw in there. Natalie kept quiet as he worked, getting the dinner ready, preparing the choices of potatoes, checking the meat dish in the oven. She helped him lay out the plates when he asked, grabbed a couple of items from the pantry for him, and slowly he adjusted to her presence once again. She helped him take all the dinners out to the awaiting guests and even managed to do it with a smile on her face.

* * *

Once dinner service was over, Rupert started the task of cleaning up while Natalie was in the dining room making sure they'd brought everything through.

When the hatch flew open and one of the Garcia kids' faces appeared the other side, he smiled but wished he'd locked it shut. 'What can I do for you, young man?' He wasn't so young he was about to start running toy cars or trains up and down the countertop the other side, but he looked interested in the kitchen until he produced something shiny in his hand.

'What have you got there?' Rupert went over to see Katy's necklace laying in the palm of the boy's hand. 'Where did you find that?'

'My mom found it in our bathroom. I told her finders keepers, but she said to go tell you or the lady.'

'Katy. And you will make her day if you go give it to her. She'll be out front in the lounge, I expect.'

He didn't hesitate. Off he went and Rupert had to admit he was relieved it seemed his sister had nothing to do with it. Even though it had been unlikely, he still hadn't completely dismissed the thought and now he felt bad for being suspicious.

When Katy came in not long after, she was smiling and put her fingers to the necklace, already back in place. 'I must've put it on in such a rush after my shower that I didn't do the clasp up properly. I'll be more careful in future.' And with a smile she added, 'I told the young boy that extra ice cream might come his way.'

'Sure thing,' said Rupert.

'I also need to let you know that there are three guests who have just this minute requested three dinners. I can tell them no. They're well aware of the lack of notice but Mr Brown thought his wife had booked, Mrs Brown thought he'd done it, and their daughter looks about to keel over after being dragged around the city all day.'

On a sigh, he eyed the cloches lined up on the far counter. 'Looks like us three will have to have something else.'

'That won't be a problem.' There was that sexy smile again and he hoped her happiness might be because of his presence as well as the finding of her necklace. 'There's an Italian place I've been meaning to try for ages.'

He was about to suggest they order together when the moment broke as Natalie burst into the kitchen so quickly that the door flew open hard and knocked Katy on the back.

'Oops.' Natalie groaned as she came in with a pile of plates and cutlery. 'Sorry about that.'

Katy rubbed her arm. 'Not the best place to stand, I suppose.' And if she was pissed, she hid it well.

'The worst place to stand,' Natalie agreed, giving Rupert the impression she was still annoyed about the so-called accusation. And she only took a moment longer to spot the necklace on Katy. 'You found it.'

'I did,' said Katy. 'And I never accused you of taking it, Natalie.'

'Whatever,' said Natalie as though she didn't give a toss.

When Katy left, Rupert wasted no time. 'Are you kidding me with the attitude?'

'She *was* in the way. And the way she asked me felt like an accusation.'

'That's not really the point, is it? Just watch yourself, kiddo.'

'Don't call me kiddo. I'm twenty-eight.'

'Yeah, well, start acting like it.'

'So much for a holiday away from it all.' She'd muttered it and probably meant to do it under her breath, but he hadn't missed a single word of her complaint.

'Your holiday ended when I found out why you came to New

York, so don't push it.' He glared at her before he plunged his hands into filthy dish water. 'Do I need to remind you that you're here because you're in trouble, trouble that I might add you've brought on yourself?'

He'd expected her to yell back at him, to take off her apron, throw it down on the counter, and go upstairs to pack her things, declaring she didn't need her big brother to lecture her. But instead, her eyes filled with tears and when she opened her mouth, nothing came out. She set down the plates without much care at all, sending the cutlery tumbling off one side into the sink. A tear spilled over onto her cheek and he took his hands from the water, dried them off, and picked up the cutlery before she could.

'You need to sort yourself out, sis,' he said when he stood up again.

'I know,' she croaked.

He dumped the cutlery back on top of the plates and pulled her into a hug. That was the thing about family, certainly the Gray family: mild arguments were frequent and some of those evolved into full-blown fights, but no matter what, they never stopped loving or being there for each other.

'You look exhausted, Natalie.' She looked drained and right now it really registered with him.

She sniffed against his chest. 'I'm so tired, Rupert.'

He'd noticed her napping this afternoon on the sofa when he went on his break and it had saddened him that the girl he remembered wasn't this snappy, detached person who'd descended on him with problems. Natalie was usually bubbly, fun to be around, carefree, and could bring a smile to his face without much effort at all. The Natalie he knew would've been best pals with Katy about five seconds after she came in through the front door.

'If you need to talk to me, you know I'll listen.'

She looked up at him and seemed about to take him up on the

offer, but when Katy came through to grab a cloth, she clammed up.

'Spilt juice,' Katy explained as she ran a cloth beneath the faucet over the empty sink rather than the one next to it that looked set to overflow.

'Why don't you have an early night?' Rupert told his sister when Katy left them to it.

'I can still help you finish the clean up; you're letting me stay, after all, and paying me. You're a good man, Rupert. Best brother ever.'

'The only brother you'll ever have.'

'One's enough,' she teased, a hint of the Natalie he knew in there somewhere.

'All right, if you could wipe down the countertops, that would be a big help.' Unfortunately his day was far from over. 'I need to get to the markets and my suppliers.'

'Tonight?'

'I go every day if I can – fresh ingredients, nothing like them. But I'm afraid there's no main meal left for us tonight, so are you happy with takeout?'

'Sure. I'll go get it if you like.'

'That would be a big help, thanks sis.'

He took off his apron and hung it on its hook before he mentioned the tables in the dining room that still needed his attention.

'I can do those,' Natalie told him.

'Thanks, that's great. And I promise after that you can relax. We all can.'

In the communal lounge, Rupert found Katy chatting to guests as she fixed their drinks and when she had a moment to come over, he explained what Natalie was doing. 'I'll go out and get supplies now but won't be long, then if you let me know the details

of that Italian place you'd like to try, my sister said she'll go pick up
the takeout.'

'Great. And I'll make sure I've at least swept the hallway on the
first floor – someone seems to have dropped a load of cookie
crumbs,' she said in a low voice so as to maintain their professionalism and discretion when guests were around. 'But I might leave
the mopping of the downstairs hallway until really early tomorrow
morning before the breakfast rush starts.'

'Happy to do that when I'm up.'

But she wouldn't have it. 'I'll do it; you have enough on in the
mornings.'

'True that.' He hovered a moment. 'Was your boyfriend happy
with the coffees?'

'Former boyfriend,' she smiled. 'And yes, very happy.'

And so was he when he headed away from the inn. He
could've stayed chatting to Katy for hours but instead swapped
conversation with her to ingredient talk at the markets with
suppliers while he sampled cheeses at one place, seasonal fresh
fruit at another. He even found himself whistling all the way
back to the Inglenook Inn, despite the heavy bags he was
carrying.

* * *

The moment he arrived back at the inn, his elated mood
plummeted.

He closed the front door and followed the voices of Katy and
Natalie who were in the communal lounge. Thankfully all other
guests were absent, whether out and about in the city or in the
apartments above he had no idea, but he was glad nobody else
witnessed this.

'If you're not going to help, at least go up to your apartment and get out of the way,' Katy snapped. He'd never seen her lose her temper before but right now she looked and sounded furious.

'What's going on?' He hovered at the foot of the stairs to make sure they weren't interrupted, at least not until they'd both calmed down.

'Ask her,' Natalie said, pointing at Katy.

But Katy was shaking her head, walking away from Natalie and she looked Rupert's way. 'I know she's your sister, but—'

'What would you know about sisters or brothers anyway?' Natalie bit back. 'You don't have any of your own, so you have no idea about either of us.'

'Natalie, that's enough,' Rupert said firmly and before he could send her out of the room, she stomped off and up the stairs like a child.

'I'm sorry.' Katy slumped at the desk, head in her hands. Was she crying?

But he didn't want to ask because he sensed that if she was, she didn't want it to be pointed out.

'What she said, about siblings,' Katy began, looking up at him, eyes filled with tears but none of them spilling over, 'I—'

He interrupted her. 'I wasn't gossiping about you, just that we got talking yesterday and Natalie asked about you. I told her you were from around here, you were an only child, your dad lived in the city. I'm sorry if you didn't want me to tell her anything about you.'

'No, it's fine, it's not that.' She pulled herself together and it made him wonder how often she had to pull herself from being upset one minute to professional the next. It couldn't be an easy thing to do.

'Do you want to come and talk in the kitchen?'

But she shook her head. 'I'll stay here, I'm honestly okay.'

He indicated the bags. If she wasn't going to go with him, he'd come back. 'Let me dump these and we'll talk.' As quick as he could, he went into the kitchen and unloaded refrigerator ingredients but left what needed to go in the pantry. No rush, not like the situation unfolding at the front of the inn moments ago. And he felt responsible when Natalie was his sister and clearly the source of Katy's problems.

'Right, what happened?' he asked the minute he got back to the lounge, where Katy was on her own now. At her confusion, he prompted, 'With Natalie.'

'Oh, right.' She seemed to have to shift her thinking somehow. 'I lost my temper with her when I found her sitting in the dining room.'

'I asked her to clean the tables.'

'I know you did. She had a cloth but the tables were still filthy. I showed the Garcias back in there as they wanted to play board games and I ended up having to make them wait while I wiped down and dried all the surfaces. Natalie had disappeared pretty quickly and I didn't want to create a scene by going after her. Once I'd settled the Garcias, I found her sitting in the lounge and I'm afraid I lost my temper.' She looked up at him with a small, wary smile. 'I bet you never thought you'd be refereeing between two women at work.'

'Definitely wasn't in my job description,' he answered softly. 'Mind you, I'm kind of used to it at home.' He attempted a smile to make her feel better.

But Katy went over to the sofa and slumped down, defeated. 'I don't usually lose my temper like that. This job is actually pretty wonderful, the inn too, but...'

'I get it. Natalie's hardly your average employee and I suspect half of it is because she's my sister, the rest because she doesn't particularly have a vested interest in this place or the job.'

'She said she didn't feel very well but I still had a go at her.'

He sighed. 'She's got things going on, which is not an excuse to be rude in any way. I'll have a word with her about that.' Again. 'And after tonight, she'll go stay at my place but I still want her to come help out here. We need the extra pair of hands.' And he couldn't imagine letting her loose with an apartment of her own, space to do exactly how she pleased.

'It wasn't that she didn't help, it's that I thought that job was done and then found myself having to do it. This place is looking dirty already and I can't get a cleaner in. I've tried to find someone – you'd think it would be easy.' She shrugged. 'And it's not just finding someone, it's vetting them to make sure they're suitable. When I interviewed for the job, Darcy explained how highly Sofia thinks of her staff which also tells me she likes to make sure she gets the right people working for her.'

He liked how she'd been able to sum up his boss, even though the pair had never met. 'For what it's worth, I think you're right not to hire just anyone. I mean, we've got enough to contend with supervising Natalie.'

That got a smile out of her, a gorgeous smile that reached her eyes and made her cheeks go a little pink.

'Besides,' he carried on, 'this place could do with a better clean but it's hardly filthy. It's good enough thanks to us staying on top of it. And my sister... well... all I can say is thank you for tolerating having her around. You could easily tell Sofia it's you or her and walk out on me.'

'I'd never do that.'

He'd sat next to her on the sofa with one arm resting along the back of it and realised this was exactly how her former boyfriend had been sitting this morning when he'd seen them together. He stood up. 'Now seems like a good time to order that food.'

'Rupert, about what Natalie said, the comment about me not understanding either of you...'

'She was just hitting out, trying to find your Achilles heel. Accusing you of not understanding what it's like to be a sibling was a low and pathetic blow.'

'It's just—'

'Don't overthink it. I'll go finish putting away the groceries in the pantry and order the takeout.'

She took a moment to let it go and then told him, 'I'll head to my apartment and grab the takeout menu for you. I was looking at it yesterday.'

'That's the spirit.' He only hoped they could get through dinner without any more clashes.

They both went their separate ways and when Rupert came back along the hallway, he thought he heard Katy talking in the lounge until he saw her come down the stairs. They both looked in to see Natalie sitting at the desk on the telephone.

Rupert watched Katy head over to her as his sister scribbled something down on a piece of paper. He'd wondered why she hadn't used her own phone when she hung up the call and announced proudly that they had another booking.

Natalie looked from her brother to Katy. 'What? I thought you both wanted me to pull my weight. So that's what I'm doing,' she huffed but changed her tone at Rupert's warning look. 'Nobody else was here.'

Katy jumped in. 'Thank you, Natalie. Are those the details?' She put out a hand to take the piece of paper Natalie had been scribbling on.

'I've written down the date as well as the name and the phone number of the guest, someone called Mrs Cheddington. I said someone would call her back to confirm.'

'Is this a five?' Katy squinted, looking at the piece of paper. She could read the date perfectly but not the phone number.

Natalie looked at where Katy's finger pointed. 'It's a three.'

But clearly it wasn't because when Katy handed them the takeout menu to peruse as she tried to return the call, Rupert could tell from Katy's face she was having little success.

'I've tried a five and a three, neither works.' Katy's voice was even. 'Did you ask for a deposit?' she asked Natalie.

'I'm sorry, no.' Her gaze went to her brother and to Katy. 'I thought I was doing the right thing.'

'It's fine, I'll just do caller ID.'

But a minute later, after no joy, she asked Natalie, 'And was it for one person?'

'Four... she definitely said four.'

'Are you positive?' Rupert asked her.

'Yes,' Natalie groaned. 'I am capable of answering a phone. I thought I was doing everyone a favour.'

'You did, thank you,' said Katy.

Rupert sent a smile in her direction to express his gratitude.

Katy had a look on the computer. 'The only apartment available on that date is the top-floor suite. Did you give any prices?' she asked Natalie.

'I didn't know any.' And then she added, 'They did ask about food and I told them how good the chef was.'

Rupert nodded his thanks. 'I appreciate the vote of confidence.'

Katy swished away any worries. 'I'm sure they'll call back again when we don't return their call. I'll book the apartment out tentatively anyway and fingers crossed we'll hear from them soon.' With a reassuring look in Natalie's direction, she picked up the takeout menu. 'Food?'

'Food,' Natalie smiled in return.

Was it too much to expect a truce on the horizon?

When Natalie left to pick up the order, Rupert and Katy both sat back on the sofa.

'At least she didn't ignore the phone,' Katy said, both of them looking at the fireplace and the vast flower arrangement; neither of them with much energy left, at least until they'd eaten.

'Good point. That might have wound me up even more than her taking the wrong number.'

He hoped from here on in it would be smooth sailing with Katy and Natalie. He didn't want to drive Natalie away and for her to go back to whoever she'd been hanging out with in Vermont and at the same time, he really didn't want to drive Katy away either, not only because he needed her to help him run this place but also because he was beginning to feel more strongly than he'd felt about a woman in a really long time.

11

KATY

Katy woke the next morning before her alarm, conscious she was going to be mopping floors, a task she wanted done before anyone else stirred. The Italian takeout last night had been pleasant and Katy had even seen a slightly calmer, friendlier side to Natalie, although she'd been relatively unforthcoming about her life in Vermont. By the time Katy headed upstairs to bed, she'd still found herself wondering how much longer Natalie was going to stay here in New York. She was helping out, sure, but Katy sensed she wasn't the only one who knew they'd manage better without her around. Rupert would never say it, though; he had strong family values and already it was something Katy admired about him. She liked to think she had similar principles, but even if she did, her family had fractured in ways that seemed beyond repair.

She drank a glass of water and went straight downstairs where she did a once-over with a broom to start with – sweeping the hallway was far quieter than using the vacuum at this early hour – then filled a bucket with hot water and floor cleaner and grabbed the mop. She started at the front entrance and would progress all the way along the floorboards to the kitchen and dining room and hopefully do it without anyone interrupting her, partly because she wanted it to stay clean and dry before anyone else walked on it, but also because she was doing the job in a scruffy pair of tracksuit bottoms and a spaghetti-strapped top – not the sort of attire she wanted guests to see.

As she worked, she thought again of the sting of Natalie's words about her not understanding brothers and sisters. Natalie probably hadn't thought much of what she'd said but the words had certainly stayed with Katy. And she'd tried to tell Rupert the whole truth yesterday, but he'd mistaken her need to talk for over-sensitivity at his sister's remark when it was so much more than that.

When Rupert had asked her a while back whether she had any sisters, she'd answered with an honest no. But when he asked if she had brothers, she'd said that it was just her. And while that was the case and had been for some time, it covered up the truth about David.

Over time, Katy had pushed her brother out of her mind and rarely brought up his name if she could help it. The first time she'd talked about him in a long while was with Shaun the other day. She'd told Shaun about Natalie and the conversation Katy had heard in the basement and Shaun had asked Katy whether she was struggling with Natalie's presence because it was a reminder. He'd been spot on. Natalie's troubled life was a double-barrelled reminder, not only that David was a drug addict but also that even though she'd tried – they all had – Katy had never been able to stick by her sibling in the way Rupert was doing for his sister now.

Katy had loved her brother, she still did, but she didn't love the person he'd become, the pain he'd caused their family. And so, over time, it had become easier to not talk about him and to try to move forwards. When Katy had overheard the conversation between Natalie and Rupert, the way Natalie said she wasn't an addict, it had brought back so many memories of hearing the same words coming from David's mouth time and time again, the lies he'd told, the shiftiness. She'd immediately catastrophised and had visions of Natalie doing drugs at the inn and dragging her and Rupert down with her. She knew from bitter experience what a drug habit could do, not only to the addict but to those around them.

Katy realised now that she was pushing on the mop so hard in her frustration that she was in danger of hurting her neck from all the tension and she eased back a bit, dipping the mop back into the water that had already turned murky.

The worst thing about David had been his selfishness and the way he brought trouble to their doorstep. Her mind spun back to the day the police had turned up one sunny afternoon as she and their mom sat on the porch swing, laughing about the racoon that had sneaked in the open kitchen window and stolen the last doughnut. It had dragged it away but in doing so, the jam from inside had oozed everywhere – all across the countertop, down the side of the dishwasher and along the windowsill. Katy had laughed, saying she hoped he wouldn't be disappointed with the lack of jam when the little trash bandit got it back to wherever he was taking it.

Their laughter had been cut short when they saw a police car pull up outside the house and the officer looking their way. He'd opened up the back door to the patrol car and David had got out. He'd been found hanging around with a group of well-known drug dealers and while a few of them had been arrested, David had shown no signs of having used or possessing anything. The officer delivered a stark warning to David and to Judy about getting involved with those people and Katy suspected he was a dad himself by the way he spoke when he warned them to put a stop to this before it escalated.

But David didn't learn any lessons that day, it seemed. He might well have been doing drugs already by that point, but no matter whether he had or hadn't, that's the path he either started down or continued along. He began to spend more and more time away from the house, started to lie, steal, not come home half the time, leaving their parents worried sick. And Katy had hated what he'd done to their family. Her mom had made excuses for him; Katy got it, she wanted to believe in her son and for a while, Katy tried to be like she was. But in the end, all she began to see was the lies he told, the resistance to letting any of them help, that he'd had choices just like everyone did and he'd chosen to go along a path he seemed reluctant to change.

Katy shifted the bucket along the hallway of the inn now, the water getting murkier and murkier as she got nearer to the kitchen entrance.

To this day, Katy's heart still broke knowing her brother had robbed her family of so much happiness when they were intact, a unit, all together and healthy. And one of the worst things David had ever done was not turning up to their mom's funeral. Her dad had held himself together that day and, at one point, when Katy had looked across at him as he held tightly to her hand, she'd wondered whether it was actually for the best that David hadn't come. Their mom had died without ever reconciling with her own son and Katy had done her best to track David down in the weeks before her death, knowing she didn't have long left. But he'd kept a low profile and although she'd found out where he was staying, and sent him notice of the funeral, he still hadn't showed.

Whatever problems he had, Katy wasn't sure there was any excuse in the world for not being there to bury your own mom.

Katy finished the mopping and emptied the spent water down the sink in the kitchen, careful to leave the area around it splash free and totally clean, the way Rupert always did.

Happy she'd managed to do the floors entirely without inter-ruption, she was glad to see the floor was drying already thanks to the open window in the lounge – she'd used a step stool to climb up and give it a decent shove. She tiptoed in only the dry patches, which were bigger and bigger by the time she got to the foot of the stairs and headed to her apartment. She hadn't quite made it through her apartment door when she came face to face with Rupert, who'd just come out of his.

'That's the most informal outfit I've ever seen you in.' His eyes teased, his mouth tugged at the corners.

'I wanted to do the mopping before I got dressed and before anyone else was up.'

'You've already done it?'

'Yes, and it dried quick enough. Watch out towards the kitchen as it might still be a bit wet there; that's where I finished.' She frowned. 'It's way too early even for the markets, isn't it?'

'I'm going for a run.'

'You're a runner?'

'When I can – not as much as I should do, but I need it.'

She almost asked whether he needed it because of Natalie but they'd all had such a pleasant evening last night that she didn't want anything to ruin that. 'I've got my dad stopping by too, so thought I'd better get a head start on things.'

'What time's he coming?'

'Mid-morning, he said. I thought it would be a good time – after the breakfast rush and morning chores but before check-out or check-in and before dinner.'

'I'll make you up a morning tea platter.'

'You don't have to go to any bother.'

'It's my pleasure, Katy.'

Uneasy beneath his gaze, she said, 'I'd better get inside before any guests see me.'

'Oh, I don't know...' He had one hand on the top banister ready to go down the stairs. 'I kind of like it.' And with that, he was off.

Katy smiled through her shower and had time for breakfast given the crazy hour she was up – she'd even had the forethought to bring some muesli up to her apartment from the kitchen last night as well as a small jug of milk. She couldn't eat Rupert's luxury breakfasts the whole time she was here, there was such a thing as too much good food, especially if he was making a morning tea platter for her and her dad. Knowing Rupert, it would be generous in its quantity.

Katy didn't stop all morning after she returned downstairs. The phone seemed to ring non-stop with enquiries, one cancellation and one booking for a guest who'd only left last week and had already decided they were coming back at the same time next year.

Katy was adding a collection of leaflets to the rack in the lounge when her dad arrived. The door to the inn was unlocked and sometimes left open wide if one of them was around, and today being so beautiful, it was open at one side, welcoming guests and visitors inside the stunning brownstone.

She hugged him tight. 'It feels like forever since I saw you.'

That got a laugh. Dressed in shorts and a T-shirt to make the most of the weather, he said, 'You've not been gone long, but I know what you mean.' He handed her the bouquet he'd held out of the way while they hugged. 'These are for your room; I bet you haven't had a chance to spoil yourself yet, have you?'

She took the beautiful arrangement of fresh, pink peonies. 'Thank you, Dad. And you're right, I've been so busy that I haven't. I even went to the florist to keep the flowers around the inn looking nice and fresh, but it went out of my head to pick some up for myself. And I spend very little time up there – it felt like too much of a luxury when I thought about it afterwards.'

'No such thing, not for you.' He had his arm around her again as she led them into the lounge.

The phone rang and while Katy answered the call, it gave Wade a chance to take in his daughter's new workplace. She confirmed the rates of the top-floor apartment with the potential guest and by the time she was free to talk to her dad, he was sitting on the sofa smiling.

'That phone has been ringing non-stop all morning,' she told him.

Wade was looking all around the room. 'I'm not surprised. This inn really is quite something. How did we never know this was here? Your mother would've loved it.'

In the early days of Stephanie, Katy had mentioned Judy whenever she felt like it, whether Stephanie was around or not, even though Wade sometimes seemed uncomfortable doing so. Katy had told herself that Stephanie should be fine with it because she knew what she was getting into; she knew Wade's history. But over time, Katy had mellowed a little in that regard – she'd begun to realise that the reason why Wade didn't mention Judy too much in front of Stephanie was out of respect. And if anything, it made her love him that little bit more and it made her proud he was so considerate. And so she'd kept talk of her mom mostly to when it was just the two of them.

'Mom always chose smaller inns and independently run places,' smiled Katy.

'That she did. I remember her booking one particular hotel in Florida for us one year and it was described as boutique and family owned. Little did we realise until we got there that it would be like staying with the family. They were loud, argued all the time, and your mother ended up checking us in to a big fancy hotel for the last night. But this place...'

'I'm glad you love it.' In her short time here, Katy had noted that close to every single guest who came through the front doors complemented the inn on its welcoming ambience, described it as personal and a home away from home. Those who didn't say much were usually the business clients who most of the time were so busy and wiped out after their work that all they were after was a comfy bed and clean sheets.

Katy inhaled the scent of her flowers again. She'd kept a hold of them while she was on the phone. 'Come on, let me give you a tour of the inn and I'll see if there's a vase in my apartment for these.' Having fresh flowers around was a habit she'd got from her mom, who always had vases of flowers dotted around the home. Katy and Wade had carried on with the tradition after she passed away. It made Judy feel that bit closer to them.

'The owner or manager won't mind?'

'I'm kind of the stand-in manager, remember, along with the chef and his sister, who turned up out of the blue.'

'Sounds an interesting arrangement.'

'You could say that.'

By the time they headed back downstairs, her dad had had the full tour, including her apartment, where he'd noted Samuel's position in the centre of her pillows. She'd found a cream vase on the shelf and left her flowers ready to welcome her back once she finished her working day. No matter how tired she was, she knew the sight of them would make her smile.

Chatting away, they found Natalie sitting in the lounge, scrolling on her phone. She stopped when Katy and her dad went into the room.

Katy introduced the pair, but Natalie didn't hang around.

'The sister?' Wade waited until Natalie was long gone before he asked the question. He'd sat down on the sofa. 'She seems nice.'

'Yeah. She's not too bad.' She wasn't sure how genuine she

sounded, probably more so than she might have done before they had dinner together last night and the atmosphere thawed a bit.

Rupert came through and didn't hesitate to introduce himself to her dad. 'Natalie told me Katy had a visitor. It's good to meet you, sir.'

'Likewise. I hear you're quite the chef.'

The way he said it implied, at least it did the way Katy heard it, that she hadn't been able to stop extolling the virtues of this man every time she got the chance. But if Katy tried to play down the compliments she'd given him during her brief conversations with her dad, she suspected she'd only make matters worse.

'Well, you can let me know if you agree after you have the morning tea platter I prepared. It's more of a lunch platter, really.'

Wade patted his stomach. 'Not going to say no to that. I went for a run before I came here and only had a banana.'

'I'm glad to hear you have an appetite,' said Rupert and to Katy, 'The platter is in the fridge. I can stay in here for an hour.'

'Are you sure?'

'Of course, take a proper break. You were up early enough working. Go and enjoy the food, relax in the dining room while you've got it to yourselves. I've opened up the balcony doors; it's a beautiful day. And I'll come get you if I need you.'

With his kind smile and compassionate nature, Katy realised how difficult it must be for Rupert to bring his sister into line. When she'd heard them talking, he'd been firm, but deep down he cared and that streak was always going to win through. He was willing to accept others' faults, namely Natalie's, and Katy only hoped his sister would realise how lucky she was to have him on her side and willing to do what he could for her.

In the dining room, the breeze was already circulating, bringing the sounds of New York inside even at the back of the inn.

'You make yourself comfortable, Dad. I'll go get the platter.' She gestured to the door in case her dad preferred it closed.

'I like hearing the city; reminds me why I moved here, the life,' he winked.

She was glad he'd made the change; he'd needed it and she was still smiling as she went off to the kitchen to get the platter. But when she pushed open the door to the kitchen, which gleamed with its stainless steel and polished countertops, she found Natalie inside and, worse, Natalie picking pieces off the platter in the refrigerator.

'What are you doing?'

Natalie rolled her eyes in the way that already had Katy on edge. 'What does it look like I'm doing? I'm eating. I'm hungry.'

'And you didn't think to check with anyone before you helped yourself?'

'You all seemed kind of busy in the lounge.'

Katy leaned across her and took the platter from the refrigerator, the food wrap loose at one edge. She hadn't done too much damage other than scoffing a few grapes, by the looks of things.

'Is it for the guests?' Natalie asked.

'No, it's for me.'

Natalie waited a beat before she said, 'So you've got my brother making your lunches now.'

Katy had thought after last night they were in a much better place, but it seemed she was wrong. 'Natalie, I hope we can get on while you're here, but you have to make an effort too.' She almost added that that meant no snarky remarks but she couldn't be bothered with an argument, so she picked up the platter and left.

'Everything all right?' Wade had grown quite adept at reading her moods.

'It's all good, almost dropped this, that's all. I'd have felt terrible.' Just as Wade had got better at reading her moods or knowing what she was thinking, she'd got more skilled at covering up her feelings. She'd had to do it with Stephanie around, especially in the early days of her dad's new relationship when Katy had really resented the intrusion. She still wasn't entirely happy about it, but she supposed she'd got used to having another person around so much.

Wade took the plate his daughter handed him as well as the cutlery she'd wrapped in a napkin. And when Natalie came in, having assumed they'd gone to enjoy the platter in the lounge, Katy suspected, she didn't even utter a word, just huffed and walked out.

'She was probably coming to clean up or something,' Katy lied.

He wasn't stupid. 'You're not getting on with her.'

Katy sighed. 'No, I'm not. She turned up out of the blue and despite helping out a bit, I think she still forgets this is her brother's place of work.'

'Rupert seems calm enough.'

'I think he's a saint putting up with her antics.'

'Oh?'

She swished away her remark. 'Maybe I'm just getting stressed, wanting to do this job right and prove I can, worrying she'll get in the way.'

'You always wanted to do the best job, something I am very proud of.'

'Thanks, Dad. Now dig in.'

His eyes bulged. 'I think I'm hungrier now I've seen this.'

'Me too. It's spectacular, isn't it?'

The platter was way too much for the two of them – Natalie probably could've easily shared it and there still would've been lots left over – but that wasn't really the point. Rupert had done a professional job, as always. A variety of cheeses and crackers had been arranged alongside a small pot of sweet tomato and chilli chutney. Grapes – some purple, others green – lay in bunches next to kiwi fruits he'd cut in half and made to look like opened up flowers, there were triangles of waffles stacked in a row, one behind the other, with a little pot of cream and another of maple syrup. Strawberries and blueberries added even more colour and the slices of lemon drizzle cake looked mouth-watering.

When her dad had had a couple of crackers with chutney and cheese, he said, 'You know what siblings are like.' He'd clearly been eating and thinking about Natalie's appearance at the same time. 'When you were younger, you and David used to rile one another in whatever way you could – name-calling, tattling, arguing over who washed more dishes than the other one or whose turn it was to feed the goldfish.'

'They were his goldfish,' said Katy, allowing him the happier recollections. Talking about David often brought to mind memories so sour it was important to savour those that weren't.

'He said they were yours.'

'Mine died – his two remained.'

Wade laughed, going for a section of waffle he drizzled with maple syrup and a little blob of cream. 'My guess,' he said when he'd finished his mouthful, 'is that because Rupert is this girl's brother, she's pushing the boundaries. I don't know him, but he seems to have his head on straight. I'm sure he won't let it go too far.'

'Let's hope not.'

'Give her a chance, love. I know you have high standards.' And then he looked puzzled. 'Come to think of it, I haven't asked – why is she working here if she's visiting?'

Katy could've told him they were so desperate they needed her to, but she found herself saying, 'She's in a bit of trouble,' and popped a couple of blueberries into her mouth.

'What sort of trouble?'

She took a piece of the lemon drizzle cake and put it on her dad's plate for him and then put another piece on her own before she admitted, 'The sort of trouble David was in.'

After a beat, he said, 'I can see why that might be getting to you, love.'

It was. She was already worried that whatever Natalie was mixed up in would bring trouble Rupert's way.

'Rupert will be all right, I'm sure.'

'Dad, you only met him for all of about a minute.'

'I'm a good judge of character. And your mom would've liked him too.'

'She'd have liked his cooking,' Katy grinned. 'How do you feel about him, Dad? David, I mean.' They rarely talked about him now and that was largely down to her avoiding the topic as much as she could.

'He's still my son, still your brother, he's still family. I love him as much as I love you.' He put down his half-eaten piece of cake. 'But I don't love the things he's done, particularly not showing up for your mom's funeral.'

At first, her dad hadn't wanted to move out of the family home because their house in Scarsdale was the only place David knew where to find them. But the longer time went on and they continued to hear nothing from David, the more Wade realised he had to move their lives forward regardless.

'I couldn't help David when he didn't want to be helped,' said Wade. 'And I know you don't like to talk about your brother too often.'

'Sometimes I want to,' she said.

'But it's hard…'

'So hard, Dad.'

'Then let's leave it for now; we can talk more another time.'

'I'd like that.' She smiled. 'And now we need to address the elephant in the room.'

He understood and began to laugh. 'Don't call Stephanie that.'

At least it broke the tension. Who would've thought Katy would prefer to talk about her dad's upcoming nuptials? But compared to discussing David, it wasn't anywhere near as painful.

'It's sudden, Dad.'

'Not really. We've been dating a while.'

'Not just the decision: the wedding day too.'

'You've had no time to get your head around it, I know, and I'm sorry. But Stephanie and I didn't see the point in waiting and it means her closest friend can be there. You are coming, aren't you? Even though this job is demanding?'

The look on his face had her quickly reassuring him. 'Of course I am, I wouldn't dream of missing it. I've already booked the time off.' But his relief didn't last when she added, 'You're changing.'

His look of surprise faded as his face softened. 'I'm sure I am. All of us are, Katy.'

'I don't want us to lose anything else.'

He reached for her hand. 'Neither do I. And you're not about to lose me. But change isn't always bad. There's no one right path. Remember that, not just for me but for yourself too.'

All of a sudden, she was thrust back into a memory from her childhood of sitting on the sofa next to her dad when he came in from work. She'd come third in the school's spelling bee that day and had been disappointed. Her mom had made cookies, her mom had talked to her, but it was her dad she'd sought comfort from later on in the form of leaning her head on his shoulder as they sat and watched TV. He knew how hard she'd worked to learn her words and he could tell that Judy had helped but she still wasn't convinced. He'd told her that day that he was proud of her but that she must remember life was full of circumstances where you had to manage expectations, where you set goals. He explained that humans weren't infallible – he'd got her to spell the word after he told her what it meant. She'd always set high goals, expected a lot of herself and he'd made her realise that day that she could make mistakes in life; in fact, mistakes were all a part of it, a part of learning who you really were and who you wanted to be.

Katy had forgotten until now that it wasn't always her mom who did the talking – Judy might have been the better of the pair at lengthy conversations, at talking around a subject and covering all the ground they needed to, but her dad was pretty wise and under-standing too.

'I'm worried about all the running you've been doing, Dad,' Katy admitted. She might as well come right out and say it. 'You never did it before.'

'Before Stephanie, you mean.'

She opened her mouth but couldn't deny that was exactly what she meant. Her shoulders slumped. 'I can't lose you, Dad.'

'And I've told you, you won't.' He shook his head, refusing the mere suggestion. 'Would it make you feel better if I get the once-over with the doctor?'

'Yes,' she said without delay. She almost smiled at the relief until she realised that wasn't the only thing bothering her. 'I'm worried you're doing all this – the running, the drinking milk-shakes, the healthier eating – well, that it's all for her.'

'For Stephanie?'

She nodded.

He gripped her hand a little tighter. 'Katy, I'm my own person, but yes, I took up running at Stephanie's suggestion.' He didn't let her pull her hand away when she tried as though she'd just been proven right. 'I had lower back pain, I felt old, I was spending too many hours sitting, and I needed something extra for my mind and my body. Stephanie suggested hiking and we've done that a few times and of course I have golf, but then she asked why I didn't try running. Once I started, I was hooked.' His eyes lit up. 'Just like that, Katy, I really loved it and to be honest, I wonder why I never took it up sooner. Stephanie came with me a few times.'

'She did?'

'Much like you, she worried it would be too much, even though it had been her suggestion. I think she thought I might try a light jog once a week and was surprised how often I wanted to get out there, the distances I began to cover. It didn't take her long to realise I was absolutely fine.'

'You really like it that much?'

'I really do. And as for the milkshakes – Stephanie urged me to try one with some magic ingredient or other – can't remember what it was – and at first, I drank it to please her, but then I began to enjoy them. I guess tastes evolve.'

'Oh, Dad, you must think I'm being ridiculous.' She wiped at the side of her eye, remembering she was still in her workplace, she was an adult.

'Not at all. It's a big thing to get your head around, your dad in a new relationship.'

'Are you really sure being married to Stephanie is what you want?'

'Of course.' And if he hadn't waited a beat to answer the question, she might well have believed him.

She sat up straighter. 'You have doubts.'

'No, I don't.' He puffed out his cheeks and then put up his hand, his index finger and thumb about an inch apart. 'Well, maybe just a tiny bit. But that makes me human, doesn't it?'

'Yes and no.' She didn't want to upset him, but she'd always liked to get things out in the open wherever she could. 'Dad, you're really good at being able to tell when something is bothering me, and it's the same the other way round. I don't think you're telling me everything.' A thought hit her. The thought that this had nothing to do with Stephanie and everything to do with her. 'Is it because you're worried I won't handle you marrying again?'

'I know you, Katy, and while it won't be easy, I know you'll adjust. You're already beginning to, I hope.'

She nodded. Because she realised that while she wasn't entirely comfortable, she was starting to make sense of it all.

'And we really are happy, Katy.' But he added, 'I can't quite put my finger on what it is. Perhaps it's just jitters, but in the last week, Stephanie has been... aloof.'

'What do you mean, *aloof*?'

'Just little things like the odd hushed phone call, nipping out at weird times and being evasive about where she's going.'

'Those are really minor things, Dad. Perhaps you're getting nervous. Marriage is a big step.' She couldn't believe she was the one talking him out of having doubts. She should be leaping on any kind of negative and running with it in the hope he'd change his mind. Or maybe sitting here with Wade and a high level of honesty on both of their parts was helping her to see that this wasn't her decision to make. He was changing but perhaps he *was* right to do so. And if it was a mistake, then maybe that was his mistake to make.

'Perhaps I am.' He finished his cake. 'Putting my worries aside, this lemon drizzle reminds me that Stephanie suggested you might like to organise a cake for us. She thought it was a nice way to get you involved. It's very short notice but then again everything is last minute. And it doesn't have to be a proper wedding cake, just something tasty and enough for a dozen people. If you're too busy, don't worry. It was just a thought.'

She leapt in with, 'Dad, I'd love to.'

'You would?'

She nodded and smiled. 'I really would.'

'Stephanie requested no nuts.'

'Consider it done.'

'We'll reimburse you too.' He held up a hand to stop argument. 'I insist. And we both agreed we'd love a surprise, so pick something and run with it. You know both of us love most sorts of cake.'

'Unless it has nuts around the edge,' Katy smiled. She remembered the pair of them bringing home cake for Stephanie's last birthday. It had been pouring with rain and they'd obviously not checked inside the box in their haste to get back to the apartment and when they opened it, it was the correct sponge and filling but the baker had decorated the edges with chopped nuts, something Stephanie really didn't like.

Katy and her dad spent some time talking about what plans had been made for the wedding and by the time Wade had talked about the venue, the minimal guest list, which, Katy was glad to know included Shaun who was close to the family, and food choices they were going for, he seemed a little better. But Katy still had niggling worries. She hoped it was just jitters on Wade's part and that Stephanie wasn't up to anything, because she didn't want her dad hurt. He'd had too much of that in one lifetime.

Katy showed her dad out and went into the lounge to see Rupert. 'Thank you for giving me that time,' she said to the back of his head. He was in the desk chair, facing away from the room and looking at the ceiling. 'And the food was amazing.'

He spun round and smiled. 'I'm glad. I've been rushed off my feet in here.'

She began to laugh. 'Looks like it.'

'Only just sat down, I promise you.'

'I'll take your word for it. Now, what can you tell me about the best place to get a decent cake for a dozen people at short notice? I mean, I know there are a ton of bakeries in Manhattan but I don't want to mess this up.'

'All right, rewind a bit.'

She reminded him about the time off she'd requested for her dad's wedding and then recapped Wade's request about the cake.

Rupert went over to the rack of leaflets and plucked a flyer from the bottom row to hand to her. 'Can't go wrong with this guy.'

She looked at the name. 'Finn. He's good at cakes?'

'Brilliant at them.'

'Must be if Sofia has his bakery details on display.'

'I met him for the first time when he came here to the inn one year.'

'He was a guest?'

'Not in the usual sense, no.' With a smile, he said, 'It's a long story of a big thanksgiving meal held at the inn for a group of friends, a story where he came along and created plenty of drama. He turned up young, free, single, and troubled and now he has a totally different career and he's fallen in love.' Rupert shrugged. 'This inn has a few love stories.'

'It would appear so,' she smiled, hoping she'd hear more of that story some day.

He pointed to the flyer she was holding. 'Go see Finn. He'll sort you out.'

When Rupert left to go to the markets, Katy got on with some more cleaning. All the shelves and the bar top in the lounge needed attention and so she dusted those as well as around the fireplace and the desk. She used glass cleaner for the inside of the windows, which had a surprising number of fingerprints on them. She updated the guest profile database with their most recent guest on the top floor so that if she checked in again in the future, they'd know that she liked to have fresh fruit and no cookies, and a selection of herbal teas rather than coffee.

A request for fresh towels on the top floor had come through –
usually guests could choose to have fresh each day or hang up wet
towels to be kinder for the environment, but it was entirely their
choice – and so Katy went back to the basement, found a large bath
towel plus a medium-sized as well as a hand towel. She wondered
where Natalie had disappeared off to and thought perhaps she'd
piggybacked Rupert's visit to the market. With any luck she had
and might even help him carry the shopping back.

Once Katy had delivered the towels to the top floor, she headed
back downstairs, but as she rounded the top of the staircase near
Sofia's apartment where Rupert and his sister were staying, she
noticed the door open. She went to check he hadn't left it that way
by mistake. It was an easy thing to do – sometimes she forgot she
wasn't coming out of her bedroom to a house but an inn with
multiple guests who came and went as they liked.

She was about to reach out and close the door when she
spotted Natalie through the open gap. She wasn't standing in front
of her but rather it was her reflection in the big walled mirror.

Katy pushed the door open because there was no mistaking
what Natalie was doing. 'What the hell are those?' She nodded to
the pills on the palm of Natalie's hand.

Natalie immediately put her hand and its contents behind her
back. 'Get out!'

'Not until you tell me what you're taking. What is it?'

'It's none of your damn business, that's what it is!'

'I'm in charge here as well as your brother.'

'And this is a private space – and it's a sodding vitamin, so just
get out.'

'Bullshit is it a vitamin.' She knew the signs. Those dark circles
beneath Natalie's eyes, the secrecy, the desperation behind her
voice that nobody discover what she was up to.

She'd seen it all before with David.

'Please, just leave me alone.' Natalie sounded different almost immediately, not defensive, more like she'd given up. It was the utter hopelessness of an addict.

'This is your brother's workplace, Natalie.'

Natalie sniffed and Katy wondered how she did it, how those tears had the power to render others sympathetic when all she should feel was anger that Natalie was doing something untoward. In a softer voice, she suggested, 'Why don't you try talking to Rupert?'

And then Natalie seemed to remember to put up the wall again, the suit of armour she usually wore around Katy and most likely everyone else. Katy had seen the same with David. There was denial, there was detachment, as though he'd separated his life from theirs.

'This is none of anybody's business but mine,' Natalie hissed, and she advanced on Katy so much that Katy backed up and out of the apartment before the door slammed in her face.

12

RUPERT

Rupert pounded the chicken with the mallet to tenderise it before he'd make schnitzel for tonight's dinner. He'd just added seasoning when Katy came into the kitchen to put some glasses into the dishwasher.

'You didn't tell me how it went with Finn at the bakery. I take it you've had a chance to go since I passed on his details the other day.' He squirted soap into his palms, ready to give his hands a good wash. 'Earth to Katy,' he said when it seemed she hadn't heard.

'Sorry,' she said. 'What did you say?'

He washed his hands twice after handling the raw meat and repeated himself.

'It went well,' she smiled. 'He showed me some photographs of cakes he's made before, he really is very talented.'

'What did you go for?' He fed some day-old bread into a food processor ready to make into crumbs for the schnitzel coating.

'Chocolate cake – I know Dad and Stephanie both love it. And I made sure it has both milk and dark chocolate in the design as Dad prefers dark, Stephanie milk.'

'Sounds like the perfect choice for them. Did you get to taste any?'

'He hasn't made it yet.'

'I know that.' She was being strange. 'I mean, did he give you samples? That's what they usually do to make sure you're going for a flavour you really want. I've been in there when I'm passing, even when I've no intention of buying a cake. I think Finn knows that, though.'

'I'm sure he does.' She left him to it.

Perhaps it was tiredness that had made Katy a bit out of sorts, Rupert decided. He'd been feeling it himself lately, but at least Natalie was at his apartment now, which meant she was no longer here full time to clash with him or Katy. The only problem with the arrangement was that with Natalie not living under the same roof and him not being able to run upstairs and tell her to get a move on, she'd been late starting here, twice already. But to give her credit, Natalie had made up for her lack of punctuality each time by working hard – answering phone calls, ordering taxis for guests, going out to source fresh flowers and replenishing all the vases at the inn. She'd given the front steps a good scrubbing, even though Rupert could tell she'd hated every minute and he'd seen her leaning against the railings more than once. Rupert was hoping that this temporary job and the hard work it entailed would do her good because the less she thought of this as a holi-day, the more likely she'd be to sort herself out, whatever was going on with her, and the less likely she was to get in with another bad crowd and do any more so-called experimenting with illicit substances.

Rupert looked at the clock in the kitchen as he whizzed the bread in the blender to chop it into fine pieces. He'd have to call his sister yet again if she wasn't here soon. It wasn't even an early start this time. She'd worked later last night and he'd told her she wasn't needed until late afternoon today, but she was almost out of time for that to be the case. He should've been more specific.

Katy popped her head around the door as Rupert put the breadcrumbs into a Tupperware container. 'Mind if I head out just before dinner service? I can cancel if not.'

'It's fine by me. Natalie can stay in the lounge while I'm in here, it's all good.' It was usually the lull at that time anyway. 'Are you going somewhere nice?'

'Just coffee.' And before he could ask who with, she said, 'I assumed Natalie wasn't in today. I thought perhaps she was out sick. That's why I was checking with you whether it's all right for me to take off.'

'She wasn't due in until late afternoon.'

Her eyes went to the clock in the same way his did again and he took his cell phone from his back pocket. 'Maybe I should check where she's at, she might be on her way.'

'I'll go ahead and clean apartment two.'

He dropped his chin to his chest in defeat. 'I'm sorry,' he said, looking back up at Katy. 'I'd forgotten Natalie was going to do that.' The person who checked out had pre-arranged an extra-late check-out to match up with their flight times and he and Katy had thought it would be fine but now realised even with Natalie here late afternoon, they were pushing it because the new guests would check in in an hour.

'Not your fault. But could you hover between here and the lounge for me while I do it? I can poke my head over the banisters every now and then but I'm unlikely to hear much with the vacuum going.'

'Will do.' He clicked on his sister's name but the call went unanswered. Three times.

No way was he leaving a voicemail.

He made a fourth attempt and this time she picked up and she sounded terrible.

She croaked as though she hadn't had a drink of water in hours. 'Oh God, is that the time? Shit. Rupert. Shit. Sorry. I tried to get up, twice.'

'Hang on, I'm not so much of an ass that I don't accept people aren't well. And none of us want to catch whatever you've got. What have you got, by the way?'

'Well, I just puked, does that help?'

'Yup. You rest up, have plenty of fluids, I'll call you again later.'

'Sure,' she managed again and she sounded so bad he didn't want to keep her.

He put his cell back in his pocket and had a quick check that no guests were lurking downstairs needing help before he cleaned the kitchen, washed up everything he'd used so far, and wiped down the surfaces. Dinner prep, no matter how much you'd done in advance, took time but he could put it off another hour.

Once Rupert heard the desk bell ding from the lounge, he went out to find the new guests had arrived already and he settled them with coffees and a slice of coffee cake each while he went to check on the apartment.

He found Katy in apartment two, her blonde hair haphazardly falling out of its clips as she lay across the mattress, trying to tuck in one side of the bottom sheet that didn't seem to want to behave.

'The guests are here,' he told her. 'They're happily settled in the lounge with an Americano each. I threw in some cake too.'

'Well done and I'm almost finished.' She puffed at the exertion of making the bed.

'And Natalie is out sick.'

She stopped what she was doing. 'Do you need to head out and check on her?'

'I think I'll avoid her since there's vomit involved. She's best to sleep and drink fluids and I'll call her later.'

'I'll cancel my plans and stay here.'

'Wouldn't hear of it.' Natalie had let them down and he knew Katy hadn't had a break all day. 'You're only a phone call away, right? And now the guests are here, it's less of a panic.'

'Rupert, I'll reschedule, it's no big deal.'

He didn't hesitate for long. 'All right, thank you.' When she grappled with the sheet again, he took one side and her the other and between them they had it stretched enough and on in seconds.

'Keeps you fit,' she laughed once they'd finished and between them they'd piled on all the pillows and arranged them. 'I bet cleaners never need to go to a gym.'

He spotted the wide-based, ceramic fruit bowl. 'I'll fill this with a selection of fruit and bring it back up.'

Katy closed the door behind them before tugging the clips from her hair. She ruffled the blonde waves. 'Do I look a total mess?'

He felt as though he'd been invited to look her up and down and really would love nothing more. 'No, you don't look a mess. Oh, wait.' He reached out and pulled a piece of cotton from her hair and the action jolted him when he realised how intimate it was.

'Thank you.'

He stopped before they headed downstairs. 'Natalie really did sound sick.'

'You don't have to convince me.'

'It's just the pair of you have clashed a fair bit since she came here, but she really doesn't mean any harm.' When Katy said nothing, just nodded her acknowledgement, he couldn't let it go. 'She's trying. She apologised. Can't you try to get on? She won't be here much longer.'

Katy leaned against the banister. 'I haven't been here very long myself.'

'It feels like you have.' He realised what that sounded like. 'I mean that in a good way.' There, he'd coaxed a smile, a real one.

'I'm a professional, Rupert.'

'Likewise.'

She hesitated but then, 'I don't want to get mixed up in anything that might ruin the inn's reputation, or yours, or mine.'

'You're not making much sense.'

Again, she seemed unsure whether to say anything but after a breath admitted, 'I heard you that day, you and Natalie.'

'What day?'

Katy had a look up the stairs, down the rest of them to make sure they were on their own, and then led him into a corner away from all apartment doors. 'I'll say this quickly and we can get on.'

With the fruit bowl still in his hand, he nodded.

'I heard you talking with Natalie in the basement, you told her your mom told you she'd been taking drugs.'

He slumped against the wall. 'You heard that?'

'I did.'

'Then you'll have also heard her say she promises she isn't an addict.' Doubt was written all over Katy's face.

'That's what they all say, unfortunately.'

'I believe her.'

Katy tried desperately to find the right words. 'Just be careful, Rupert.'

She cared, she actually cared, and he didn't mind it one bit. 'I will be, promise.'

'There's something else.'

And when she told him she'd seen Natalie in Sofia's apartment with pills in her hand, pills she'd hidden from view, his heart sank.

'Katy, I—'

'I thought you should know, that's all.'

'Thank you.' There was only one thing to do now. 'I know you just cancelled plans...'

She read his mind. 'Go. Go see her, talk to her, whatever you need to do. I'll be fine here.'

He indicated the fruit bowl before he took off down the stairs. Natalie was lying to him and so once he'd replenished the fruit, he'd be paying his younger sister a surprise visit.

No way was he going to put up with this.

13

KATY

The heavens had opened and Katy dealt with the big golfing umbrella Rupert brought back with him and Natalie beneath it. Admittedly, Natalie hadn't looked at all well as she came inside and sent daggers Katy's way, but obviously Rupert had no sympathy given what he now knew. And evidently he'd decided she wasn't all that contagious but rather covering something up.

Katy stayed out of the way of Rupert and his sister until dinner service which she helped with, avoiding getting too close to Natalie, who was assisting Rupert in the kitchen. Once that was done, she was back to the front of house and found another couple of umbrellas to give to two guests heading out, undeterred by a bit of spring rain. She handed them to the guests at the door to the inn and for a minute or two hovered at the top of the stoop when they left. The scent of rain filtered in as Katy watched the goings on outside: the sea of colourful pieces of material bobbing about as people tried to stay dry, a man running past with his jacket over his head, a desperate pedestrian hailing a taxi in an effort to avoid the downpour. The sound was soothing and calming, rain pitter pattering against the windowpanes in the lounge, hammering the steps from bottom to top but not quite up to the doorway where she stood.

She closed the doors and used an old towel to mop up the wet floor. She suspected she'd be doing that a few more times tonight.

When Rupert came along the hallway, she asked after his sister. 'How is she?'

'I believe that she isn't well, but I don't think she's contagious, especially given what I know. I couldn't leave her at the apartment and keep my mind on working here. I needed her to come back with me.'

'I understand.' She didn't want to make this any harder on him than it already was.

The way he slumped down on the bottom step of the staircase suggested he didn't have the energy for much apart from functioning to do the basics right now. 'I took a look around the apartment for myself and as far as I could see, she isn't hiding anything.'

Katy didn't want to tell him that drug addicts tended to be quite proficient at hiding things – the more practice they got, the better.

'She despises me for that, by the way.'

'I'm sure she does.' She sat down next to him. She wanted to tell him that she knew what it was like not trusting those you loved but this wasn't the moment to talk about David. It wasn't an easy topic to address, let alone go into detail about. There was pain from what David had done, guilt at having not tried harder with him than she had. And it didn't matter whether those feelings were justified or not, they were still there.

'She insists you were mistaken.' He had his hands clasped together on top of his thighs. 'Katy, I don't want this to come between us.'

'It won't,' she assured him. But there were so many reminders of David in all this. David had always denied any drug use, to them, probably to himself half the time. The drugs themselves probably did half of it, didn't let you see straight or a way out, turned you against anyone who gave a damn about you, made the user paranoid.

'Where is she now?' Katy asked.

'She's washing up the last of the big pots for me in the kitchen.'

'And you really don't think she's sick?'

'Not properly, no. She'd vomited once this morning and I called shortly afterwards but when I got to the apartment, she was sitting up eating a bowl of soup and said she felt a lot better. I let her tell me that when she thought I was just there to check on her rather than search the place as though she's some kind of criminal.'

She reached across and put her hand on his forearm and for a moment, he looked at her fingers against his darker skin. 'Let me know if there's anything I can do but I sense it's best I stay out of her way for now.'

'Yeah, probably.' He looked strung out, as though he'd just got given a second job and the workload was about to edge him towards tipping point.

Rupert's cell rang at the same time as they heard a couple more guests coming down the stairs.

Katy stood up to talk with them while Rupert took his call. The guests informed her that they weren't in the least bit intimidated by a little rain – they were from Seattle where it rained like you wouldn't believe, apparently. And so Katy handed them just the one umbrella when they said they'd share and bid them a good evening as they headed out into the depths of Manhattan.

Rupert came back to her as he hung up his call. 'It never rains but it pours,' he said.

She thought he was referring to the weather outside but judging by his face, it wasn't. 'What's up?' Please don't let this be another Natalie drama for him, more trouble coming their way.

'That was my mom. Her dad, my grandpa, broke his arm in two places – up a ladder at his age and lost his balance, could've been a lot worse.'

'Is he going to be okay?'

'He's a bit shaken and sore but other than the arm, everything seems intact.' He made a semi-theatrical groan that had Katy laughing. 'Sorry, but he's been told to act his age before. At almost ninety, he won't listen.'

'He sounds a character.'

'The best.' He spoke softly, the worry evident.

'Do you need to go home and see him?'

'Don't panic, I wouldn't do that to you.'

She hadn't even thought about being deserted with the inn to be in charge of; she'd been thinking of him and his obvious love for his family. She wondered what it was like to have so many of them in his life.

'I'll keep in touch by phone and do a FaceTime with him once he's home. He's got all the latest gadgets – he swears it keeps him young.'

'Good for him.' She was still smiling when Natalie came through to see her brother and she, of course, gave Katy a familiar death stare.

'I've washed and dried the pots,' Natalie announced. 'I need to use the bathroom. I assume that's all right with you.' She glared Katy's way.

'Don't be rude,' Rupert warned. 'And of course you can use the bathroom.' He dug the key to his apartment from his pocket and handed it to her. 'When you come back, if you could dry up the glasses and put them away, that would be great.'

She muttered something but neither of them registered what it was and when she was out of earshot, Rupert said, 'I bet you didn't bank on a stressed-out chef and his wayward sister when you signed up to work here.' His tone suggested he was trying for a joke but Katy could tell it concerned him more than he was letting on.

'She doesn't look too good.'

'She doesn't but she knows she has to be on her best behaviour and that means not being rude to you.'

'I can take it.'

'You shouldn't have to. I promise I'll make sure she puts a stop to the attitude.'

When he headed off to the kitchen, Katy went down to the basement to fold the sheets that had been in the dryer but when she came back again, Rupert was hovering in the hallway and looked about to go upstairs and get his sister.

'She not back yet?'

'I might have to check on her.' He had one foot on the bottom step as though he wasn't sure whether it was a good idea or not.

Their talking must've conjured her up, however, because she rounded the top of the stairwell.

'Took your time,' Rupert muttered when she got down to their level.

'I don't feel well. You know that.'

'That'll be whatever substance you decided to take.'

With an edge of fury in her voice that she thankfully did not raise, she said, 'I told you I haven't taken anything. And you...' She looked at Katy. 'Stop sticking your nose in other people's business and making stuff up.'

'Watch your mouth,' said Rupert as Natalie began heading to the kitchen.

That had her stop in her tracks. She turned and glared at her brother. 'Nothing is worth this shit. I can't do this.'

But he stood in front of her as though he was going to block her whatever she tried to do. 'Oh no, you don't. Mom does not need you at the moment, she's got enough going on. You're staying here.'

'What's going on with Mom?' The accusatory tone was replaced by concern.

'Nothing. Grandad hurt his arm, that's all, fell off a ladder. He's going to be fine.'

Natalie groaned. 'He's been told time and time again about that, when will he learn?'

At least the siblings were talking as they headed back to the rear of the brownstone. Katy had time to catch her breath and she put all the sheets away, helped a guest with their sodden umbrella by shaking it out for them on the stoop before putting it in the bucket just inside the door. She answered a couple of calls asking whether they had vacancies on Fourth of July weekend – they didn't – and when a guest came down to enjoy a whisky and cola at the bar in the lounge, she made him his drink and listened to him talk about his day, how he'd spent the entire time in an art gallery and while it had been bright sunshine when he went inside, it certainly wasn't by the time he ventured out.

Rupert and Natalie came out of the kitchen an hour or so later and Natalie hooked her bag over her shoulder while Rupert took out one of the umbrellas to hand to her. 'Are you sure you can't stay for chocolate and fudge brownies?' He said it in a way that got a smile from Natalie, and Katy wondered whether it was a recipe he'd made at home before for his sister. 'I can walk you home to the apartment if you like.'

Natalie looked about to agree but when she spotted Katy wiping the bar top in the lounge, her demeanour changed. 'Worried I'll make a detour to a drug den?' she called out, definitely more for Katy's benefit than her brother's. She shot the umbrella he'd given her high into the air at the top of the stoop and left them to it.

'Sorry, I should've kept out of sight,' Katy grimaced. 'Are you happy with her going back to yours?'

'Obviously I'd prefer her not to be going via a drug den,' he joked. 'But yes, I thought it might be best all round.'

Katy took that to mean for her as well and silently thanked him, even though she sensed Natalie would be back tomorrow with more snappish remarks and bundles of attitude.

'What are the chocolate fudge brownies for?' Katy, happy to move the topic onto brighter things, checked her watch. 'Can't be dessert, too late for that.'

'I thought I'd make them for anyone coming in out of the rain this evening – a bit of home comfort we can offer. You know what it's like, especially if you get wet and don't have an umbrella – I know at least one guest who went out without one.'

He was considerate. This was so much more than a job to him; it was as though a part of his soul was wrapped up in the inn and she admired it. She found herself saying, 'If I go out in the rain, can I have a brownie?'

At least it erased the frown and he replaced it with a smile that reached the brown eyes that looked right at her now, teasing, tempting. 'Go on, then.'

'You're going to make me go out?' The front door was closed again but Rupert stepped forwards and opened it for her using his free arm to gesture for her to walk through.

She looked at the umbrella bucket. It was empty. 'There aren't any umbrellas.'

His eyes danced. 'This will tell me how badly you want one of my widely talked-about brownies, gooey, fresh from the oven with fudge, all dense, moist.'

'My mouth is watering.' She stepped forwards. 'And I really want a brownie.'

She was going to make a run for it and suddenly it seemed fun, a release from all the tension Natalie had brought with her. 'Here goes!' She only got to the top step when he pulled her back inside, so close her chest was almost against his.

'I was joking,' he said, eyes dancing with mischief as he looked down at her.

'I wasn't, I was going to do it.' She watched the rise and fall of his chest, the sound of rain beside them as they stood in the open doorway. She looked up at him and her voice barely a whisper, confessed, 'I really wanted a brownie.'

He reached a hand up and for a moment, she was sure he was going to put it against her cheek. Maybe he was and had second thoughts because he seemed regretful that instead his hand found the edge of the door and he closed the front entrance of the inn.

They made their way to the kitchen and all of a sudden, Katy wasn't as relaxed in his company as she had been before, but it changed when he suggested what they do next. There were three trays of brownies, two large and one much smaller, and he took out two forks, passing one to Katy before setting the smallest tray between them on a cooler rack on top of the counter.

'I say we go straight in,' he smiled, hair at the front flopping against his forehead to one side, a way to hide his frown whenever he needed it to.

'Straight from the dish?'

'Let's live a little.'

'Living on the edge,' she agreed, as he was the first to plunge his fork into the gooey mixture and pull out a generous portion.

She did the same and the moment she put the brownie in her mouth, she put a hand across her lips. 'Oh, my goodness... this is divine!'

'It is, even though I say so myself.'

'This is also very bad,' she said between mouthfuls. 'I'm eating dessert and I haven't had dinner yet.'

'No law that says we can't do dessert and then dinner,' he shrugged. 'Chicken schnitzel all right for you?'

She eyed the brownie pan they'd made a decent dent in already. 'Maybe a very small portion.'

'Done.'

All they shared for the next few minutes were the brownies and looks of pleasure at what they were eating and perhaps the mutual company.

'Dinner in an hour?' he checked once they were done, patting a taut stomach beneath his chef's jacket. 'Give this a chance to be digested.'

They'd demolished the entire contents of the smallest pan and she began to smile. 'I think it's the perfect advert for perfect brownies, you know.'

'What is? My stomach?' He set down his fork in the tray now they were done. He took out a big knife and began to slice the brownies in the other tins before they were completely cool. When he looked up, she just laughed. 'Tell me... is it the smell?' he asked as he turned the tray around to do the slicing the other way.

When she pointed at the side of his face, he swiped the wrong side with the back of his hand. 'Gone?'

'Nope, still a smear of chocolate. Like I said, it's a good advert for this place and the desserts you make.' But she was laughing and more so when he lifted out the first brownie and set it onto the waiting plate. 'You've also got some by your ear. How did you manage that?'

The second one he lifted hovered before it reached the plate and instead he put it in his hand and advanced towards her. 'I think you should advertise this place too.'

She'd backed up so much, she was almost pressing against the door as he got close enough to put a little bit on her cheek.

Katy was laughing hard but protesting. 'I'm front of house, I have an image to portray.'

His hand was hovering, ready to put more chocolate on her, when the bell from the lounge rang. 'Saved by the bell,' he murmured. His face was so close, it wouldn't have taken much for them to kiss.

'I'd better see to that.'

'Yeah.' His eyes dipped to her lips and up again.

Katy stumbled out of the kitchen and brushed down her skirt and blouse before finding a guest in the lounge who truly was soaked through and had lost the key to their room. Katy handed it back to them – she'd found it when she was cleaning earlier. 'You must've dropped it on the stairs.' She knew it wasn't only a sugar rush giving her the buzz she felt right now but the whole encounter with Rupert.

'Something smells good,' the guest declared, now the worry of the key had gone.

'It's chocolate brownies, the chef made them for anyone who's interested this evening.' The usual practice was to let guests know, either by popping a note under their doors upstairs or telling them when they came back to the inn.

Almost an hour later, Rupert came to tell Katy that her dinner was waiting for her in the dining room. For now, it seemed guests were settled and the lady who'd come in earlier had taken brownies up to her apartment to enjoy in front of a movie.

'Let me open these doors,' he said when Katy went into the dining room to where there were two dinners waiting – hers and his. He'd taken off his chef's whites and instead put on a charcoal T-shirt and jeans. 'If it was a fine evening, we could've sat at the bistro table in the courtyard, but the sound of the rain and fresh air will be nice enough.'

Katy swallowed. It sounded a bit like he was trying to arrange the perfect date and it caught her off-guard. It shouldn't have, given the way they'd been in the kitchen – without guests to see to, she might have sat for the entire hour daydreaming about what might or might not be going on between them. Shaun was right: he'd said Rupert was interested, but Katy hadn't thought he really was until tonight, until the way they'd flirted with one another.

'I think I approve of dessert first,' Katy smiled when Rupert sat down opposite her. 'But this looks wonderful.'

They both made a start on their dinner, the golden chicken schnitzel seasoned just right, crisp on the outside but tender inside, the portions not too enormous either.

Rupert stopped all of a sudden. 'I totally forgot... wine?'

'Wine? Isn't that frowned upon while we're working?'

'So is scoffing an entire tray of brownies, but didn't stop us before, did it?' He raised his eyebrows. 'And I wouldn't do it if I couldn't imagine Sofia doing the very same thing after a long, tough day.'

Rupert disappeared off to get a bottle of wine and two glasses. They'd left the door to the dining room propped open in case they were needed, but Katy found herself hoping more than she usually did that they wouldn't get any more interruptions. She'd known this was demanding when she was offered the position, but right now Katy knew that what made those hours tolerable had a lot to do with how much time she got to spend with this man.

Rupert poured them each a glass of red and he waited for Katy to try it. 'What do you think?'

'I'm no wine aficionado.'

'Doesn't matter.'

'I like it – fruity, like berries from a forest.'

The creases that showed at the sides of his eyes when he smiled were there again. 'It's from a winery in Vermont. And it's a family favourite. One of my sisters got married at the winery where this wine came from.'

She nodded her approval. 'You've got a big family.'

'A big, *crazy* family,' he elaborated good-naturedly.

'What are they like?'

'Well, you've met one of them.'

'Tell me about the rest.'

He seemed to like that she was interested. 'Well, you already know I have four sisters... Natalie is the youngest, then there's Cameron, who is thirty, then twins Amy and Maisie, who are thirty-two.'

'Your household must have been chaos growing up. Your parents deserve some kind of award for so many kids born so close together.'

'Mom takes it all in her stride, usually. Do you know she was initially worried she'd never have kids? That soon changed to concern she'd never stop.'

'Is your dad still around?'

'He is, and he and Mom are a great partnership. I'm never quite sure who's in charge, I think both of them, and sometimes Dad and I escape for male time to keep our sanity. We went camping a lot as kids or out fishing on the lake. The girls weren't always mad about outdoor pastimes, especially Cameron, but it was nice, just the two of us.'

'You must miss him, being here in New York.'

'Yes and no. He's not far away and he and Mom are both in good health. I'm lucky. Mom's dad is still around, or at least he will be if he starts taking a bit more care of himself and doesn't keep going up ladders, and he lives down the road from my parents in Vermont so we see him a lot.'

'That's nice; you sound like you're all close.'

'We are. What about you? Your dad seems pretty great.'

She'd almost finished the wine and leaned back in her chair to see down the hallway to ensure nobody was trying to get their attention. 'He is. We're really close, more so since Mom died.' She twirled the stem of her glass as she set it on the table. 'When Dad decided to leave Scarsdale behind and move to the city, I think it was the best thing he could've done. He came out of his shell a bit, you know?'

'I can see how change would be good.'

'It really was.' And at his words, it helped her to see that perhaps the small ways in which her dad was changing since he met Stephanie weren't necessarily a sign of anything bad either. At least that's what she hoped. For the first time, she didn't want Stephanie to simply go away; she realised she wanted things to work out for the pair of them. For them to be happy. 'We adored that house but it was the home my dad chose with his wife, a family home, and without her there, it was never going to be the same.'

'And you moved with him.'

'I was already working here in Manhattan, so it made sense. But I've been trying to move out on my own ever since,' she laughed.

'Not that bad, is it?'

'Not at all, I've loved being there at his place, but I need to be independent and he'll want his space too. Especially now he's getting married again.'

'What's his fiancée like?' He poured her more wine as if he pre-empted this not being the easiest of topics for Katy.

'She's nice.'

He stopped mid-pour, looked at her and then finished pouring before putting the top back on the bottle. 'That's the most non-committal response you could've come up with.'

'I didn't sound very convincing, did I?' she laughed. 'It's taking me time to get my head around it, that's all, and until recently, I thought this marriage might well be a mistake.'

'And now?'

'I think... she's good for him. He seems happy but I suppose part of me will never see him with anyone other than my mom.' She covered her eyes momentarily with her hand, embarrassed. 'Admitting that out loud doesn't sound very mature, does it?'

'I get it,' he said sympathetically. 'I can't imagine either of my parents with anyone else. It would be weird. But as you say, he seems happy.'

'I shouldn't have any say or influence over what Dad does in his life.'

'But...' he pushed.

'You're very good at getting information out of people, aren't you?'

'It's the wine,' he grinned. And then he sat back in his chair and with one hand scratched at the stubble on his chin, almost invisible to her if it wasn't accompanied by the distinctive sound. 'Do you want to change his mind about this woman in his life?'

She thought about the question before she told him, 'Not any more. But if I'm completely honest, I did before. I was looking for reasons not to like her and not to trust her. It wasn't fair to Dad to do that, but I couldn't help it.' She shook her head at herself. 'I feel like a spoilt kid.'

'You're confusing being spoilt for caring. I think as you get older, it's only natural to do your fair share of worrying, it's part of what makes you a grown-up, learning to deal with different people and situations. It must be hard coping on your own, especially after your mom died.'

'Me and Dad had each other.'

'I meant it must have been hard without a sibling to lean on. As much as my sisters drive me nuts sometimes, I can't imagine life without them. Thankfully, we haven't had too many major disasters, but we've had times where we've leant on one another through tougher moments. It must be hard not having that.'

She opened her mouth, unsure what she was about to tell him. Was she going to mention David? This was the moment to confide in him, tell him about her brother. He was the sort of man who would understand, who would see it from all sides.

She opened her mouth to start telling him but found herself drinking the wine instead. Why was it so hard to bring up David's name?

She knew why and she hated herself for it. She'd pushed her brother away in her mind because it hurt too much to try to let him in.

'I know if either of my parents was ever in another relationship,' said Rupert, interrupting her thoughts, 'the first thing I'd be doing is asking what the others thought. We'd balance each other out because you can bet your life we'd never agree between us.'

That made Katy smile. She could imagine the big family all caring so much they wanted to be heard. She wondered whether, if it was either of Rupert's parents, would they have confided in any of their children the way Wade had in her, that his fiancée was acting oddly and might be hiding something? Katy really hoped it was only the pre-wedding jitters or simply busyness, because she couldn't bear it to be anything that would hurt her dad. Hearing his doubts in a weird way had made her realise that deep down, she did want this to work out, something she never would've thought would be the case up until the last few days.

A guest called out and waved to them along the hallway. 'I wondered about the brownies, am I too late?'

'Not too late,' Rupert called back. He turned to Katy. 'I've got this, you stay here.'

When another guest appeared the minute Rupert came back into the dining room, Katy leapt up. 'I'll get this one, you sit.' She stopped when they were level in the doorway. 'Wait, do I have red wine on my lips?'

His eyes lingered on her mouth before looking up and into her eyes. 'Your lips look just fine to me.'

Katy hurried down the hallway to the lounge where a guest had had a disaster with their suitcase that had broken at the bottom and was in no state for repacking. 'I can get rid of it,' Katy assured them. 'You'll have to treat yourself to another.'

'I told my other half this one wouldn't last. At least it broke here and not at the airport tomorrow – imagine all your intimate items spread out across the airport floor,' she laughed as she handed over the case before asking advice on the best place to buy one.

Katy recommended several retailers and added, 'They're open first thing. And my advice is to choose a nice bright one, much easier to spot on the carousel.'

The woman, satisfied she had a solution to her luggage problem, headed off to her room before Katy went back to Rupert. The breeze from the open doors had cooled the dining room so it was noticeable now when you came from the front of the inn.

'More wine?' Rupert offered.

'I think that'll do me, but it was good to relax.'

He held up his phone. 'Sofia must've been spying on us – she emailed me and has suggested a FaceTime call soon, whenever convenient. She says she's not checking up on us, just thought it would be nice to have an update.'

'I suppose it's a little weird that I'm here in her inn and she's not met me yet.'

'She'll love you. And I'll take the request to do the FaceTime call as a good sign. If she's thinking more about us and this place, I suspect it means her daughter is a lot better. She said she might even be able to come home to New York in a couple of weeks. Which means...'

Katy's heart sank. She'd miss the busy days, the endless things to have to see to and the responsibility. 'I'll be out of a job.' She almost suggested he did pour the wine. She'd been so busy in the role, she'd only thought about getting through, not what happened when she actually reached the other side. She supposed she should start looking out for something else soon.

'But with a lot of experience.' He picked up both empty glasses by their stems. 'I'm looking forward to just being the chef. I thought my days were busy already, but helping with cleaning and being a handyman has been a bit crazy. I'll miss you, though,' he added as they passed into the kitchen and he went over to the sink to wash the glasses. 'Do you promise to stop by now and then?'

'Of course.'

'Any idea what you'll do next?'

'None at all. I haven't been looking since I came here – too busy.'

'Agreed.' He returned her smile. 'If I know Sofia, you'll be her first port of call for any help,' he went on as he set the first freshly washed glass onto the drainer. 'And you'll get a glowing reference for a job anywhere.'

'I think I'd like to stay in the city if I can.'

He turned then as he set the second glass onto the drainer. 'That'll be nice. Thank you,' he added as she picked up the drying cloth from nearby and dried the glasses.

'Might not be able to if I can't find anything, but I've got my resume at plenty of places; perhaps it's a case of waiting for the right thing to come up.'

'Let's hope so. The wine was nice tonight.' He dried his hands on another towel and leaned against the kitchen cabinet.

'It was. And it worked; I feel relaxed.'

He looked about to claim the same until he decided against it. 'I was feeling relaxed too but that changes every time I remember I've still got Natalie to deal with.'

'You're not tempted to send her back to your parents' house?'

'I think she's better here. I want to believe her, I want to trust her.'

'Maybe I shouldn't have mentioned anything about what I saw.'

'I'm glad you did. I needed to know.'

'Natalie must hate me.'

'Hate is too strong a word. She's mad at you, there's a difference.'

'Perhaps I was mistaken.' But she didn't think so and judging by his expression, neither did he.

'I can't give up on her, Katy. She's my family.'

'It's a lot to take on with a full-time job. And you don't owe her *your* happiness.'

He paused. 'That sounds too dramatic even in this situation.'

'Sorry, I—' She was thinking of what had happened in their family, comparing it, knowing that in the end David had refused all attempts to help him. And it had almost broken them.

'Don't be.' He took her hand. 'Don't be sorry, you're saying it because you care, because you see this is hard for me. It's kind of nice that you have my back.'

She could see he wasn't sure what to say; he was biting down slightly on his bottom lip.

She had no idea how to react either. It was as though they weren't at work, it was just the two of them, but she had to focus, if only to stop thoughts of her own family dramas resurfacing and crushing her all over again. 'I'd better go and make sure the floor is dry by the door.' She gulped, her hand still in his. 'I wouldn't want anyone to slip in rainwater if they don't see it.'

'No, we don't want that.' His voice was soft, warm, kind.

She felt the tug of his fingers against hers as she pulled away to go along the hallway. She didn't want to leave his side but rather stay here, just the two of them, and see where the evening might lead.

14

RUPERT

Over the next week, the atmosphere at the inn was settled and business was steady. Rupert longed to spend more time getting to know Katy, but they were both professionals, both had a job to do, and added to that, he still had his sister to worry about.

Natalie showed up every morning on time, although she spoke to Katy the bare minimum to receive instructions or inform of what she'd done. Rupert had found himself more than once looking between the two women, wondering whether Natalie was telling the truth. Had Katy been mistaken about the drugs or had she seen what she really thought she'd seen? Natalie had suggested perhaps Katy might be paranoid in her quest to succeed at the job she'd been newly appointed to. *Come on, Rupert*, she'd said to him the day he confronted her, *how well do you really know Katy? Certainly not as well as you know me. And that's got to count for something, right?* She'd then sworn on their mother's life that she hadn't been taking drugs since she got here and it was a phrase neither of them ever used. They'd hated it as kids and he'd cringed when she said it to him last night after he asked her again and wanted assurance that she wasn't hiding anything in his apartment. The phrase suggested she was telling the truth but then again, could she be using the words out of sheer desperation?

As Rupert and Katy waited for their FaceTime call with Sofia, Natalie came into the lounge. 'I've stripped the beds in apartment three,' she told Katy, who was at the desk at the end of the lounge while Rupert gave the temperamental window a push open.

Katy looked up from what she was doing. 'The next guests don't check in until 3 p.m. and the apartment needs a full clean. Could you please do that next?'

Rupert, perched on the edge of the sofa, was hoping Natalie would just go and get on with it, give himself and Katy space to ensure Sofia saw nothing but a smooth running of the inn in her absence. But Natalie was hovering.

'I'm not being lazy,' she began, 'but please can I sit down first, have something to eat. I know...' she looked at Rupert, 'I only had lunch a couple of hours ago, but I don't feel so good. I promise I'm not making it up.'

Katy leapt in before he did. 'There are some sandwiches in the fridge that were supposed to be a packed lunch for a guest, but they changed their mind last minute.'

'What's in them?'

Rupert shot his sister a look for asking the question.

'I can't quite remember,' said Katy, but Natalie, reading Rupert's disapproval, had already stalked off towards the kitchen.

'I'm sorry,' he said and with a shake of his head repeated, 'What's in them?' It was food offered to you for nothing, he wanted to tell Natalie. Either eat what's there or don't, but quit making a fuss about it.

'Stop apologising. Oh, and her pay should be in her account today, Sofia let me know the wages have been sorted out.'

'Perhaps that'll put a smile on my sister's face.'

But he mellowed some more when a familiar bleeping sound

came from the computer to announce Sofia's call. He quickly scooted around to Katy's side of the desk where he pulled in the chair from behind him. They had to sit pretty close, and the zingy, citrusy aroma from her hair put all of his senses on high alert.

He'd better calm down a bit or Sofia would read him like a book, even across thousands of miles.

Sofia was beaming and waving and there was the inevitable, 'Can you hear me? Can you see me? I can't see anyone... oh, that's better,' before they were all sorted.

Rupert introduced Katy, even though they'd had emails back and forth since Katy had come to work here. He felt honoured Sofia had trusted him and Darcy enough to make the decisions and go with them in her absence.

'You both look like you've got a handle on everything,' Sofia told them when they'd caught her up with what they needed to.

'Total chaos,' Rupert joked, enjoying the way Katy had to stay close to him so they were both on the screen at the same time. 'If we reposition the camera, you'll see for yourself.'

She was used to him kidding around. 'That won't be necessary. I trust you. And I'm forever grateful to you. I know chef duties don't usually extend to everything else, at least not in anything more than the odd emergency, but this is much better than closing the inn. And Katy, for you to jump on board and do such a good job, it's a relief.'

At least Katy had kept Natalie's story to herself. For that he was grateful. If she'd shared any of it with Sofia, he might well be in trouble with his boss.

'I'm loving being here.' Katy smiled so genuinely, Rupert knew Sofia didn't miss the sentiment. 'You have a gorgeous inn. How did I never know this was here?'

'Well, now you do and I'm glad you love it. I spoke with Darcy earlier... she wishes she'd kept you for herself, Katy. They're crazy busy at the Inglenook Lodge.'

'Darcy and Myles will be happy about that,' said Rupert.

Talk turned to their guests and upcoming bookings, they had a brief catch-up regarding supplies, expenses, and the general running of the place so there were no hidden surprises for Sofia when she returned.

'And so it's only the cleaning that has been a pain,' Sofia recapped. 'Not too much drama and I do hope Jill is back soon. I'll send her an email, let her know her job is waiting for her. She's loyal, hardworking, I don't want to lose her. And in the meantime, your sister is on board, Rupert. She came at just the right time.'

Rupert didn't flicker. 'She sure did.'

'Shame I can't meet her. Is she around?'

'Grabbing something to eat while she can,' he smiled.

After their catch-up, an estimated return date for Sofia in the next week or so all being well, and a bit of general discussion about how beautiful spring was in Switzerland as well as Sofia's tales of cheese fondue she hoped Rupert could make one evening back at the inn, they ended the call.

'She's as lovely as you told me she was,' Katy smiled as Rupert put his chair back against the wall, out of the way of the desk.

'She's a great boss,' he agreed before Natalie interrupted them. If she'd held back because she knew they were on the phone to the boss, Rupert could only be grateful.

'I can't find any more sheets for the beds in apartment three,' Natalie told them.

Katy got up from the desk. 'They'll be downstairs in the basement. I took them out of the dryer but didn't get to folding them up.'

Natalie waved her hands in front of her. 'Oh, no, you stay there.' Her words laced with sarcasm, she turned and headed out of the lounge and down the hallway towards the door that led to the basement.

Rupert twisted his lips together and waited until they heard the door to the basement open and close behind his sister before he looked at Katy and whistled. 'She's real mad at you.'

The way he said it had Katy laughing and he wouldn't have minded staying with her to listen to the sound some more.

'At least she's getting on with the job,' Katy added diplomatically.

'Talking of which, I'd better get into the kitchen and make a list for the markets. I started a list last night but always good to do a quick check after breakfast when supplies have taken a battering.' He usually headed out earlier but today had needed to hang around for Sofia's call. 'I'll go out soon if it's okay with you?'

'Of course. I'll get on too. Now Sofia has given the go-ahead, I'll order those new cushion covers to replace the worn ones in apartment two.' She was rambling and he liked it; it was as though she too was aware of the spark between them that could ignite at any moment. 'After that, I'll do an inventory of the top-floor apartment now our guest has checked out, make sure nothing is taken.' She scrunched her nose up a little in thought and he wanted to reach out and touch it. 'I hate this part, it's like we don't trust our guests.'

'Most of them are fine, but not all of them are.'

'I've been in the business long enough to know you're right – it just feels worse at an inn like this. For big hotel chains, it's almost run of the mill – not that it should be – but here it feels more homely, like it shouldn't happen.'

'But it still does.'

Rupert left Katy to get on, and in the kitchen made his list. Natalie stayed out of the way, hopefully doing what she should be doing, and by the time he headed out to the markets, he felt more relaxed than he had in days. He was sure whatever Natalie had been mixed up in was something they could put an end to before it spiralled out of control and she could go back to being the carefree sister he got on so well with. She and their parents would make up. Natalie would head back to Vermont and everything in New York would return to how it once was.

How it was with the addition of Katy in his life, he hoped. Surely when she said goodbye to this job it wouldn't be goodbye to him too.

* * *

Back at the inn, Rupert started dinner preparations for eight people – more than usual, which was perhaps because of the rain that over the last few days had felt relentless.

Once dinner prep was done, he turned his creativity to a dessert experiment. He'd picked up the ingredients and wanted to try out a twist on a key lime pie, using a couple of handfuls of blue-berries in the mixture. Once it was cool, he was going to top it with meringue, but he wasn't sure whether it would be too much with all those flavour combinations together. Only one way to find out, he guessed.

It was a quick dessert to make with its gingersnap cookie base and zesty filling and he soon had it in the oven. And by the time he put the pie into the refrigerator to chill, Katy had come in to update him discreetly on his sister.

'She's done a great job with apartment three,' she said softly. 'She's in the lounge now, I made her a coffee and got her some magazines.'

'She's at work, you know.' He frowned, but in truth appreciated the kindness. Natalie wasn't a bad person, she just made wrong decisions sometimes. Then again, didn't they all?

'She still looks really tired. Are you sure you don't need to get a doctor to check her out?'

'It's probably having to work with me that's done it.' He managed a tentative smile. 'You haven't seen anything untoward, have you?'

She shook her head.

'And you'd tell me if you did?'

'I would. Promise. As much as I wouldn't want to interfere again, especially when those looks of hers sometimes threaten to turn me to stone, I would.'

He chuckled. 'Did she at least thank you for the magazines and coffee?' At the look on Katy's face, he deduced, 'Don't tell me, she did, but begrudgingly.'

'You know your sister well.'

When they heard a voice say, 'Knock knock,' from the other side of the door, Katy went to see who it was and found Mrs Turbot, who was staying with her sister in apartment five. 'I know I'm late, but is there any way Margo and I could book in for tonight's dinner?' Rupert heard her ask Katy.

He went over to the door and stood behind Katy to see their guest.

Katy turned a bit too quickly, not realising he'd already come up behind her and ended up with her head on his chest. She looked up at him and it made him want to put his hands on either side of her face and savour the proximity.

'Can we fit in two more?' she asked, still so close he wanted to touch her.

'It's just this rain...' Mrs Turbot went on, oblivious to the chemistry between the pair in the kitchen, the chemistry Rupert had at last decided wasn't just in his imagination. It had made his workdays a lot more pleasurable, but with Natalie still there and Sofia not back yet, he didn't want to do anything to upset anyone. He also didn't want to ask Katy out and be turned down, which might well happen when they worked together, even if Katy was interested. She was a true professional and he knew he had to be too.

'We got soaked just now,' Mrs Turbot explained, 'so rather than have dinner out and then Radio City Hall, we thought we'd eat here, taxi to the show, and then taxi home.' She guffawed. 'Listen to me saying *home*.'

'It feels like that, doesn't it?' Katy smiled at their guest.

If Rupert was a guest himself, he'd bet money Katy had worked here for years rather than picking up the reins in an emergency and the absence of the boss.

'That should be fine, Mrs Turbot,' Rupert assured her.

'Oh, thank you, you wonderful man.' She opened her arms and Rupert wondered for a moment whether she was going to try to hug him, kiss him even.

Thankfully Katy was in her way and when Mrs Turbot retreated down the corridor, it had them both laughing. 'You were my protection then,' he confessed.

'I think she wanted to hug you. Look out for her this evening.'

'I might have Natalie do the fetching and carrying to the dining room. I'm not sure I can face Mrs Turbot and her sister. Her sister hugged me to thank me for breakfast the other day. I don't mind grateful guests but it's a bit much when it gets physical.'

'Take the flattery,' she said with a smile. 'They mean no harm. And are you sure you've got enough to do dinner for them too?'

'I do. It means we don't get any, though.'

'I can live with that.' She briefly closed her eyes. 'Not that I don't appreciate your cooking. I love it. Your cooking.' She was tripping over her words and the way she did it felt as though perhaps he would stand a really good chance if he eventually asked her on a date. Part of him didn't want Sofia to come back because he loved seeing Katy every day and being so close to her; the other part longed for his boss to take over again so they could move to being something more than colleagues.

'I'll let you get on,' said Katy, back in control.

But he was following after her along the hallway. He'd use the excuse that he wanted to nip to his apartment, but really he wanted to check what his sister was up to.

When they got closer to the lounge and heard Natalie's voice, Rupert followed Katy in there. But rather than her sitting relaxing with the magazine and a coffee as he'd expected, Natalie had moved over to the desk and seemed to be finishing up a phone call.

'Who was that?' Katy asked her.

Natalie picked up a piece of paper and handed it over. 'A guest. I took the details.'

'Thank you.'

Natalie shrugged. 'I was only sitting here, after all, and you two were busy.' She quirked an eyebrow that Rupert really didn't appreciate.

'You can take a couple of hours off if you like,' Rupert told his sister. 'Back here by 6.30 p.m. for dinner service.'

'Sure.' She managed a smile his way.

'Have you called Mom yet?' It was one thing having her here, but she couldn't stay at the expense of making peace with the family.

'Not yet.' It was all she said before she left.

Rupert turned to Katy. 'I don't know about you, but I could use a decent coffee and not one I have to make.'

'Want me to head out and grab a couple?' She scrunched up her nose when she caught sight of the rain beyond the window.

'I need to let my dessert set so I have time. The fresh air will do me good, I think.'

It had seemed like a good idea, but despite the raincoat, he still got wetter than he'd predicted with a wind that blew sideways.

'You're drenched.' Katy met him at the front door to the Inglenook Inn, handed him a towel, and took the tray with the two coffees. 'You should've taken an umbrella.'

'Too much hassle.' He gave his hair a good rub before wiping up any drips on the floor. He went into the lounge to dump the spent towel in the tub behind the bar.

Katy was clutching her coffee already and made an appreciative groan at the first sip. 'So good.'

He sat down next to her on the sofa. 'Mom called while I was on my way back here – another reason I was glad not to have an umbrella. I don't fancy my chances holding onto one and answering a cell phone at the same time. I mean people do it, but I'm not that coordinated.'

'How's your grandad?'

'On the mend, doing very well. Natalie called him, apparently.' That had pleased him to know his sister could put aside whatever else was going on and check in with a family member when bad things happened. It was part of their family ethos – didn't matter how big the argument, what words were said in anger, they still showed up for each other. 'And Mom didn't mention Natalie other than to say she called Grandad, so perhaps she's calming down. It'll make it easier when Natalie tries to talk to her if she ever does.'

'She will, I bet.'

'Yeah...' He sat on the sofa next to Katy, who was gazing longingly at the fireplace. 'What's on your mind?'

She turned to him and smiled then looked back to the fireplace. 'Days like this, with the rain pouring down, make me think of the colder months. I'll bet this lounge is really cosy come fall.'

'It sure is.' He savoured a gulp of coffee. 'This room is cosy in the rain too, don't you think?' She murmured an agreement, but his mind was on his sister. He wondered whether he was trying to tell himself she wasn't doing anything untoward when he said,

'Knowing Natalie, she'll have walked a block at most and found a good coffee shop to sit in for a while. That or she's gone to the library.'

'Your sister likes books?'

'Always has. She was mad for them as a little girl – she'd go with Dad, dragging the little wooden trolley he made behind her down to the local library and bring back a whole collection. She even set up one of those miniature mailbox-sized libraries at the end of the driveway when she was a teenager and started it off with a couple of her own books so local kids could do swaps. She keeps it going to this day. She goes to second-hand bookshops to stock up sometimes, make sure there's a variety of titles in there to suit all tastes.'

'That's nice.'

'Doesn't sound like the Natalie you've met, right?'

'I didn't want to say...'

'Don't worry, I get it. She's not been easy since coming here.'

'Do you read much?'

He shook his head. 'I've never had the concentration span unless it's a cookbook, but with those I'm more likely to go through it and then leap out of my chair to go get more ingredients to experiment.'

'You must love being a chef?'

'I do, but it took a long time coming.'

'How did you start out?'

'As a kitchen porter – pot washer,' he added to explain what the role really was in simple terms. 'It was at a restaurant in Vermont and it was as basic and hard work as it sounds. Fast paced, high pressure, busy, all the adjectives you would expect except in reality the environment was even more insane than I thought it would be. The head chef was highly strung, strict, didn't stand for much error, but it's why the restaurant was so highly regarded. I started to watch the way he worked, observe the produce that came into the kitchen, watched the creations from those basic raw ingredients to the exquisite dishes that went out on the plates to diners. The more I saw, the more I liked. I applied for apprenticeship after apprenticeship near home and found absolutely nothing.'

'And that brought you to New York?'

'I decided I might have more luck here, so I found a similar kitchen porter job in Manhattan with a view to applying for bigger and better positions along the way. It didn't quite work, unfortunately. Nobody wanted me.' The way her head tilted as he spoke suggested sympathy. 'Yeah, yeah, get the violins out. But I kept on working and then knowing I had to do something, I began working for a catering firm so I got experience in cooking, at least. It wasn't the same environment, it was slower but with just as high expectations. I enjoyed it but the firm went bust. My next move was a café. I was only really doing breakfasts there, but I could be creative with it. And then finally, a job advert came up for here at the Inglenook Inn. I haven't looked back since my first interview, which was more of an informal chat. All Sofia wanted to know was whether I was cut out to cook for her guests and so she had me make her dinner and dessert two days in a row and she was happy.'

He recapped some of Sofia's story: how she was divorced and Darcy had not only managed the inn for her but introduced her to knitting as a distraction from the stressful change in her life.

'Darcy seems a good friend now.'

'She is. We should go out to Inglenook Falls some time and visit her at her inn.'

'I'd like that.'

When a guest cleared his throat behind them, Katy automatically put a finger to the corners of her mouth to check for coffee, he assumed, before turning her attention to the guest, who wanted to confirm check-out time for the following day.

When the man left them to it, Rupert picked up his empty cup. 'Fancy being my taste tester in Sofia's absence?'

'What's on the menu?' She crossed her fingers. 'More chocolate brownies?'

'Not this time. It's my twist on a key lime pie. All that's left to do is make the meringue topping.'

'Well, then, I'd be crazy to say no to that. I'll empty the water out of the umbrella bucket and be right in.'

Rupert went off to the kitchen with a spring in his step and realised that today Natalie had been far more civil to Katy.

Was it too much to hope that the two women currently in his life might actually be able to see eye to eye for the remainder of their time here at the inn together?

15

KATY

Katy joined Rupert in the kitchen as the rain continued to batter the Inglenook Inn and every other brownstone on the street. 'It's a shocker out there. I'm glad I'm not out in it.'

He held up his phone. 'Text from my sister to say she's almost back, but as predicted has hunkered down in the coffee shop ready to make another run for it.'

He seemed to be a lot more relaxed about Natalie, and Katy for one was glad his sister was making an effort to be a bit more pleasant to her. It didn't even matter if it was all for show; it eased the tension, whatever the reasoning behind it.

She watched Rupert whipping up egg whites to stiff peaks before he added the sugar slowly. He looked across at her more than once and each time, her insides did a little jump, as though she wasn't even a grown-up but a young girl with an enormous crush.

His attention went back to scraping the mixture onto the top of the pie that looked set. According to Rupert, it had the perfect amount of wobble.

'No distracting me,' he said as he slotted the pie beneath the grill. 'A few minutes is all this will need, and I'll finish it off with the torch.' With the pie beneath the heat, he picked up the tool to show her what he meant. 'A chef's best friend.'

He took the pie out soon after and did as he'd told her, directing the torch so its flames created a deep, rich, golden effect to the peaks of the meringue topping. He pulled a couple of spoons from the drawer and stopped at her expression. 'What is it?'

'We can't ruin it, it's too pretty.'

'This is a test, remember. And, if it's any good,' he shrugged, 'I'll make another.'

'This is becoming a habit.' She held her spoon up ready to sample the dessert, the moment reminiscent of the brownies a few nights ago.

'I won't tell if you don't.' He dug in his spoon to scoop out the right amount of base, pie, and topping before holding the spoon out ready for her to taste. 'I need to know your verdict on the blue-berries. I wasn't sure about those.'

'You're staring,' she said, conscious of his focus and the fact he was still holding the spoon, but she suspected she might drop the pie if she was holding it.

'I want to see your reaction, watch your face.'

And now she really didn't want to try it. To have him watching her felt intimate, like things were heating up between them, and she wasn't sure she was ready. She'd felt the same way sitting close to him as they spoke with Sofia at the desk and when they'd sat together on the sofa as though they were more than colleagues. And she was well aware of the casual glances between them both that were growing in frequency and intensity.

Rupert was still waiting for her to try the pie, the spoon in front of her now. 'Close your eyes, really think about it as you taste it.'

She did her best to act as though this was the most natural thing in the world. She opened her mouth and soon felt the cool spoon on the top of her tongue; flavours hit her taste buds as she closed her mouth and took in the piece of pie.

'Good?'

She opened her eyes to tell him it was better than good, that it was the right amount of tart, that the blueberries added a different taste dimension. But her focus shifted before she could say anything and rather than looking at Rupert, she found herself meeting Shaun's gaze. He was standing in the doorway to the kitchen and she could tell he was thinking about how he'd predicted the chef's feelings for Katy way before she had.

Rupert looked confused at her sudden silence and inability to focus until he turned around to see the other man.

'I hope I'm not interrupting.' Shaun was having trouble keeping the smile from his lips, Katy could tell. 'I did text you a few minutes ago.'

'Sorry, I've been...'

'Working?' Shaun quirked an eyebrow Katy's way. 'I'll wait in the lounge.'

'I'll be there in a sec,' she called to him as he retreated. She turned to Rupert. 'I'm sorry, would you mind?'

'Not at all, go ahead. But your overall verdict on the pie is good?'

'It's very good. The blueberries definitely belong, the ginger base was delicious.'

She headed out to see Shaun, who was waiting in the lounge looking out of the window. When he turned around, she held up a warning finger. 'Don't go there.'

He kept his voice low. 'What did I interrupt in the kitchen?'

'Nothing.'

'Oh, come on, that wasn't nothing.' He nudged her. 'He's interested. He'll make a move soon, I bet you. Especially now he's seen me. I'm the competition.'

She shook away the suggestion for now. 'What can I do for you, Shaun? I honestly am working.'

'I know you are, but I wanted some advice. Your dad got in touch, invited me to the wedding.'

She put a hand on his arm and gave it a squeeze. 'You've always been special to our family.'

'Trouble is, I've no idea what to get him as a gift.'

'You don't have to get him anything.'

'I don't have to, but I'd like to. Your dad is a good guy, I want to wish him well. So if you could give me advice, the coffee is on me.'

Katy turned when she heard someone come in the front door to the inn. Natalie, who managed what could be deemed a smile before she headed in the direction of the kitchen.

'Is she behaving?' Shaun asked when they were alone again.

'Rupert thinks so.' And when she saw his expression, she said, 'You don't need to worry, it's all in hand.'

'I hope so, Katy. I know it's hard for you, what she may or may not be up to.'

Rupert came out of the kitchen with his sister, and while Natalie headed up the stairs, Rupert suggested Katy go out on her break now.

She wasn't going to argue. She went up to her apartment to freshen up, found her purse and a portable phone charger, and pulled on a lightweight coat. She found her own umbrella too before she went back down the stairs.

She was surprised to see both men standing at the front entrance to the Inglenook Inn as though they were two buddies catching up. But, when Rupert turned to face her, it didn't look that way at all.

He passed by her without a word. Less than thirty minutes ago, Rupert had been feeding her key lime pie and watching her with an intensity that made her skin feel prickly with anticipation, and now he could barely look at her.

'Everything okay?' she asked Shaun. 'You didn't try to make him jealous, did you?'

'Not at all. Come on, I need some ideas and coffee will help.'

They found a café a couple of blocks away and Katy ordered a hot chocolate while Shaun went for coffee and a big slice of carrot cake.

'Not for me, thanks,' she replied when he tried to coerce her once again into having cake.

'That's right, I forgot, you were already having something sweet in the kitchen when I arrived.' And before she could deny it, he added, 'Just be careful there. With his sister, I mean.'

'It's nice of you to worry, it really is, but it's all in hand.' She smiled. 'Now let's talk gifts.'

'I was thinking how much he loves golf – I could get him a lesson with a pro, throw in dinner too.'

She shook her head and swallowed her mouthful of hot chocolate. 'First of all, that's incredibly generous of you. And second of all, you've got the perfect gift, you didn't need my help at all.'

'I guess I wanted to see you anyway.' In case his intentions were misconstrued, he leapt in with, 'When I spoke to your dad about the wedding, you know, thanked him for inviting me, said I'd be honoured, he told me he was worried about how you were coping with all of this.'

'His marriage?'

'That, but more the reminders of David with this girl at the inn.'

She hid behind her hot chocolate while she thought of what to say. 'I can't say it's been easy but it's manageable. And there are always reminders, Shaun. Someone mentions a sibling and I think of David, I heard someone call his name on the street the other day, a week ago I saw a kid with a bright-blue backpack just like David had in high school.'

'I remember that bag,' he laughed. 'It was old and worn and I think your mom sewed it up more than once, the thing was falling apart.'

'He loved it. I've no idea why.'

'I suppose it's like those orange sneakers I had throughout my senior year. Awful things, they stank, but try telling me to get rid of them.'

It was her turn to laugh then. And this was nice, sharing something about David, their past, the memories that Katy usually avoided. Perhaps having Natalie at the inn had stirred something up inside of her but, maybe rather than be a bad thing, it might even be good.

'And you're really okay about the wedding?' Shaun put a generous forkful of carrot cake into his mouth.

'I think so.' She'd forgotten how much the pair got on. Shaun had been in their lives for so many years, and despite their break-up remained a firm friend. 'It was always going to be difficult, but I'll get there. It might take me a while to fully get my head around it, that's all. And Dad and I have talked some more.' She only hoped Stephanie wasn't still being aloof, that there wasn't anything she was keeping from Wade.

'While we're on the subject of relationships,' Shaun began, 'I've been seeing someone. Early days,' he added, before telling her about the woman who worked at the same company as him who he'd been out for dinner with and was planning on taking to the Hamptons.

'I'm pleased for you, Shaun.'

'And I am for you.'

'Rupert?' She paused. 'We'll see.'

'Ah, so you admit it.'

She maintained her silence and only responded with a smile.

'Like I said, just be careful as far as the sister goes.'

With an eye roll, she told him, 'You don't need to be concerned. This isn't David.'

'It's not, but you said yourself that Natalie's situation reminded you of what happened with your brother and I would hate to see it cause problems for you.'

She was about to insist that it wouldn't, that she was sure Rupert had it under control and perhaps Natalie would be on her way soon, when it suddenly dawned on her. 'Wait, did you say anything to Rupert at the inn while I was getting my things?'

His hesitation was enough of a giveaway. 'I was going to tell you.'

She put her face in her hands.

'I was trying to help.'

'I told you about Natalie in confidence and now he'll think I'm gossiping.' Her chest rose and fell distinctly. 'What did you tell him exactly?'

'Just that you went through a hell of a time with David and that if his sister is involved in drugs in any way, shape, or form, you don't want to be anywhere near it.'

'And what did he say?'

'Weirdly, not a lot. Apart from, "Who's David?" And as soon as I said he was your brother, presuming Rupert would have heard the name before, that's when I realised I'd put my big size elevens right in it.'

She stood, grabbing her bag from the back of her chair.

'You're going?'

'I have to.' No wonder Rupert had barely looked at her when

she left. They'd talked, she'd had ample opportunity to tell him about her brother and now, not only would he think she'd been gossiping about his family, he knew that she'd lied about her own. To him, it must seem like David had been in trouble and they'd turned their backs on him and even denied his existence. It was the total opposite of what he was doing for Natalie.

She couldn't waste time; she had to get back to her job, and as soon as dinner service was over, try to salvage some of this. The friendship she'd built, whatever else was on the horizon, might now not even be a possibility. Not when Rupert would see her as a liar and a woman who turned her back on her own flesh and blood.

* * *

Rupert was in the lounge answering the phone as she came through the door. He mumbled that the person the caller wanted was back and promptly held out the phone until she walked towards him to take it.

She covered the mouthpiece right away. 'Rupert, can we talk?'

He looked at her as if it was the most absurd thing she'd ever suggested. 'I don't think so.'

'After dinner service. Please.'

But he didn't bother with a response and so she took a deep breath and dealt with business; it was all she could do right now. The call was a guest thanking her for being so welcoming earlier that week and for the small touches in the apartment. Katy barely heard a word but briefly managed to remember to prompt the caller to leave a review on their website.

Nervously she headed for the kitchen, unsure what reaction she'd get. Dinner service would be underway in an hour or so and she checked the dining room first – it was all sorted. Places were set, napkins and cutlery ready, and the back doors were closed for now, even though the rain had stopped. It was a judgement call in the spring it seemed – one day it was nice to have them open for the breeze, another day it was too wet or too windy and more of a nuisance.

She peeked through the crack in the hatch. She could just about see Rupert working away. He looked so content in his domain, she couldn't upset him right now, not any more than she already had. And so she headed back towards the lounge, but stopped as she passed the door to the basement because she heard a sound.

She opened up the door. She could hear crying, she was sure of it.

Carefully she made her way down, calling out, 'Hello,' as she went, her hand sliding down the handrail. She'd never get used to how steep this staircase was; it didn't matter how many times she used it, it still required full concentration.

'Hello?' she called again and that was when she saw Natalie on the floor.

The first thing she thought of was a drug overdose. But when she got closer, Natalie wasn't out of it, she looked like she was in pain. Katy had seen David on drugs and this wasn't the same, not at all.

'What happened?' she asked.

Natalie was crying, repeating over and over, 'It's my fault.'

'You fell over?' Katy looked at her body on the floor, but nothing seemed amiss. Falling was the only explanation. 'What have you hurt?' When she didn't get an answer, she pressed on. 'Can you get up, Natalie?'

'It's my fault, I wished for this.'

Wished to fall over and hurt herself? 'Natalie, you're not

making much sense. Have you taken something?' She had to ask, had to know what to do from here.

'Oh, fuck off!'

Katy felt her rage rise and was about to tell Natalie as much when Natalie reached out and grabbed a hold of her arm. 'I'm sorry, I'm sorry, please don't leave me on my own.'

'What happened?' she asked again.

'Promise you won't tell my brother.'

'Don't tell him you're hurt?'

And that was when Natalie clutched her tummy yet again and curled more into a ball. Katy spotted the blood on Natalie's pale-blue summer skirt; it must've seeped from her underwear. And everything fell into place. The exhaustion, the nausea, the hunger pangs.

'Natalie, are you pregnant?'

She sobbed, she nodded.

'I need to get you up.' Katy took charge and reluctantly Natalie stood up, still mumbling again that she'd brought this on herself.

'Please don't tell Rupert about this.' Natalie clutched Katy's arm and it was beginning to hurt, but the girl was in pain, scared witless.

'Does he know you're pregnant?'

'No, and he mustn't. Not ever.'

Katy didn't want to point out that he'd know when a baby appeared in the months ahead, although blood wasn't a good sign, and neither were the painful cramps that made it hard to help Natalie over to the bottom of the staircase.

When Natalie begged again not to tell her brother, Katy told her to wait there.

'What are you going to do?' Natalie sat on the bottom step the best she could.

But Katy didn't answer because how could she explain and stop Natalie's panic when she had no idea herself?

All she could do was take the steps as quickly as she could, call a cab, and head into the kitchen to think of something, anything, that would allow Natalie to escape the inn without her brother knowing.

16

Katy had found Rupert in the kitchen mid-souffle-making and when he didn't turn around at her entrance, she'd backed out. She couldn't do it. Natalie had to take priority and she'd think of an excuse later.

Thankfully, Rupert hadn't emerged from the kitchen by the time the cab arrived and Katy helped Natalie down the front steps and gave the driver the destination.

But Natalie reached out to her before she could go back up the steps and into the inn. 'You're not coming with me?' she begged.

'I... I can't, this place.'

A horn honked behind the cab at what looked like customers taking their time to get in and on their way. Katy held up a finger to indicate they'd need one more minute. She looked back at the inn, she looked at Natalie. 'I'll grab my bag.'

Luckily for them, the cab driver was patient, or perhaps he didn't care about holding up traffic when his meter was cranking up the entire time. He waited. Katy leapt in a minute later and sat right next to Natalie, who reached for her again, clutching hold as another cramp almost overwhelmed her.

'It really hurts,' she whimpered.

'I'll bet.'

'I'll get you there in no time,' the cab driver told them. He had to be a father with this level of understanding. Some cab drivers wouldn't have let them in the cab in the first place if the fare looked too much of a hassle.

Katy knew she had to call Rupert and he picked up on her second attempt.

'Where are you?' he barked.

'I'm with your sister.'

'My sister?'

'She hurt her ankle on the steps, I think it needs checking at the emergency room.' She had her eyes closed as though it might help her think of excuses and sound as though she was telling the truth.

'So you just left?' He swore.

'I made a snap decision.'

'Is she badly hurt?'

'No, it looks minor.'

And then sympathy gave way to frustration as he grumbled, 'Can't she do anything right?'

'I'll get back as soon as I can.'

'Yeah.' And with that he hung up.

'He's fine without us for a while,' was all Katy told Natalie, who looked more frightened than anyone Katy had ever seen.

When the cab pulled to a stop outside the emergency room, Katy was ready to stay in the vehicle and go straight back to the inn. But when Natalie realised her intention, she kept a firm grip on Katy's arm. 'Please,' she pleaded.

Katy hesitated only for a second then pulled out her purse, paid the driver, and took Natalie inside.

* * *

While Katy was waiting for Natalie to receive the medical attention she needed, she texted Rupert rather than call him. She wasn't sure she'd manage to lie again and he'd sounded so pissed earlier. Her text was truthful when it said they'd had to wait to be seen, she just didn't elaborate on anything. And his replies were at least civil.

Katy waited at the hospital for hours, until a nurse came to find her and tell her she could go and see Natalie now. She wondered whether Natalie had described her as a good friend rather than the woman who'd been interfering in her life since she arrived in the city.

Katy followed the corridor along past the nurses' station to the room at the very end and gingerly approached Natalie's bedside but didn't sit down. And when Natalie turned her head so she was looking at her, she asked, 'How are you feeling?'

'I lost the baby.'

'I'm so sorry.' She didn't know whether Natalie wanted her here or whether the nurse had been the one to decide that for her. 'I wasn't sure if you wanted to be on your own.'

'I could use some company.' She tilted her head towards the chair, which Katy took to mean she could sit down.

When Katy looked at her again, Natalie was focusing on the ceiling light rather than looking at her.

'Are you in much pain?' Katy asked.

'Not as bad as before, but I've been warned I'll likely have some more cramping. Pain relievers should help.' She shook her head, tears in her eyes. 'Every cramp will just be a reminder there's no baby any more. But perhaps this was just meant to be.'

After a pause, Katy asked, 'How far along were you?'

'A little over twelve weeks.' Her voice came out small.

They sat in silence for a while and Katy didn't push her to talk. She simply waited.

'It was just starting to become real,' Natalie admitted, looking Katy's way. 'The day before I left Vermont, I had a scan – another reason for Mom not to trust me when I'd been out for the afternoon and wouldn't tell her where I was. But seeing my baby that day, that was when I knew. I wanted to keep it.'

When Katy nodded and said nothing, Natalie didn't let her get away with it. 'I just admitted I wasn't sure I wanted to keep my baby; you're not going to ask me why?'

'It's none of my business.' Katy waited for a nurse to bring in the jug of water and a cup and pour a measure for Natalie, who had managed to pull herself more upright against her pillows. 'Can I call anyone? The father?'

Natalie ignored the question and tried to take a sip of water, but tears prevented her from drinking as her mouth formed a different shape and her hand began to shake as she began to cry.

Katy took her cup and passed her the box of tissues instead.

She pulled one out to wipe beneath her eyes and then blow her nose. 'You didn't tell Rupert, did you?'

'I didn't, but you should. You can't keep this from your family, you'll need them.'

'None of them have any idea I'm pregnant. Not even my sisters. I mean, what kind of fucked-up family can't share a thing so huge with each other?'

'I'm guessing you've got your reasons.' Katy waited before she added, 'You and I got off to a bad start, but I'm here now, I'm the only one who knows. You could try talking to me. I'm not a bad listener.' At least, she'd tried to be for David. She just hadn't managed it. Perhaps she could in some way make up for it now by being there for someone else's sibling.

After another wait, Natalie relented, perhaps realising Katy was her best, or only, option for now. 'I suppose this was all going to come out sooner rather than later. I was just trying to work out how I felt first and foremost, you know?'

'I understand that completely.'

She frowned, shook her head. 'You must have thought me lazy when I wanted to rest so often, you must have thought me ungrateful – I know Rupert did – at the inn when you offered me sandwiches and I checked what was in them. It was because I knew I had to be careful what I ate in case it wasn't good for the baby. Even though I was contemplating not keeping it before that scan, as soon as I knew I was pregnant, I tried to take good care of myself and...' Her voice caught, she couldn't even say the word *baby* again. 'I guess there's no point worrying about any of that now, is there?'

Katy covered her eyes. 'I feel terrible that neither me nor your brother saw it. We pushed you and pushed you.'

'No, you didn't. Not really. I was working, and if I was you or my brother, I would've reacted the same, thought the troubled sister was trying to shirk her responsibilities.' The phrase made her voice shake because she'd been trying to do the very opposite by the sounds of things. Her mind had been on her pregnancy and her baby.

'Does the father know?' Katy asked.

The question opened the floodgates of emotion. 'No, and the bastard was never going to. I don't even know his real name.' With a crumpled tissue in her fingers, she told Katy, 'By the way, those pills you saw me with? They were prenatal vitamins.'

'I'm sorry, I jumped to conclusions. I can't believe I did that to you.'

'I guess given what Rupert obviously told you, it was understandable. But the drugs my family assumed I took? The drugs I said I'd been experimenting with?' She kept looking at Katy, her face drained of colour. 'I took a drug all right, but I didn't take it on purpose.'

'You didn't? Then—'

'My drink was spiked.'

Katy, stunned into silence, just listened.

Natalie was still shaking her head. 'You guessed it, I was the stupid girl who went out on a date with someone she met over the internet and woke up hours after the date not remembering much about it at all, let alone places I'd been or the name of the guy. Which I doubt was even real. I willingly met up with him, I remember kissing him and agreeing to go somewhere, but after that, I don't remember much apart from my sister's husband taking me home. And even the memory of that is foggy.'

'Don't tell me—'

'That asshole is the father? Yes, he is... or at least he was.' The tissue was in shreds now, there was nothing for Natalie to tug apart any more. 'I got pregnant by the kind of man who does that to a woman. And even crazier, I ended up wanting the baby.' She gave a cold laugh at the ridiculousness of it all. 'So you'll see, that's why I never denied the drugs in the first place, it was easier to let everyone think I'd been partying and experimenting than have to confess how utterly stupid I'd been. I hate the thought of my family knowing that I had sex with someone whose name I probably never even knew, not for real. The thought of it makes me feel sick.'

Katy stood up and leaned across to reach for Natalie's hand. 'You did nothing wrong. Absolutely nothing. Do you hear me?' And, before Natalie could argue against the claim, she repeated herself until Natalie, taken aback at the support being offered, burst into tears, huge sobs consuming her entire body.

And all Katy could do was comfort her. There were no words

right now. Nothing she could say that would take any of this pain away.

All she could do was hold her tightly and tell her that everything was going to be okay.

* * *

By the time Katy got back to the Inglenook Inn, it was past midnight. She'd be up again before 6 a.m. and she was shattered. She put her key into the lock of the front door and stole inside as quietly as she could. She felt like she needed a good long shower, but she didn't want to disturb anyone else and the thought of a bed right now was too appealing. She'd left Natalie at the hospital; they were keeping her in for the one night. She was shattered through her ordeal and the recollection of not only today's events but the night of the date rape and everything since. Katy had been an unlikely confidante, but Natalie had poured her heart out tonight, having kept all of this quiet for so long.

Katy headed for the lounge to ensure everything was off. Rupert would likely have done it all, but he'd also have been exhausted and on his own, so it was the least she could do to make doubly sure everything was as it should be. When she'd left Natalie at the hospital tonight, Natalie had been slipping in and out of sleep already, but one thing she said was perfectly clear. And that was her request that Katy tell Rupert everything now. Somehow the confession to Katy had paved the way for her to want to tell her family and Katy was glad she'd been able to help. She also, weirdly enough, didn't mind being the one to have to tell Rupert. The revelations were going to be hard for a brother to hear and Natalie would need his support rather than having to manage his reaction.

Katy, over at the desk, switched the computer off because it had been left on. She picked up an empty glass from the bar top and another from behind the leaflet rack, but as she went to creep out again and go to the kitchen, she gasped in shock when Rupert sat up from his reclined position on the sofa.

Her hand against her chest, she took a deep breath in and released it slowly. 'You scared me.'

He looked at his watch. 'It's gone midnight. Where's Natalie?'

'Still at the hospital. She'll stay in for the night.'

He rubbed his eyes with the heels of his hands. 'For a mild ankle injury?'

Katy had intended to tell him everything in the morning but with him sitting here in front of her now, she knew it couldn't wait. And so, instead of taking the used glassware out to the kitchen, she went behind the bar and took out two fresh glasses.

'What are you doing?'

She poured out two measures of brandy and handed one to Rupert. 'You're going to need this.' When he looked doubtful, she told him to drink it in one.

He obeyed and then she took the glass and refilled it. She hadn't touched her own yet. 'I need to tell you something about Natalie.'

'No, Katy. I've told you, I think it's best you don't give advice about my sister given—'

'Please stop talking, Rupert, let me say what I have to say.' Her abruptness shocked him enough that he did what he was asked. 'Natalie told me something and she wanted me to talk to you about it. Can we sit down?'

As they sat at opposite ends of the sofa, she told him the whole truth about his sister and what had happened to her right from the date she went on one night and the drink spiking through to the miscarriage today.

Rupert had set down his drink long ago, leaned forwards, arms resting on his thighs, and now he put his head in his hands. When Katy realised he was crying for the pain of what his sister had endured, she put a reassuring hand on his arm and told him she'd give him some time and that tomorrow he should go see his sister. Natalie needed her brother more than ever now.

17

RUPERT

It was Katy's turn to manage the Inglenook Inn on her own today because Rupert had barely slept a wink, one eye on the clock so he could get up at the crack of dawn and be at the hospital for visiting hours.

He was the first visitor to arrive and the moment he saw Natalie lying in her hospital bed, her face crumpled; he only just managed to not allow his to do the same. He'd cried last night, knowing what she'd been through, how she'd felt she couldn't tell anyone. Despite what he claimed about being a close-knit family, each of them able to turn to another in times of crisis, it seemed he was blinkered because they hadn't been that for Natalie this time. And knowing so saddened him more than anything.

Rupert held his sister in a tight hug the same way he'd held her when she fell out of their tree house when she was eight and thought she'd broken a leg, the way he comforted her after she had her wisdom teeth removed and worried the puffy cheeks were there to stay and would make her look like a chipmunk forever. He'd used the reminder of the last memory to coax her out of her tears of sadness, anger, grief, and more towards realising she would smile again, that her family were there for her no matter what.

'You should've told me,' he said, holding both of her hands as he sat on the edge of the bed. 'I've been an ass to you, making you work, watching your every move.'

'I didn't give you much choice,' she sniffed, accepting his offer to help her sit up in bed. She was due to be discharged today and hopefully the doctor wouldn't take long to come round.

'I know you like your space at my apartment, but I'd like to take you back to the inn, you can stay with me for a few days. I want to keep an eye on you. And not because I don't trust you but because I'll worry otherwise.'

She began to smile, a smile that said they were okay, that she knew he was here for her. 'Do I get a choice?'

'No, you don't.'

'I feel like I need to sleep for a week,' she admitted.

'Then that's what you can do.'

'You'll miss my help.'

He chuckled. 'Of course I will.'

'Hey, I wasn't that bad.'

'No, you weren't at all. Your help was appreciated.'

'Every part of it?'

'Don't push it,' he laughed.

'Rupert, are you sure you want to take me back to the inn? If I were you and I'd brought all this drama to your door, I'd have me packed off back to Mom and Dad's the minute I get the okay from the doctor.'

'After everything you've told me, I understand why you came here now.'

'You do? You don't think I should've gone to Amy, Maisie, or Cameron?'

'I don't and I get why you preferred to come here. It's far away, I have no spouse, no kids, you thought you'd see me, be in an entirely different place and perhaps be able to get your head sorted.'

She looked down at her fingers, clasped together on her lap. 'Didn't quite work out that way, though, did it?'

'Life rarely does.'

After the nurse poked her head around the door to tell them the doctor was on his rounds and should be there within the hour, Natalie told him about Katy and how she'd been there for her since yesterday. 'I misjudged her. She's actually kind of pretty great.'

He'd thought so too until he found out she'd not even admitted to having a brother. He'd come over all superior and assumed it meant she held little value when it came to family, that they'd turned their backs on David, that she thought he should do the same with Natalie as she was in trouble. But he'd leapt to conclusions, he could see that now, when really he knew nothing of Katy's situation. Not only that: this latest drama for Natalie went to show that even a seemingly perfect family could be messed up in ways you never realised. Last night, Katy's face and voice when she'd told him everything had shown him she wasn't the sort of person who found it easy to walk away from family, friends, or people who needed her, not unless she felt she had no other choice. And he needed to let her explain if that was what she wanted to do.

'I made Katy come here to the hospital with me,' said Natalie. 'I was scared, Rupert.'

'I'm sure you were.' His voice caught and he cleared his throat. 'I'm sorry for everything that happened to you. If I ever find out who that guy was...' He'd dropped her hands and his fists clenched, his fingernails leaving indents in his skin. 'I'll kill him.'

'I'd settle for you handing him over to the police,' she said softly. 'I don't want my brother getting in trouble on my behalf.'

'Will you go to the police?'

'There's little point if I can't remember his name, don't know where he lived, and it's too late to take evidence, surely.'

'You can't remember anything?'

'Not a thing. He covered his tracks well. Which means he'll likely be doing it to someone else. And I really hate the thought of that. The thought that someone else...' Her voice trailed off.

'Why don't you talk to Randall? He'll help.'

Her face fell. 'I don't think I can. Reliving it is horrible. And personal. I don't know if I'm strong enough.'

He squeezed her hand. 'Yes, you are, you're one of the strongest women I know. Just like your sisters, just like Mom. Please, Natalie. You can't let it go unreported. For what it's worth, I think you'll regret it if you do that. A lot of women must shy away from telling anyone out of shame, fear they won't be believed, belief they've left it too long or can't remember enough to make a difference.' He shuddered the way he did whenever he thought of the guy who'd done this to her, to his sister. 'If you don't want to tell Randall everything, then ask him to have another officer come see you.' He dipped his head so that she looked up at him rather than at her fingers. 'Promise me you'll do that when you're home.'

He got a nod in response and that was all he could ask for right now.

'I'm glad Randall found me outside the bar,' she admitted.

'You've no idea how glad I am about that too.' His sister Cameron's husband was a cop but more than that, he was a good man. He always wanted to do the right thing. 'Do you think he's mentioned it to Cameron?'

'Do you think Cameron would keep something this big to herself if he had?'

'Good point.'

'I hated keeping this from all of you guys, you know. But I didn't see any other way. It was too much, too big a thing and I didn't know how to even begin.'

'You know you have to tell Mom.'

'I know. But not yet, I'm not ready. I think I'd like to rest up a bit and then go home to Vermont.'

'You'll tell her face to face?'

She shrugged. 'Not sure yet.'

'How about I tell her?'

Her gaze lifted suddenly to his. 'You'd do that for me?'

'Of course I would. I understand why you had Katy tell me. It meant I could process before I saw you rather than you having to cope with my reaction.'

She managed a smile. 'That's exactly why I did it. I'd like Mom's support, but it'll be easier if she can process the facts first. It's going to be a shock, and I'm not ready to go into lengthy explanations or be someone else's support person as they try to get their head around it all.'

'I'll wait until you're on your way back to Vermont and then she doesn't have to worry for days on end until she sees you.'

'Thank you, Rupert. You're a good brother.'

'I can't believe it's taken you so long to realise,' he tried to joke, but her happier expression at his remark didn't last long and when he saw her fingers tugging at the skin on her opposite wrist, he asked, 'Can I ask you something else?'

'If I say no, will you be quiet?' One look told her that no, he wouldn't.

'Were you really going to keep the baby?' he asked.

'Not at first. I thought about getting rid of it, it's all I thought about, but then I don't know, something in me shifted. I bought a bottle of vodka one night, intended to either get very drunk or better still it would cause me to lose the baby, but I sat there for almost an hour, open bottle in my lap, and I couldn't do it. I knew the answer to my problems didn't lie in the bottom of a glass, as I knew that not being pregnant any more wouldn't obliterate what happened to me.

'The next day, I went and bought prenatal vitamins. I thought I'd buy myself some time to decide what to do. But as well as taking care of myself and the baby, I was also looking into clinics where I'd be able to get a termination should that be what I wanted. I'm not proud of it. Imagine if Mom knew, Rupert. Mom, the woman who has a big family and wouldn't dream of ever doing the same.'

'If Mom knew the entire story, she would understand why you were thinking that way.'

'I slowly began to realise that it wasn't my baby's fault what happened, he or she was a part of me, as well as a part of a man who was capable of such a thing.' Her voice wobbled. 'I brought this on myself. I wanted to get rid of it at first, somehow the universe knew, made it happen. That's why I lost my baby, isn't it? It's my punishment.'

He moved closer to her and this time took both of her hands in his. 'You know as well as I do that that simply isn't true. It happened because it happened, not because of how you were thinking. You know what I've been wrestling with in the cab up here?'

'What?'

'I wonder whether it happened because I kept nagging you to work, made you go up and down the stairs all those times, heaving the vacuum cleaner, scrubbing floors. If I'd let you rest more—'

'Rupert, that's crazy!'

'Exactly. And so is blaming yourself. Neither one of us did anything that made this happen. It just did. And it's horrible.'

Her face crumpled and he cradled her in his arms again.

When the doctor appeared, she wiped her tears away with the back of her hand.

'I'll give you guys a few minutes,' said Rupert before he looked to the doctor. 'How's the coffee here? Do I want to grab a cup from the vending machine?'

The doctor pulled a face. 'I wouldn't recommend it.'

'Right you are. I'll save it for when I'm back at the inn.' He'd get Natalie settled and then he'd grab two large takeaway coffees from the café on the corner of the next block, one for him, one for Katy, and then he'd set aside his own family turmoil so he could apologise to Katy for being so judgemental and refusing to give her a chance to explain. He owed her that much.

He only hoped he hadn't messed things up between them for good.

* * *

Rupert paid the cab driver and then, stepping out onto the sidewalk first, took his sister's hand to help her out of the vehicle.

'I'm not an invalid, Rupert.'

'You've had a bad time.'

'And I appreciate you looking out for me, but all I want is to get back to normal.'

He opened his mouth to tell her that this wouldn't just go away, the pain of what happened to her, losing her baby, it all needed to be dealt with, but for now he could see she needed to be on her own and curl up in bed.

Katy was in the lounge on the phone and he raised a hand in greeting before taking Natalie straight upstairs. And when he was sure he couldn't get her anything and promised he'd check on her in a while, he went back downstairs and out to grab the coffees.

Rupert stood in line at the café. If he let himself think about that guy, what he'd done to his sister, it would drive him crazy. He wondered not only how their mom would react but their dad. Someone doing that to his little girl, it was unimaginable.

But she was safe now. And she wasn't doing drugs, that was a relief, at least.

He scooted back across the street and, balancing one takeaway cup on top of the other, he opened the door to the inn as Katy finished up on the phone.

He set her coffee down at her desk. 'Peace offering,' he began, 'for the way I've been: not letting you talk to me, grouchy, whatever labels you want to give me.'

She just looked at him. Maybe an apology wasn't going to get him anywhere. Maybe they were just colleagues and that's all they'd ever be.

'Thank you for being there for my sister too,' he pushed on. 'I'm sorry I made assumptions about you, the way you were with your family.'

This time, she waved both hands in front of her to stop him talking. Okay, worse than he thought.

'Rupert, we've got bigger things to worry about.'

'What do you mean?' He'd been about to enjoy his first sip of coffee.

'Remember how your sister took a booking for the Cheddingtons a while ago?'

'Not really. Refresh my memory.'

She recapped – family of four, one night, arriving Wednesday.

'We have room,' he said, 'so what's the issue, they're not coming?'

'Oh, the Cheddingtons are coming. They called to confirm today. Except the Cheddingtons aren't a family of four, they're a company. And they don't want a room, they want a corporate dinner, the full works for fourteen people, at 6.30 p.m. Tonight.'

'Shit.'

For the last couple of years, Sofia's business clientele had grown not only for overnight stays, but also for corporate dinners hosted on occasion at the inn. They usually got some magazine coverage of the events courtesy of Darcy's friend Holly, who had plenty of contacts. They'd hosted Thanksgivings, Fourth of July events, luncheons, and corporate meetings. Any guests staying at the inn and not involved with the event would usually be offered a choice of nearby restaurants at a generous discount to make up for the fact they couldn't eat at the inn, but it was easy enough to do that and so far none of their guests had ever minded.

What wasn't so easy to do was organise a last-minute corporate dinner.

'What did you tell them?' Rupert asked.

Katy closed her eyes and opened only one of them as she replied tentatively, 'I told them yes. I mean, I didn't know what to do, you were with Natalie when they called, I didn't want Sofia to miss the booking and get a bad reputation. They were so complimentary, knew other corporates who'd been here, they paid the deposit which I pretty much made up off the top of my head with the help of the last three corporate bookings. I took those figures and worked out a rough guestimate of deposit and balance. And they already said that they were using tonight as a trial as they might want to book a party here in the fall,' she babbled on. 'This will be the perfect chance to see if the inn was the right venue.'

'Okay, Katy. First of all, breathe.' He waited for her to stop panicking. 'And second of all, you did the right thing.'

'But...'

'You did. It was the right thing for the inn.' He puffed out his cheeks. He wasn't too sure it was the right thing for him at the moment, not with everything else going on. And he didn't want to leave Natalie on her own for too long, no matter whether she insisted he didn't need to make any more fuss.

'Do you think we can do it?'

He liked the way she said *we*; it grounded him, stopped his own panic from rising. 'I usually plan these things days and weeks in advance.'

'I'm sorry.'

'Don't be. Here...' He picked up the other takeout coffee and handed it to her. 'We'll drink these and start planning now. Better late than never.'

Flustered again, she said, 'I haven't even asked how Natalie is.'

'She's doing okay, all things considered. She's going to sleep. Can we—'

'If you're going to ask if we can not yell at her for taking incorrect details then consider it done. It was a mistake, easily made, I'm not going to be saying anything to her.'

He pulled up a chair next to her at the desk. 'Thank you. I appreciate it. And everything else you've done.'

'Any time,' she smiled.

* * *

Between them, Rupert and Katy organised for guests who'd booked in for dinner at the inn this evening to go to one of two restaurants with a hefty discount on their bill, and they notified everyone that the dining room would be closed for the corporate clients as was the usual routine but that the communal lounge would still serve drinks and light snacks. Katy got back in touch with Cheddingtons to double check for any food allergies, of which there were none, and they made a rough plan for the menu. Rupert valued Katy's input, given his head was all over the place.

When they thought they were ready, Katy had a moment of doubt. 'Are you sure about this, Rupert?'

'We can't let Sofia down. That's why you didn't cancel when you realised what had happened. You're invested in this place,' he encouraged, because it would need the pair of them to see this through. 'You want us to do well, which means we will.'

'I wish I had your confidence. Are you sure you don't want to try to get an extra member of staff?'

'No need. We've got this.'

'All right, then. You get to the kitchen and make a list of everything you need from the markets.'

'I'll check on Natalie first.'

'Sure. And I'll check on her again when you're out.'

'Thanks, that's a worry off my mind.' And then he added, 'You and she are getting on.'

'She's growing on me.'

Before he went upstairs, he said, 'You and I still need to talk, Katy.' He longed to apologise as he'd intended, to explain how wrong he was to judge her when he didn't know the whole story.

'And we will. But, for now, let's focus on making tonight a success.'

A corporate booking for fourteen people was no walk in the park, but do it the right way and they'd generate extra bookings and good publicity.

18

KATY

Rupert had been at the markets for quite some time and Katy was already beginning to fret at how close they were to the arrival of the corporate guests. They had a few hours but still, she'd rather have him here and know everything was underway.

While the inn was quiet and Rupert still wasn't back, Katy headed upstairs to check on Natalie. She crept into the apartment and peeked around the doorway of the second bedroom. Natalie was sound asleep, or at least Katy thought she was until she stirred.

Katy grimaced. 'Sorry, didn't mean to wake you. I said I'd check on you while your brother is out.'

'What time is it?' She was pretty groggy.

'It's coming up to 4 p.m.' Natalie had propped herself up on her elbows and Katy went over to adjust her pillows so she could lean against those instead. 'How are you feeling?'

'A little better. I should get up, I won't sleep tonight otherwise.'

'It's going to be hectic downstairs this evening, I'd stay up here if I were you.' The plan was for Rupert to spend most of his time in the kitchen with Katy going between there and the dining room as well as front of house. It was going to be demanding but with

Rupert's belief they could do it, Katy had the confidence they'd manage.

'I wasn't going to be a nuisance.'

'That wasn't what I meant at all.'

'Sorry...'

Katy smiled. 'I guess it'll take us a while to be nice to each other.' She was pleased to see Natalie took it in the jovial way she'd intended. 'All I meant was that it will be busy and a bit high pressure for us but mainly your brother as the chef.' She reiterated the corporate booking, omitting the details of how it came about.

'So this is a big deal?'

'Apparently yes, for the inn; they get good write-ups and word-of-mouth as well as satisfied clients if we pull it off.' She crossed her fingers on both hands to grab every bit of hope she could.

'It sounds last minute.'

'Kind of,' she shrugged. 'It's a booking that got a bit confused, that's all; we only realised it was happening when the company called this morning.'

'I feel bad I can't help out.'

'Don't. Your job is to look after yourself.'

Natalie picked up the glass beside her bed and finished the rest of the water.

'Let me get you another.'

'I'm not incapacitated.' And with that, she swung her legs gently out of bed and stood. 'It'll do me good to walk around. I might make some toast.'

It was a good sign she was on the mend. 'I expect Rupert will come up when he's home from the markets,' Katy said before she headed for the door.

'Tell him to focus on work, that I'm okay, that I'm even eating.'

Katy smiled. 'That might work.'

'He needs to focus tonight; that's an order from his little sister.'

She began to laugh. 'I'm pretty sure I never got to boss him about when we were younger, so I don't know why I think it'll work now.' A smile spread tentatively across her face, whether because she was still unwell and grieving or perhaps because she wasn't sure she could say this to Katy. 'My brother likes you, you know.'

Hand on the door handle, she was ready to leave. 'I like him too.'

'No, I mean he *likes* you.'

'We're not in the third grade.' And at her teasing look, Katy added, 'I'm going now.'

Natalie didn't hide her amusement. At least she still had a bit of a sense of humour and Katy didn't mind one bit.

* * *

When Rupert got back to the inn, Katy was there to open the front door for him. 'How on earth did you carry everything?' She knew he usually liked to walk and his strong forearms and biceps were testament to the loads he usually lugged back all that way.

'I got a cab, too pushed for time.'

Katy followed him into the kitchen where he dumped everything onto the countertop as she updated him.

'Natalie is good. She's even got up and made something to eat.'

'Great. I'll check on her in a minute.' He began to unpack the groceries, moving faster than usual given the time pressure, organising ingredients in different areas on the counter tops as he went, she assumed according to what course they were applicable for. He'd gone through menu ideas with her and they'd looked at previous corporate menus to make the final decision. Katy had sensed he didn't especially need her input, but she knew from experience that it was always nice to bat ideas around for something so major.

'She said to tell you to concentrate on tonight's dinner, that you needed to focus – and that's an order.'

He stopped for a moment and looked at her with an expression of amusement. 'She said that?'

'Yeah, and then decided you'd never be bossed around by her.'

He carried on what he was doing but said, 'I'll go up later on then. You're sure she's good?'

'Very, I promise, Rupert. Now, what can I do?'

'I've got everything under control.' But when he caught her eye, he looked relieved. 'Actually, I could use some extra help.'

'Now why was it so hard to say that in the first place?'

'Not used to it, I guess.' He pulled a blue and white striped apron from the drawer next to the fridge and handed it to her. 'Put this on, I'll prop the door open so we can hear if the bell goes out there.'

She fastened the apron. 'Entrée first, I assume?' She watched him take out utensils.

'Nope. Dessert,' he grinned. Despite the pressure of the situation, this was clearly where he felt his most comfortable. His kitchen. His domain. 'Eton mess is first, or at least part of it. I want to get the berry sauce sorted and everything ready to go.' Pulling open the door to a cupboard, he counted some of the glassware at the front.

'They're cute.' She peered over his shoulder to see what looked a bit like shot glasses but slightly larger.

'Cute, but only twelve of those.' He moved to the next cupboard and totted up what was inside. 'These will do.' And he pulled out a few at a time, between his fingers, setting the elegant cylindrical vessels with angled tops on the counter. 'Big enough but not so large the dessert will be lost.'

'What do you want me to do?'

'If you could wash the strawberries for me?' He grabbed the

colander from its hook on the back wall. But the bell dinging from the lounge had other ideas. 'You go,' he assured her. 'I'm used to all of this, remember.'

'Not last minute.'

'I've done enough last-minute dinners... at least that's what I keep telling myself.'

By the time Katy returned, Rupert had washed the strawberries, hulled them and heaped them into a blender jug.

'I wasn't exactly much help, was I?' she grimaced as he added icing sugar.

'I don't know... you could press the button now?'

She did the honours, whizzing the ingredients until Rupert was satisfied the mixture was smooth enough.

He put the jug into the fridge. 'This part is ready early but juggling the different elements to dishes and courses is the most efficient way to work.' He emptied a punnet of blueberries into a colander and handed it to Katy.

Katy washed the berries and he indicated to empty them onto kitchen paper. 'Do all these berries go into the dessert?'

'Some will, others will be used to garnish.' He had a few more raspberries set aside, she noticed, and he put the blueberries with those next to the dessert glasses he'd lined up along the counter out of the way of the main work space. He picked up a bag. 'Now I've cheated a bit here.' He showed her the contents.

'You don't make the meringue?'

'Ordinarily, yes, but tonight, it's the speedy way. Pre-made meringue. But...' he held up a finger to make his point, 'the meringue is from Finn at the bakery, so I know it's good.'

'Fair enough.'

He pulled out a piece of white meringue. 'Here... a meringue kiss from me to you.' He cleared his throat and looked away, realising what he'd said. 'Try it, give me your verdict.'

Katy popped it into her mouth. 'It's light, airy, gets my seal of approval.'

'You sound like a food critic, or you sound like Sofia, both of which is good in my kitchen. I need opinions to help me get the best dishes.'

'Happy to oblige. Has Sofia ever rejected anything?'

He laughed as he took the chicken out of the fridge. 'Not too many things, thankfully, although she has her own likes and dislikes. She tried my potato salad once and neglected to tell me she can't stand dill – I'd added it already. She didn't quite spit it out, but I reckon she came close.'

Katy accepted the offer of another meringue kiss and this time, Rupert didn't use the words but rather took one out of the bag and held it out to her.

'Are you making extras of the Eton Mess desserts?'

'You know me, always extras just in case. And this time, I'll make double the extras I usually do. Then, if we pull this off, we'll get to enjoy the fruits of our labour – literally – when everyone has gone. I don't care how tired I am. The stress of this will fire up my appetite.'

She wasn't sure he really needed her in here now but still offered to help some more. 'Give me something to do before that bell rings again.'

He pointed to the other bag he hadn't yet unpacked. 'Pull out the celery and the carrots – the entire lot needs to be washed and then diced.'

She took out the ingredients and looked around. 'Knife?'

He pulled one from the block he'd been obscuring by his position and passed it handle first to her. 'It's sharp on a whole different scale to knives you likely have at home.'

'Oh, you don't know Stephanie,' she laughed. 'When she started seeing Dad, she came over to cook him a meal and couldn't believe the knives we were using. She was straight online to order a prime set of Sabatier knives, which are now a permanent fixture in our kitchen.' She realised he'd turned to look at her for a moment.

'And what about Stephanie?' he asked. 'Does it feel as though she'll be a permanent fixture?'

'Given they're getting married tomorrow, I'd say so.'

'You think it'll last?'

'I hope so.' And she really did. She was even beginning to get used to the idea. She carried on washing the vegetables and dropped the carrots and celery into the colander as they were cleaned. 'I want my dad to be happy. I need to trust he knows what he's doing. I keep telling myself all I have to worry about doing is showing up and providing a great cake.'

'That's the spirit. And your worry is normal; we worry about our family, we want what's best for them.' He was still watching her. 'I know it's the same for you. Again, I'm—'

'We don't have time to talk about it right now, but I know.' She added a smile to show she really did.

She moved the vegetables over to the chopping board and started to dice them while Rupert plucked garlic from a special container, onions from where they were hanging, and a couple of green peppers ready for prep. At the sound of him chopping, she turned and began to laugh. 'My goodness, you chop and dice at the speed of light!'

'I've had a lot of practice.'

'I'm still on my first carrot!'

Between them, they got the prep for the main dish of chicken goulash well underway. Rupert had told Katy he would've liked to impress tonight with slow-cooked lamb and a baked cheesecake for dessert but it wasn't possible with time constraints. And luckily they'd run through the menu selections on the phone with the client, who'd been delighted with everything.

He took out the paprika from the pantry. 'I know we don't have time to talk much tonight, Katy, but I just want to say how glad I am that you were there for Natalie. I still can't believe she kept everything to herself. That I didn't see there was something more going on with her.'

'You're not psychic. And I get why she kept it to herself.' She carefully dried the sharp knives that Rupert had washed because they didn't go in the dishwasher. 'I can barely say *date rape* without feeling sick to my stomach. Sorry,' she added quickly at the way his body tensed. 'Now's not the time.'

'I started the conversation,' he said solemnly. 'I'm just glad she's talking now. And it's you I have to thank for that.'

'Let's keep moving,' she encouraged with a smile. 'We can't afford to slow down.'

As he took out a large cooking pot for the main dish, Katy asked whether he'd spoken to his mom about Natalie.

'My sister wanted me to wait until she's recovered and on her way home. She figured it'll worry the family less that way.'

'Sounds wise to me.'

'Could you pass me the flour?' he asked Katy as he poured a measure of oil into the cook pot he'd placed on top of the hob. 'It's in the pantry, top left, plain flour will do.'

She found it for him and he weighed the correct quantity on the scale, shaking the packet to get a little more out when it came up short. He poured it into a bowl and after seasoning it, he moved over to the other section of counter to chop the chicken.

Watching him, Katy realised something. 'You don't seem to have a problem talking and working at the same time.' She'd not been keen to have a conversation in the kitchen, but he seemed far more comfortable with it than she was.

'It's a well-honed skill. And sometimes conversations happen best when you're doing something else totally unrelated.'

'I'd make mistakes if I talked too much.'

'Well, tonight, just keep an ear out for my instructions and we won't go far wrong. It's a team effort.'

She felt relieved he was the most relaxed of the pair of them when he was in charge of the food. 'What's next?'

'You're enjoying this. Should I be worried I'll be out of a job soon?'

'Not unless Sofia suddenly wants her guests getting eggs on toast or pancakes and pretty much nothing else. And you saw my chopping skills... slow!'

It wasn't long before the chicken was coated in the seasoned flour and Rupert began cooking the meat in batches until all the pieces had turned a rich golden colour on the surface.

With no interruptions from the guests, Katy scooped up handfuls of the chopped vegetables and added them to the cook pot at Rupert's prompt after he'd put all the chicken back inside. 'What are you serving it with?' she asked as he added tomatoes, paprika, and whatever else was required for another of his culinary sensations.

'Tagliatelle for this one.'

'Are you sure that's not too messy for corporate?'

'It's not a first date for anyone. I'm sure we'll get away with it.'

'Imagine having spaghetti on your first date,' she giggled as he put the dish into the oven.

'If you eat it properly, it's not a problem.' At her bewilderment, he mimed using a fork and hooking spaghetti to twirl on a spoon in the other hand.

'Not the way I grew up eating it, believe me. Me and my brother used to have competitions at who could slurp the loudest and get the most splashes on their face.' She was laughing until she realised she'd inadvertently brought David into the conversation for the first time in years.

'Do you miss him?' Rupert washed his hands and then took out the trays of scallops from the refrigerator.

She couldn't look at him when she admitted, 'More than I realised.'

He went to her side and put his hand on her shoulder until she looked up at him. 'You know it's never too late, don't you?'

And with tears in her eyes, she managed a nod. 'I hope it's not.'

However, from past history, she knew this was about more than what she wanted or her dad wanted or what anyone needed. It had a lot to do with David and up to now, he'd never shown an interest in being a part of her family again.

And if he did, could she forgive him for not being there for their mom in her darkest of days?

19

KATY

Considering the panic she'd found herself in when she took the phone call from Cheddingtons, Katy remained calm as she showed their corporate guests through to the dining room on arrival with the offer of an aperitif. She kept thinking how composed and methodical Rupert had been in the kitchen, in his comfort zone, and thinking that way had her able to go through the motions with a smile on her face. She was even relaxed enough to make small talk with the CEO of the company who, as it turned out, was from Scarsdale. She poured wine, topped up glasses of water, and answered questions about the inn itself when she was asked. She wasn't sure who got the deciding vote about booking a future event or accommodations but everyone at this table mattered, every guest.

'One minute until showtime,' Rupert told Katy when she checked in with him. He'd begun to line up plates with crumbed creamy scallops near the hatch.

'Aren't you nervous?'

'Of course not.' After he'd set the last of the portions down, he whipped off the chef's jacket and put on a fresh one as well as the chef's hat.

'Hang on a minute.' A bit of his fringe was poking from beneath the front of the hat and she stood on her tiptoes and pushed it inside the material. 'Now you look the part.'

'You mean I didn't before?' he teased.

Flustered, she told him, 'You go into the dining room, talk to the guests; they've been raving about the smell of the food, how they need to meet you. I'll pass the entrées through to you for service.'

In the dining room, there were compliments coming Rupert's way as he recapped what the courses would be and Katy smiled, listening to each and every one as Rupert went to and from the hatch until every place setting had an entrée. She went into the dining room and dealt with top-ups of drinks before she and Rupert left the party to it and headed out of the dining room with the biggest smiles yet.

'I can't believe this is going so well,' she said the moment they were out of earshot of their guests.

Rupert took a breather before he'd have to return to the kitchen. 'Couldn't have done it without you.'

'Tonight could've very easily been a total disaster.'

They were both locked in a stare, neither of them saying a word, neither noticing that Natalie had come downstairs.

'What are you two whispering about?' Natalie asked.

'Never you mind.' Rupert took a small step back from Katy. 'How are you?'

'I don't feel too bad, but from now on, can we please stop fussing?'

Rupert opened his mouth to say something but relented. He looked content that Natalie was better than she'd been earlier and it only served to make him look a bit more relaxed, despite the stressful circumstances all round.

'I thought I'd order takeout, eat in the dining room,' Natalie announced.

'Can't tonight I'm afraid, sis,' Rupert informed her quietly. Everyone in the dining room seemed in such high spirits, their chatter had increased in volume ten-fold since they'd arrived.

She put a palm to her head. 'I totally forgot. Katy did mention it. Kind of a big deal from what I understand. Are you pulling it off?'

He made a noise, as if to say of course they were, it was a breeze, before they stood back as the CEO came out to ask where the bathroom was.

'The door at the end, Mr Cheddington,' Katy said, pointing in the right direction, 'You can't miss it.'

He thanked her and when he went on his way, Natalie was looking puzzled.

'I'll head to the lounge,' said Katy. 'I'll be back soon to check on everything and everyone. Rupert, shout if you need me.'

'Will do. You all right there, sis?'

'Do not tell me to go back to bed,' Natalie told him.

Hands in the air in defence, he told her, 'I wasn't going to, don't worry. You actually do look a lot better, more colour in your cheeks.'

Natalie, placated by his comment, looked at Katy. 'There's something familiar about that name.'

'What name?' Rupert asked.

'Cheddington.'

It would've been better if Rupert had simply gone back to the kitchen and Katy could've distracted his sister and her curiosity.

And then Natalie put a hand over her mouth. 'Cheddington

was the name of the booking I took. But it wasn't a corporate party. It was for four people.'

Rupert stayed quiet, but Katy shook her head. There was no point trying to cover it up now. 'Cheddington was the right name, but it was never for accommodation; it's the corporate dinner.'

Her face was almost as pale as when Katy had found her in the basement when she said, 'You mean I fucked up?'

'Ssshhhhhh...' Rupert and Katy said together as Mr Cheddington came back and went into the dining room.

'I am so sorry,' Natalie went on. 'One phone call and I couldn't even get that right.'

'Doesn't matter now,' said Katy.

'What can I do to help?'

'You can go rest, so I don't worry,' said Rupert, who was anxious to get back to his kitchen.

'I can rest and help.'

'Are you sure you're up to it?' Katy asked.

'I've taken painkillers for the cramps, but they're nothing like they were. And I need the distraction, please. At least give me a sitting job. I'll sit in the lounge at the desk, keep an eye on things.'

Katy looked at Rupert. 'Not a bad idea, it means I can help you more. I think, given how lively it's getting in the dining room when we're not even on the first course, you'll need me by the time the cheese platter comes out.' She'd seen more than one work party turn into chaos, out of fun rather than anything bad, but still, hard work for the staff trying to keep everyone happy and make sure those high spirits didn't get out of hand.

'Okay, but let us know if you need us and no running around after guests,' he told his sister.

And when Natalie smiled at her brother's agreement, Katy told her to be sure to ring the bell when she needed to.

* * *

Operations at the Inglenook Inn ran smoother than Katy had predicted given the way this booking had come about. Natalie had managed front of house and answered guest queries and fixed drinks at the bar for those who wanted a nightcap when they returned from wherever they'd been.

By the time the cheese platter had been demolished and the event drew to a close, a little before 11 p.m., Natalie had gone up to bed. Katy and Rupert were still on top form with the guests, but the second she and Rupert put the last of the party into a cab, waved them off, and closed the double doors of the inn behind them, Katy leaned against the wall. She closed her eyes. 'I'm pretty sure I could fall asleep right here in this spot. That was...'

'Exhausting, stressful, chaos...' said Rupert, '...exhilarating, fun, and a buzz,' he added. Katy could hear the smile in his voice; she didn't even need to look at him.

'That's a lot of adjectives to process.' And when she did open her eyes, Rupert was watching her.

'It's nice here at this time of night, peaceful, even though you can still hear the city beyond those doors.'

'I love the city, the whole vibe of it.' Conscious he couldn't stop watching her, she said, 'Your sister really stepped up tonight. She looked happy at the desk chatting with guests; I think it took her mind off things a little bit.'

A small smile crept onto his face. 'I think you're right.' And Katy knew enough about him to know that he was a man who'd do anything for those he loved.

'I'd better do all the checks.' Katy ventured into the lounge to make sure there were no glasses, mugs or side plates either on the bar top or side tables. She switched the computer off and made sure that the window at the front of the brownstone was closed. 'Is there anything more to do in the kitchen?'

'It's all done apart from washing the fancy glasses we served the port in alongside the cheese platter and I can do those in the morning.'

'Thank goodness for that.'

When she turned, Rupert was behind the bar. 'You having a nightcap?' she asked. She was worn out, but the glint in his eyes told her he might be buzzing too much to go to sleep yet.

He held a glass aloft. 'Interested?'

'Actually, I am. And don't we still have those Eton Mess desserts?'

His eyes lit up. 'I'd forgotten about those. You go get them, I'll fix the drinks. Cognac?'

'Anything,' she said, and she meant it.

She got the desserts and between them they stood at the bar and demolished them within seconds. They talked about her dad's wedding tomorrow and the cake she'd chosen for the celebrations that would be delivered by Finn, the baker Rupert had recommended.

'Totally worth it,' she approved, her spoon clinking against the glass as she put it inside the empty vessel and went over to the sofa.

She flopped down, groaning as the furniture's softness almost swallowed her whole. 'You amazed me tonight by keeping the kitchen so in order between courses.' She thanked him for her drink when he brought it over to her.

'Not my first rodeo, my friend.'

'I know, but... well, I don't know how you do it. It's stressful.'

'You work in hotels, you must know stress.'

'I do, but I don't cook at the same time. If I'm cooking, my focus needs to be solely on that.'

When she went quiet, Rupert turned where he was sitting so he could face her. 'I owe you an apology.'

'Rupert, I'm the one who lied, who failed to admit to having a sibling, I'm the one who has done the exact opposite of what you've done with Natalie.' She gulped at the thought of the comparison between them both, their seemingly different values. 'You took your sister in, helped her. I... we... turned our backs.'

'I expect that's not really true.' When she didn't answer, he said, 'I leapt to conclusions, Katy. I don't know anything about you, your family, what happened. And I'm pretty sure I simplified what happened with the limited information I had to go on and that was wrong of me.'

Clutching his cognac, he encouraged her to talk to him. 'Tell me now, tell me what happened with David.'

'We didn't simply turn our backs, you're right.'

'Thought I might be,' he said with a nudge and a small smile of understanding before he went over to the bar and brought back the bottle of cognac to top up her glass.

'It's a bit late for a long story.'

'I'm buzzing, couldn't sleep yet if I tried.'

'You sure you want to hear?' And when he nodded, she started at the beginning after a hefty swig of her drink for courage.

'David was a pretty normal kid. We had a fun childhood – the usual scrapes, making a fort in the backyard, s'mores over the campfire with Mom and Dad, trick or treating costumes every Halloween. But then, just out of high school, David began to change. His best friend Martin was killed in a car accident. David was also in the car with two others. One of the others was Shaun and all three of them walked away with minor injuries.'

His eyes widened at the revelations. 'So that's why you and Shaun are still close.'

'Yes and no. Shaun is the sort of guy who even if you break up with him, he's still a good friend. But because he knew what happened with David first hand, it made him easy to talk to. He was there, you know. He came over to the house a lot to see my parents, talk to them, he listened to them worrying when I couldn't take much more of it. He comforted me. He comforted them. He did the same when Mom was sick; he's just always been around. Not many guys do that with no romantic involvement.'

'They do if they're a good friend.'

'I suppose he became a bit of a brother in the end. Not a replacement, but someone I could confide in, talk to, someone close in age. Perhaps he would've drifted away had the accident not happened or if David hadn't got into trouble, Mom hadn't got sick...' Her voice trailed off.

'The accident must have been hard on the survivors.'

'Worse for David.' She swirled the reddish-brown cognac at the bottom of her glass. 'He was supposed to drive that night, but had taken a few bottles out to share with the other guys and they were all wasted. So his friend had to drive. David kept saying afterwards that it was his fault, that he should've been sitting in the driver's seat, that it should've been him.'

The accident had sounded horrific from what David and Shaun had shared. She could almost hear the crunch of metal, the skid of the tyres, and she hadn't even been there, so she wasn't sure where she'd got the sounds from – television, most likely.

'David was depressed for a while and then he got a little better, then he was down again, up again, it was like a rollercoaster. He refused help and then he seemed to have turned a corner. He got himself a job as a mechanic at a local garage, hung out with an entirely different crowd. They were bad news, all a lot older than him, and the gossip mill started turning that drugs were being dealt at the garage. My dad asked David what he knew, and he said he didn't know a thing. Dad had no reason not to believe him.' She shook her head. 'It wasn't only *his* demons that David was dealing with but the wrath of Martin's mother. She was grieving, she was looking for someone to blame, and she blamed David. She knew he blamed himself and she latched onto that. She'd turn up at the house yelling and screaming at all hours of the day or night, she did it for years, even after David had left. But the times she got to see David were the worst; she'd go for him, claw at him, bash her fists against his chest. It was horrible.

'David started staying away from the house later and later for days at a time, told us he'd slept at the garage. We all knew it was because he couldn't take any more of Martin's mother. Along with the guilt he already felt, it was too much.'

'Why didn't you call the police?'

'My parents didn't have it in their hearts to do that to her. The woman had lost a child. We thought Martin's mother would soon grow tired of it. She turned up one day and must have heard about Mom, started telling me our family deserved some pain. Not long after that day, we found out that while David might not have been dealing in drugs, he was certainly using them. He stole from us, Dad caught him, he lied, he put us all through hell. And then he was gone and we had no idea whether he was dead or alive. Mom was getting sicker and sicker and was heartbroken, and it seemed all of a sudden, she couldn't get out of bed. Martin's mom turned up again after midnight one night yelling about David being a killer, the accident being all his fault, and I just lost it with her. Our family was already broken.' She hadn't realised her hands were shaking until Rupert took her glass and set it onto the coffee table. 'I yelled at her, told her we'd lost David and that Mom was dying. I asked her if she was happy now. She didn't say a word. She left. And after that, never came back.'

'It sounds tough for all of you, including David.'

She felt a tear track down her cheek and stop at her lip. 'David never even showed at Mom's funeral.' She looked across at Rupert, his kind eyes drinking her in, his patience there waiting in the wings. 'Going through burying my mom without my brother broke my heart even more. I didn't think that even was possible. I hated David a little bit for that – or maybe hate isn't the right word because I don't think I could ever hate him. He's my brother. But I was the angriest I've ever been the next time I saw him. He turned up at the house about a month after the funeral. Dad wasn't home, it was just me, and I found David rifling through my mom's chest of drawers.'

'Looking for money?'

'Actually, no. I assumed that was what he was doing, and I was about to yell at him or threaten to call the police when I saw what he had in his hands. It was a photograph album she'd made him for his eighteenth birthday – she did one for each of us when we reached that age.'

Her mind went back to that day as she told Rupert everything about it. David had been skinnier than she'd ever seen him. He'd never been a big guy, never pumped iron at the gym or been into football or hockey like some of his friends, but that day he was like a coat hanger for his clothes: the bones of his shoulders protruded, she could see collar bones that should be there but covered in a healthy layer of fat. His jeans were only just staying up and his sneakers were torn at the toes.

'What are you doing here?' she demanded when she found him in their parents' bedroom.

He held up the album as though it were obvious and he'd only come in here from his own bedroom rather than returning to the family home weeks after his mother was laid to rest.

'Why didn't you come?' she asked when he stayed mute.

He was shaking his head, his skin pale, his mouth downturned. 'Couldn't.'

'Couldn't or wouldn't?'

'Both,' he mumbled.

'You're so selfish!' Her shriek took them both by surprise. 'So fucking selfish!' Her fists pounded his chest without her realising what she was doing, they continued pounding his back as he turned to put the album down.

'Stop it, Katy, stop it!' he yelled.

When she dissolved into a flood of tears and sunk down to her knees, he didn't walk away like she expected him to. He didn't bolt and leave her to wonder when or if he'd turn up again; he sunk down with her and wrapped his sister in his arms and held her the way she'd needed at the funeral. Two siblings who'd lost the woman they adored with only memories to remain. He kept saying, 'I'm sorry,' over and over to her. She hadn't asked him what for – the drugs? The stealing? The lying? Not visiting when their mom was so sick? Not being at the funeral?

'I'm working on it, Katy,' he said as her sobs began to fade. 'I don't want to be this person.'

'Then don't be,' she pleaded. And for the first time in a long while, she saw her brother as a little boy. He was crying as much as Katy, sitting on the bed, clutching the photo album against his chest.

'Let us help you, David.' She shuffled over to where he was.

'I spiralled when I got the news about Mom.'

'Drugs?' When he didn't answer, she asked, 'Are you still on something?'

'Not as much as before.'

She sat down on the bed. Her parents' bed. The place their mom had taken her last breath. Her dad was back sleeping in here now rather than the spare room and the sheets had been washed many times, but it was as though her mom's spirit still lived on in the walls, the décor, the choice of linen. She often heard her dad crying softly in here but she'd never once interrupted him. They were all grieving but he needed his space to grieve for not only the mother of his children but the love of his life.

'Not as much as before,' she repeated. 'Well, that's just fine then.'

'Katy, I—'

'No, enough. You weren't here when Mom needed you, David. You broke her heart over and over again. She died never seeing you again. Her son.'

When he tried to walk out of the room, she darted over to him and blocked the doorway. 'How could you do it, David? To her, to me, to Dad?'

'Get out of the way, Katy. I mean it.'

'What, you're going to push me out of the way like you've pushed us all aside?' She stood back.

'I'm going, Katy. I can't deal with this. I don't want to.'

'Oh, go ahead. Do whatever you like. I'm past caring any more.'

In the lounge at the Inglenook Inn now, Rupert had listened to her, topped up her glass again, he'd waited for all of it to come out as she told the entire truth about the brother she'd kept a secret from him until now.

'I said something else before David left that day – something unforgivable.' She covered her mouth, not only to stop her lips wobbling but also because she was about to admit something she was so ashamed of. 'I told him he was dead to me.' Her voice caught as she managed to get the rest out. 'I told him that from now on, I didn't have a brother.'

She looked away; she couldn't bear to see anything on Rupert's face that would make her feel worse than she already did. 'Now tell me you misjudged me.' She began to cry. 'He walked away with the photo album; it was all he had. I watched from the top window of the house as he crossed the lawn, met with the sidewalk, and didn't turn back once.'

And this time, her shoulders heaved with the tears and the emotions that that day brought back to her.

He pulled her against him and her head rested on his shoulder. 'I won't judge you. I have no idea what you went through, and I have no idea how a drug addict thinks.'

'But what if my words are the reason he never came back?'

'You can't think that way. And while I firmly believe in supporting your family, second chances can only be given if the person actually wants them.'

'I couldn't save him, I couldn't save David.' She felt spent from the day, the work pressure, the emotional revelations.

'David has to want to change or nothing anyone says or does will make much difference.' When she looked, he'd reached across to hold her hand and she'd been too upset to realise. Now she could feel the reassurance of his skin against hers, the tingle of anticipation it created. 'You have a bigger heart than I gave you credit for, Katy. You really do. What you did for my sister, what you tell me about your family's heartache, everything you did came from a place of sincerity, a place deep inside you with the right values and a huge amount of love.'

'I'm too tired to work through what you've said, but I think you're making sense.' Her legs were drawn up on the sofa as she curled up next to him.

'Don't write David off forever either,' he said after a few moments. 'Never give up.'

'If he wanted to get better and wanted us back, he would've shown up by now.'

'Just don't give up hope. He might want and need his family again one day.'

She murmured an acknowledgment of what he was saying, her eyes fully closed now as exhaustion overwhelmed her.

Katy was disorientated and she

20

KATY

Katy was disorientated when she woke up and she quickly realised she wasn't the only one on the sofa in the lounge. She was leaning against Rupert.

She stole a glance at her watch, which in the faintest of moonlight coming through the window she could see showed a time of three in the morning.

Rupert groaned as he stirred.

'We fell asleep,' she whispered. 'We should get to bed. We've not got long before our workday starts all over again.'

He rubbed his eyes and pushed himself to standing before looking at her in a way that suggested he'd be quite happy to stay here with her for the rest of the night. 'You know, this could've made for an interesting scenario if we'd been woken by one of the guests.'

Katy had already switched off the computer and she turned off the softly glowing lamp that had obviously worked its magic to lull them both to sleep. The nightcaps and the emotions of the evening, as well as the tiredness, had probably helped too.

They crept slowly up the stairs and outside Katy's apartment, she stopped before Rupert could keep going.

They hovered there in the still of the night until Katy knew what she wanted to do.

She took a step closer to him rather than opening her door. She stood on tiptoes and planted a kiss on his cheek. 'Thanks for tonight.'

He seemed surprised she'd kissed him but eventually managed a smile and said softly, 'Right back at you. Teamwork.'

'I didn't really mean that.'

And this time, it was he who kissed her, just once, right on the lips, lingering for a moment. When he pulled away, he murmured, 'I know you didn't. Goodnight, Katy.'

'Goodnight, Rupert.'

* * *

The alarm clock was a rude awakening at 6 a.m. Breakfast service started at 7 a.m. today and Katy found she barely got a moment alone with Rupert. The only thing they really managed to exchange was the odd look of understanding that things had shifted between them, in a good way. And when Katy was in the kitchen, filling a jug of fresh water to set in the lounge, Rupert didn't have time to stop but managed to put a hand on her waist when he stretched past her to get something from the top of a cabinet. The touch sent ripples of electricity through her body, and she wished she could have more.

But all too soon, it was time for Katy to get ready for the wedding.

She came down the stairs into the hallway and Rupert whistled before biting down on his bottom lip and checking no guests were in the vicinity. 'Wow.' He took in her outfit, the ocean-blue silk dress with a split up the side that showed her leg if it moved in the right way.

'Quiet,' she smiled. 'We're colleagues.'

'You know I want more than that, right?' He moved closer and she suspected the only reason for any distance between them at all was because they were at work.

'The way you're looking at me now suggests that might be the case.' She took a step towards him but they sprang apart when Natalie came through from the direction of the dining room and cleared her throat to announce she was heading into the lounge.

Katy adopted a little more professionalism. 'You're sure you're all right without me for a while?'

'Katy, it's your dad's wedding, of course we'll be all right here.'

'He's got me,' Natalie called over from where she was tidying the leaflet rack. 'And before you ask, yes, I'm okay.' She said it in a way that suggested they'd asked it one too many times.

Rupert smiled at Katy, eyes only for one another until Natalie cleared her throat again, this time louder.

'All right,' Katy smiled. 'I'm going. I'll leave you both to it.'

'I hope it goes well,' Rupert told her, and he lingered at the door when she left. She wondered whether he was watching her and couldn't resist turning around to check whether that was the case.

He was.

Katy faced the right direction again with the biggest smile on her face and only just avoided getting entangled with a double leash, two Chihuahuas and their dog walker.

The venue wasn't far – her dad and Stephanie had chosen to have a small ceremony where they had their first ever date. And when she arrived at the cute Italian restaurant with a blue canopy over the door and curly gold writing announcing its name, Shaun was coming from the opposite direction.

He smiled at her and held out his arms. 'You look amazing, Katy. As always.'

'As do you,' she said after they'd hugged. He always had looked good in a suit.

'You coming inside?' he asked when she lingered.

'In a bit. I need a minute. You go ahead.'

He picked up on her need to be alone, to gather thoughts for this change coming for not only her dad but their family.

She wasn't sure whether Shaun had announced her arrival but less than a few minutes later, Stephanie came outside to see her. Wearing a white, knee-length, lacy dress with bead detailing, her hair twirled up elegantly and dotted with fresh pale pink flowers, she looked radiant.

'Stephanie, you look absolutely stunning.' Katy would've said it no matter how she felt, but in this moment, she realised this union was happening; her dad had altered his life and rather than fearing it, she wanted to embrace it. Looking at Stephanie now, a combination of nerves and excitement at marrying the man she loved, Katy felt acceptance settle.

Stephanie kissed her on her cheek, an air kiss so as not to ruin her lipstick. 'Your words mean a lot to me. Thank you.'

Katy figured Stephanie had come out to encourage her inside but as Katy began to go towards the door, Stephanie pulled her back. 'Not yet, I need to talk to you.'

Standing to one side next to terracotta pots, Katy asked, 'What's up?'

'I need to tell you something.'

'Right...'

'Wade said to keep it quiet until today – he didn't know whether you'd be able to handle it, then he didn't want to get your hopes up, or to have you unhappy and worried—'

'You're pregnant.' The words flew out of Katy's mouth before she could stop them.

Stephanie began to laugh and it seemed to ease the tension for her. 'Definitely not. I think me marrying your dad is enough for now.'

'I'm sorry, that was rude of me. And it's not that—'

'Katy, I really need to tell you something, so can you please let me get it out?'

Katy nodded.

But as Stephanie opened her mouth to say whatever it was that was so important, she closed it again as well as her eyes. 'I told Wade he should've come to see you this morning.'

And when she opened her eyes and looked over Katy's shoulder, Katy turned.

And this was more of a shock than anything she could've imagined today, even more so than a surprise pregnancy.

Because walking towards them with her dad was a man in a suit.

David.

* * *

Katy wasn't sure how long she stood there staring – it felt like seconds and yet at the same time it felt like forever.

For the first time in years, brother and sister stood facing one another and neither of them said a word. People passed on by – some for the wedding, others nothing to do with their party. They stood still as though their feet were incapable of doing anything else.

David was the first to speak. 'Hey, sis.'

It took her a while to say, 'You look well.'

'You look beautiful.' She noted her dad and Stephanie had gone inside. When had that happened?

A sudden breeze made her shiver. 'I wish I wasn't seeing you right before we have to go inside and act as though everything is normal.'

'Would you rather I wasn't here?' He wasn't being shirty; he sounded like it was the reaction he'd been expecting from her.

'How... I mean, when...' Her words wouldn't come out because even in her head, she couldn't form the right questions to find out how he'd come to be here today. Seeing him after all this time, seeing him when their last words had been horrible, was a lot to deal with.

'I'm sorry, for everything.'

She gulped back tears but her breath caught in the back of her throat, trying to hold them away.

David stepped to one side as someone on the street bustled past without giving much room for the two people hovering outside a restaurant, unable to go in. 'You've every right to be angry with me for everything I did.'

'Today is about Dad and Stephanie,' she said, looking up at him. He looked so well, that was a shock in itself. She realised now he was about the same height as Rupert. He'd filled out a lot since she last saw him; he looked healthy, together.

'Dad said he wasn't going to tell you I was around until he knew I wasn't going anywhere.'

'And are you? Going anywhere?'

'I hope not. At least nowhere bad.' He reached for her hand and she let him take it. 'I went to rehab.'

Katy felt her whole body sag with relief, shock, she wasn't sure which. All she knew was that David had put an arm around her and led her over to the chair just inside the front door. He crouched down to talk to her so he was looking up at her face, all the while holding her hands to help her believe he was really here.

'I stuck with it, Katy. It wasn't easy; some days I wanted to run away, but I did it, sis. I'm never going back to that life. Not ever. I got help. This is a one-way street for me. I don't want to fuck up my life any more than I have already... or fuck up anyone else's, for that matter,' he added.

'Stop saying *fuck*,' she said when a woman went out through the front door and gave them a dirty look, stuck her nose in the air, and carried on.

At least that had brother and sister laughing together. Something she never, ever thought would happen again.

'Are you ready for this?' David asked, standing.

Katy took a deep breath. 'I'm ready. Let's go be with Dad.'

'I would love nothing more.'

And for now, there were no more words, only emotions that she had to keep in check. Their family, the fragmented parts of it, was forming a new shape today. Every now and then during the nuptials, Katy and David glanced at one another, their pasts already written but the rest of their lives more promising than they had been in a long while.

21

RUPERT

When Katy returned to the inn, Rupert didn't think he'd ever seen her looking so happy. She was glowing.

He met her in the hallway. 'It must have gone well.'

'You're not in your chef's whites,' she smiled.

'No dinner service tonight; all our guests are out, it seems. I try not to take it too personally.' Instead of his usual jacket at this time of day, he was wearing jeans and a marl grey T-shirt. 'So tell me, did it all go according to plan?'

'It did.' She sat on the bottom stair and took off her shoes with a sigh of relief.

He leaned against the banister, watching her. 'You can't stop smiling.'

She looped the straps of her shoes over her fingers and went into the lounge. And her happiness melted into a heaviness of emotions when she told him David was there today.

'I couldn't believe it, Rupert.' Her voice shook, she'd paled even though the shock was over now. 'He came, he showed up.'

'I'm going to make us a coffee each. I think you need it.'

She looked into his eyes and nodded without a word.

By the time he came back with the coffees for them, she looked as though today was finally beginning to sink in. Perhaps she hadn't been able to process it at the wedding and it was only now she was somewhere familiar that she was able to do that. Over coffee, she told him everything: how she'd gone to the wedding and Stephanie had come out to see her, how her dad had arrived with her brother, how they'd talked, the ceremony, afterwards.

'After the cake was served, me, Dad, David, and Stephanie all sat together. Stephanie offered to leave us three alone but none of us wanted that.' She took a deep breath as though she couldn't believe any of this herself. 'Dad told me a while ago that he was worried Stephanie was hiding something.'

'And was she?' he asked as she sipped her coffee and briefly savoured the taste.

'It turned out that she was. David had been in touch. He turned up at the apartment when Dad was away on a golfing trip months ago. I was away at the time too and so Stephanie was staying at the apartment while the decorators did some work for Dad. She said she'd let David stay, she said she'd fully expected him to be gone in the morning, along with anything valuable he could get his hands on. But he was still there. And the morning after that too.'

'It sounds as though she's been a part of your family long before today.'

'I think you're right.' It just took her a while to see it. She turned to Rupert. 'You'd like David. I wanted to bring him here to meet you, today.'

'That might've been a bit much for him.'

She smiled. 'Exactly what he said. He's taking it one step at a time, and I think I need to do that too. But he did ask all about my job, the inn, my life – he's never been interested in much before, not for a long time, anyway. I know I need to give him space, but it's...'

'Difficult,' he finished for her. He wanted to reach out and move her blonde hair behind her ear so he could see her face more clearly.

'He's a work in progress, he says. And so much of it is thanks to Stephanie. If she hadn't let him into the apartment that day...'

'But she did.'

'It sounds as though they really talked. She said it was as though once he started, he couldn't stop. That's something else about David: he's never really been much of a talker. Not like Mom and I were.'

'He's had a lot going on, probably kept most of it bottled up and sometimes strangers are easier to confide in.'

She met his gaze. 'He said that too.'

'They don't have quite the emotional investment... or the baggage.'

'Stephanie's best friend Marnie is married to a man who has years of experience and expertise helping drug addicts. Between them they got David into a rehab programme for a few months. David had finally admitted he had a problem and more than that, this time he *wanted* to find a way out. He never did that before. I mean, he knew he needed to but never had the drive to want it enough. At least, that's how it felt. He insisted Stephanie didn't tell Dad about it at the start. I don't think he believed he could do it and he didn't want to disappoint everyone all over again. Stephanie covered the cost of the rehab without even questioning whether it might be paid back by Dad or not, she just did it, without question.'

'Says a lot about her as a person.'

'Dad has known about David's return for a few days now and he badly wanted to tell me but he didn't want to disappoint me if it didn't work. He knows what this has done to the both of us; I guess he was trying to spare me any more pain.'

'I knew your dad was a good man.' He leant forwards and kissed her on the forehead. It wasn't a time for passion; it was a time for understanding and friendship, part of what they had together no matter what else. 'Tell me one thing. It's important.'

'What?' Her eyes searched his.

'Was the cake up to standard?'

She began to laugh. 'It was perfect, demolished in no time at all. When you next see Finn, you'd better tell him I've spread the word about his baking so he might get a few customers.'

He liked that. She felt a part of his life already.

They both turned when they heard the sound of a suitcase being wheeled in the hallway and Katy puffed out her cheeks briefly.

'I'll deal with it,' he said, 'don't worry.' But to his surprise, it wasn't one of their guests but his sister. He must've been so focused on Katy that neither of them had noticed her coming down the stairs.

'What's going on?' he asked. Natalie had her suitcase, a holdall resting on top of it and her bag over her shoulder. 'You didn't lift that, did you? You should be taking it easy.'

'And I have. I've rested, I've looked after myself and this, brother, is me leaving you to it, getting out of your face, however you want to phrase it. And I didn't warn you I was leaving this afternoon because I didn't even know until about an hour ago. I called Mom.'

'You did?' Katy was at his side.

'Well, I sent her a text first instructing her to read the entire message and then call me. The wait was excruciating.'

'You told her everything?' He couldn't believe it. 'I would've done it for you, I was waiting for you to give me the go-ahead.'

'Let's just say I had a sudden urge to do it myself. I can't always run to my big brother when I'm in trouble.'

'You can and you should. But maybe not for a while,' he teased. 'Let me get over this visit first.'

She took it in good humour. 'Anyway, it was easy enough to text Mom – no interrupting, no me bursting into tears, all the facts right there in front of her for her to digest. Didn't quite work out as easy as I thought because she called, she cried, I cried, neither of us made much sense. But I suddenly found myself saying I'd go home today. And I really want to, Rupert.'

He wrapped her in a hug. 'Well, that's the first time I've heard you even hint that you want to be back in Vermont with the family. I'm glad.'

She pulled back and screwed up her face. 'Am I going to regret this?'

'Probably. And you'll miss my cooking.'

'Ain't that the truth,' she smiled.

Katy stepped forwards and wrapped Natalie in a hug next. 'We're going to miss you around here.'

When Natalie pulled back, she laughed. 'I bet you never thought you'd hear yourself say that.' And then she got more serious. 'Thank you for everything you did for me, I mean it. She's a keeper,' she winked at Rupert.

Rupert shook his head at his sister's meddling. 'Are you really sure this is a good idea, Natalie? You've been through a lot.'

'I know and I'll probably cry a thousand more times over the next few days. I'll be angry and I'll be sad. But I'll be with family and you know as well as I do that sometimes we need it without even realising.'

'Let me take you to the bus station.'

'No need, it's all in hand. But thank you.' And when a horn honked outside, she added, 'That'll be my ride.' Rupert suspected doing it all for herself today was part of her coping mechanism that didn't allow her to think too much about anything else for now, at least until she was back in Vermont.

'Thank you for all your help around this place,' Katy told her as they walked her to the front door to the inn and Rupert picked up her suitcase to take down to the cab.

'It was a pleasure.' She pulled a face as she took her sunglasses from the top of her head and put them on. 'Well, not always. I'd be lying if I said that.'

Natalie followed Rupert down the steps and while he put her suitcase into the trunk of the cab, Natalie waved back at Katy before she gave him one more hug.

'You two make a good team,' Natalie said loud enough through the open window of the vehicle for Katy to hear too. And with another wave, she was off.

Rupert went back up the steps and was about to ask Katy whether she'd like to go out on a proper date with him some time, when another cab drew up outside the inn. 'Is that...' Rupert peered closer. 'It is, you know.' He went straight back down the steps and this time flung his arms around Sofia when she emerged from the vehicle.

'Well, that's some welcome home,' Sofia beamed.

'What can I say? I'm in a hugging mood today. And this is a surprise. We weren't expecting you back so soon. Let me get your bags.' He ran around to the trunk to do the honours.

By the time he got the luggage and made it up the steps to the top of the stoop, Sofia had already headed on up there and introduced herself to Katy. She was busy recapping that yes, her daughter was going to be just fine.

'I feel as though we already know one another,' Sofia smiled again as they went inside.

Sofia stopped in the hallway, letting the ambience of the

brownstone say its own welcome home to her. 'I've missed this place.'

'You could've given us some warning,' Rupert laughed before setting her bags down in the lounge for the time being. 'I haven't moved out of your apartment yet.'

She swished her hand through the air as if it didn't matter at all now. 'There's room for us both, no rush, although I suspect you'll prefer to be in your own place, I understand.'

'And Gabriella is well?'

'She's wonderful, almost back to her old self. And her in-laws are there; it's their turn to spend time with the grandkids, so I got a flight as soon as I could when Gabriella assured me she had enough people to help her out should she need it. Between you and me, I think she might well be glad when they leave, when they get back to normal, just the four of them as a family.'

Sofia looked around and sighed deeply. 'I'm home.' After a moment, she looked at them both. 'Tell me... did I miss much?' She was walking around the lounge, one minute looking at the fireplace, the next peering out of the window onto the street. It was as though she'd been away forever and had to remind herself of every little detail.

'You didn't miss much at all.' Rupert winked at Katy, who smiled at the conspiracy.

'I knew it,' said Sofia. 'With you in charge, everything has run like clockwork.'

'That's one way of putting it,' Rupert mumbled.

'I've loved working here, Sofia.' Katy went through and towards the desk as though she'd have to hand everything over right this second. And the thought made Rupert sad this was coming to an end. 'If I could put your name down for a reference, it would be much appreciated, Sofia.'

'There's no need to even ask, I'd be very happy to do that.' Sofia came away from the window to face them both. 'And you'll stay a week or two longer, Katy?'

'Of course,' Katy nodded with enthusiasm coupled with what looked like relief.

'Thank you. I'd appreciate the extra help for a while as we all try to get back to normal. Now, what numbers do we have for dinner tonight?'

'One of those rare occasions where nobody has booked in,' Rupert told her.

She clapped her hands together. 'Perfect. Then off you go, both of you. Take the afternoon and the evening off, you deserve it. Me, I'm going to make myself a large Americano at the machine in the kitchen and drink it in here and hope to see some of my guests coming and going.'

'I can make you the coffee,' Rupert offered.

'No, I won't hear of it, you've done enough, now scoot.' She headed for the kitchen.

'I'll go get changed, then,' said Katy.

'Do you have to?' he grinned, one hand on her waist and pulling her closer. 'I kind of like that dress.'

'Oh, you do?'

'I do.' He looked into her eyes, his hands on either side of her face. 'Have dinner with me.'

'Don't you want to take your things back to your apartment now Sofia is here?'

'Good idea. I can be ready in twenty minutes. Thirty tops.'

'Sounds good to me. Meet you at the door.'

He wanted to kiss her, but he wanted to save it too, so reluctantly he took the stairs two at a time to Sofia's apartment where he stripped the beds and got the sheets from the sofa. Natalie had left the place tidy, so there wasn't much to do at all apart from put on a load of laundry in the basement and once he'd done that, he filled a holdall with his things.

He was back downstairs in less time than he'd estimated and found Katy standing at the door to the inn, looking out onto the street.

He set down the holdall and came up behind her and as he did so, she leaned against him. A man ran past with a dog on a leash, dodging a frail woman with a smile as bright as the bunch of flowers she cradled in her arm. Three kids crossed the street together, holding one another's hands.

'I'm really going to miss being here every day,' Katy sighed.

'I'm going to miss you being here too. But you've got a week or two left, thanks to Sofia. I'm glad about that.'

She turned around in his arms to face him and he didn't have to wonder about kissing her properly when it was the right time because she'd already decided. She kissed him the way he'd thought about a thousand times since she first walked into his kitchen.

The kiss lasted with both of them lost in the moment until they heard a chuckle behind them.

Sofia.

'I really did miss something when I was away,' she said, eyebrows raised. 'Is there something you need to tell me?'

Katy had buried her head in his chest and Rupert inhaled the scent from her hair as he laughed. 'Nothing to tell,' he said before Sofia saved them their embarrassment and left them alone.

Katy gripped his wrists as he threaded his hands into her hair, ready to kiss her again. He didn't want to stop, not ever. 'I wish I lived at the inn; I'd take you upstairs right now.'

'Quiet or Sofia will hear. And besides, I'm going to need a few dates with you first.'

'Is dinner a good start?'

'Dinner is a great start. But it doesn't need to be anywhere fancy. Somewhere quiet and private would be perfect.'

'I have just the place.' He planted another kiss on her lips and felt her respond immediately. 'We'll go to my apartment and I'll cook.'

'It's your night off.'

He picked up his holdall and slung it over his shoulder, his opposite arm around Katy as they walked down the steps. 'Good job I love it, then.'

She stopped when they reached the sidewalk and turned to look up at the inn, still holding the hand of the arm he had around her. 'I meant it when I said I've loved being here.'

He leaned his head closer to hers, his lips against her hair. 'The Inglenook Inn is the stuff of romance. Take Darcy and her husband Myles, for example.'

'I never did hear how that came to be.'

'It's a long story that started with plenty of drama.'

'You can tell me as we walk; we've got time.'

Plenty of time, he hoped. Because he had no intention of ever letting her go.

ACKNOWLEDGMENTS

Thank you to every single reader who has picked up this book –
and a really big thank you to readers who have followed the series
through all the way from book one! *Christmas at the Little Knitting
Box*, the first *New York Ever After* book, was supposed to be a single
title novel, but I'm so glad I made the decision to make it the start
of a series. It's been wonderful to return to the *New York Ever After*
characters and settings with book seven and finally tell Rupert's
story. When I wrote the sixth book in the series, I wasn't sure
whether I'd write another one, but there are still so many characters and stories to explore and after receiving a fair few messages
from readers asking more about the mysterious chef at The
Inglenook Inn, I couldn't ignore it any longer. He needed to star in
a novel and so *Family Secrets at the Inglenook Inn* was born.

As always, a big thank you to my family for their support, in
particular my husband who not only makes my lunch every day so
that I can write, but hears me vent when things aren't going well
and encourages me to get back to my desk. He also doubles as a
beta reader before I send the book off for the final time and won't
hold back if he thinks something in the story doesn't quite work or
that I've made a mistake.

Enormous gratitude goes to the team at Boldwood Books who
work tirelessly to bring my titles to readers all around the world in
multiple formats. I'd like to mention Tara Loder, editor extraordi-
naire, especially, for taking the book and knocking it into shape.
I'm not very good at articulating a fresh idea to Tara and I think

she might know that by now and so she tells me to go away and write the book, tells me she has faith that I can tell a good story, and so far I think we're doing well with the way we work!

The only thing missing for me with this book was a trip to New York. I'd love to get over there again and dream up another story – keep your fingers crossed for me that I can manage it some day!

Much love,

Helen x

MORE FROM HELEN ROLFE

We hope you enjoyed reading *Family Secrets at the Inglenook Inn*. If you did, please leave a review.

If you'd like to gift a copy, this book is also available as an ebook, digital audio download and audiobook CD.

Sign up to Helen Rolfe's mailing list for news, competitions and updates on future books.

https://bit.ly/HelenRolfeNews

Explore the rest of the New York Ever After series

ABOUT THE AUTHOR

Helen Rolfe is the author of many bestselling contemporary women's fiction titles, set in different locations from the Cotswolds to New York. Most recently published by Orion, she is bringing sixteen titles to Boldwood - a mixture of new series and well-established backlist. She lives in Hertfordshire with her husband and children.

Follow Helen on social media:

 twitter.com/hjrolfe
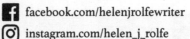 facebook.com/helenjrolfewriter
instagram.com/helen_j_rolfe

Boldwood

Boldwood Books is an award-winning fiction publishing company seeking out the best stories from around the world.

Find out more at www.boldwoodbooks.com

Join our reader community for brilliant books, competitions and offers!

Follow us
@BoldwoodBooks
@BookandTonic

Sign up to our weekly
deals newsletter

https://bit.ly/BoldwoodBNewsletter